A. M. KHERBASH

Shaula

For my husband

Author's note:

Although *Shaula* can be read as a stand-alone, it takes place some time after *Lesath*, and therefore makes references to events that took place in that novel.

CHAPTER I

"Tell me a story."

The request surprised Ben into turning away from the passenger seat's window to regard the driver next to him.

Lately, he had been going by the handle 'Pale Horse'—a name which might have better suited the willowy man were it not for the short beard and long dark hair, which Pale Horse had swept back, gathering half of it into a small knot behind his head. Sunglasses perched on his aquiline nose, and from where he sat, Ben could see the eyes behind the lens were fixed on the road—so much so that he began to doubt whether Pale Horse had spoken at all.

"What's that, sir?" asked Ben, shifting in his seat. He lost sight of the eyes as Pale Horse turned his way, black lenses reflecting double miniatures of him.

"The radio's broken and I'm just about to fall asleep here," said Pale Horse. "I'm about ready to break into a song unless you know a good story—or anecdote."

Still under a drowsy spell, Ben frowned at the unexpected request. "With all due respect, sir, asking me to think of something on the spot usually has the opposite effect: I can't think of anything off-hand."

"Fair enough," said Pale Horse, and Ben thought he almost sounded disappointed, though thankfully he refrained from singing.

Had they been in the same situation a month ago, Ben would have racked his brain to remember an anecdote or something to offer his senior, whose stellar mission record made him something of a rising star in the organization they both belonged to. But recent reports surrounding Pale Horse had been troubling. Word got around like smoke, and when Ben was briefed on this mission, he understood that his primary role was to keep an eye on Pale Horse and covertly report his observations.

If Ben had any say in the matter, he would have opined that a specialist or any other higher-ranking agent was better suited for the job. But on reflection, he considered that perhaps they chose him expressly for the purpose of not rousing Pale Horse's suspicion. All he had to do was observe, report, and let the experts handle the data. And since their mission was not likely to last more than six hours, perhaps this was the best way to go about it.

As far as Pale Horse was concerned, Ben was just an assisting partner, sent along to gain some field experience. The story was all the more convincing since Ben was a floater, with no specialty and no affiliation to any one department, often sent to wherever he was needed.

Truth be told, Ben pitied his temporary senior. Here was a man who, in his mid-thirties, should have been hitting his stride career-wise instead of being reviewed for reassignment or perhaps retirement. The former seemed more likely: if Pale Horse was no longer suited for field missions, he could still put his experience to use as an instructor or trainer. He certainly bore the flinty profile of a leader—if only he would stop smiling ever so often.

The truck sped over a pothole, jarring Ben out of his thoughts.

He heard a slight rattling, and glanced over his seat to make sure the sealed container lashed to the truck bed was still there.

"I was thinking, sir," he began, settling back in his seat, "maybe we should work on our cover story."

Pale Horse had found a wooden toothpick and was passing it from one corner of his mouth to the other. "Don't need one for a quick delivery in the backcountry."

He spoke with a slight note of contempt, as if the job itself was something of a joke. And perhaps to him it was.

Ben thought better of contradicting his senior, and with a conciliatory "if you say so, sir," turned his attention back to the endless line of trees rushing past his window.

A chain, heavy with dog tags and suspended from the rearview mirror, clinked in the early morning's gray. And just when Ben's eyelids began to droop, Pale Horse spoke up again.

"How about this?" he began with a gamesome quality in his voice. "We're two brothers smuggling some—"

"Brothers, sir?"

"Yeah," said Pale Horse, giving his junior partner an appraising nod. "How old are you? Twenty-two?"

"Twenty-four, sir, but—that's not my point. We don't look that much alike to pass as brothers," said Ben, whose light auburn hair, gray eyes, and soft features set him apart from his companion.

"Brothers—cousins—whatever," Pale Horse testily rejoined, taking the toothpick out and gesturing with it. "My point is if you want a good cover story, the simplest, most straightforward one is your best bet. It's hard to muddle. Say it right, and it's as airtight as anything. 'Nice to meet you. I'm Pale Horse. And this here is my cousin, Ben.' See?"

He turned to see the effect of this and caught the uncomfortable look Ben was averting.

"What?!"

"Nothing," Ben promptly answered. "It's just... well, it's your name, sir. I mean 'Ben' is plain and common, but 'Pale Horse' stands out a little—calls attention to you, you know?"

"So?"

"So it's the last thing we want when we're operating incognito."

"Psht! Who's gonna want to talk to a couple of hicks in jeans and plaid shirts, let alone ask us our names? We're not that interesting."

"But what if someone—"

"They won't."

Out of frustration, Ben shot back: "You know I'd be more worried about my conduct if I were you."

Pale Horse turned to regard him, and for a frightful moment Ben fancied he suspected something, if not guessed the truth. The fear passed as Pale Horse went back to looking ahead, muttering through a lopsided smile: "I keep forgetting there's no such thing as privacy in the organization."

Everyone knows you're on thin ice, Ben had almost added to emphasize the point, but thought better of it. "You don't seem much bothered by it," he instead remarked.

"I am. I cried my eyes out this morning. Why do you think I have these on?" said Pale Horse, touching his sunglasses.

"Come on. I mean the consequences..." Ben faltered,

selecting his words with care, "… they could be dire. The organization…" again he hesitated, "… well I'm sure you know they don't take kindly to insubordination."

Pale Horse's smile widened a little. "But we always look after each other, don't we?" he exclaimed, surprising Ben with a shoulder clap. The gesture was made in jest, annoying the young man, who pulled away.

"Tell you what," Pale Horse went on good-naturedly, "the name bothers you that much? Let's change it. I'll even let you pick one for me."

Ben side-eyed him, suspecting the offer was leading up to a joke. But the senior went on driving in silence, without so much as a nod of encouragement.

Just then they emerged from the forest, and under the morning sun the eastward road shone with golden luster.

"Well, it has to be something you'd answer to in an instant," said Ben, thinking out loud. "Can't go wrong with your real name."

Pale Horse scratched his scruffy cheek with one finger as he thought it over.

"I'll answer to any one of the following," he said and began ticking the names off his fingers: "Pale Horse. Jackal. Octavo. Dogdaddy. Grim."

Ben rolled his head back with a faint laugh of exasperation. "Ah, I knew this was leading up to some sort of punchline," he mumbled.

Pale Horse lifted his hands off the wheel in a slight shrug. "Hey. You asked for a name I'll answer to, I gave you five. Take your pick."

"I asked for a real name."

"They're as real as anything."

"Dogdaddy!" Ben's smile widened with incredulity. "Dogdaddy is a real name?"

"Either that or we stick with what we got."

Ben slumped back in his seat in sullen defeat. A minute later he said: "Can we make a pit stop, Grim?" trying out the new name.

Grim kept his eyes on the road, saying nothing except to give a faint smile of acknowledgement.

CHAPTER 2

Eidercrest: a tuft of a town with a modest population of a hundred and thirty-two. Once an idyllic resort town, the flow of tourists had slowed to a trickle over the last couple of decades. Then an economic crisis brought on a rash of foreclosures, evicting several families out of their homes. Local commerce began to suffer, and soon business owners followed suit, closing shops and relocating elsewhere. Not long after that, the local water supply became contaminated, leading to an outbreak that decimated the remaining population. The following two years saw the town switching over to an emergency water source, while several investigations, criminal indictments, and firings were carried out.

Nowadays, local officials assert the quality of the town's main supply had returned to acceptable levels. Yet no amount of optimism could reverse the mass departure that had taken place, more so since the area's crowning jewel, Lake Penumbra, remains marred by the incident. And while nature had already begun its slow march to reclaim empty yards and abandoned houses—with vines scaling cracked walls and sprouts shooting through boards—the lingering human population still thrived and gathered in the town's thoroughfare, or headed to the Tea Room for sandwiches and coffee.

Eidercrest, a town of a hundred and thirty-two—if you don't count the commune.

"They just showed up—oh, I'd say a couple of months ago," said the gas station store cashier, referring to the group of men, women and children that made up the commune.

"They mostly keep to the outskirts," she went on, handing Grim his change. "Plenty of abandoned property there for them to squat in. The county sheriff never bothers to look that way, let alone lift his hand shoo them away. I figure it's only a matter of time before someone complains about the declining value of real estate. I doubt it though. The town'd sooner be swallowed by moss before we see any reform. Some say they're nothing more than a cult. Who? Why the commune, of course! Well, that's what they say, but I don't buy that. Sure, some walk around barefoot, and for a while, they were panhandling on Main Street. But they seem harmless enough—except when they come in here and I have to keep a sharp eye 'n' make sure they don't walk out with unpaid goods stuffed down their— pockets or anything."

She jabbered on as she leaned over the counter, her bony elbows cradled in either hand, encouraged by Grim's "Oh?" and "Is that right?" which he murmured between sips of tea from a paper cup.

They stood talking when Ben emerged from the station's bathroom, and they continued to talk even while he loitered nearby, pretending to examine the rack of cheap sunglasses. His presence did nothing to shorten the conversation. Likely, the middle-aged cashier told the same story to any outsider who would listen; but from her tone and posture, Ben could see she took a shine to his partner and was trying to chat him up.

Not that he was bad looking: he was in good shape (if a little on the wiry side), with a certain glow of health and vitality in spite of his shabby appearance; then again, the rumpled plaid shirt and black crewneck might have lent him a commonplace charm that appealed to her. At least it served to blend him in: a couple of customers—locals from the way they greeted the cashier lady by name—passed them by, and while their eyes skimmed indifferently over Grim, their gaze lingered on Ben—fresh-faced in his pressed shirt and khakis—with a hint of disdain reserved for outsiders and wealthy tourists.

Ben turned and wandered down a nearby aisle to interrupt their line of vision. It didn't matter what they thought. He just didn't care for unwanted attention.

"If I may raise a point, sir," said Ben after he and Grim had gone back to the truck and closed the doors behind them.

"Hm?" said Grim, biting down on the rim of the lidless paper cup to pull down his seatbelt. Ben almost pointed out that there were cupholders, but his senior managed to buckle up without incident.

"Sir, in case you forgot we're not to engage with anyone unless it's absolutely necessary."

"Is this your first field mission, Ben?" asked Grim out of the blue.

"It's my second, sir. Why?"

Instead of answering, Grim dropped a plastic bag filled with sandwiches and energy drinks onto Ben's lap. "Eat up. Your empty stomach's making you nervous."

"Sir, but protocol dictates—"

"Forget protocol," Grim interrupted, heedless of the possibility that the truck might be bugged or monitored. Then again, he said it just as he started the truck, and the engine coughing to life might have drowned out his remark.

"Just follow my lead," he went on. "I got over fifteen years of experience and I can tell you a little small talk won't hurt your cover—unless you're high or intoxicated. That's my advice: no talking while you're partaking—in fact, do not partake at all while you're on the job. It goes without saying, but there should be a protocol for that: No partaking and talking. That makes a whole lot more sense than No Talking." He paused for a sip of tea before continuing. "In fact, I find excess talking a good deterrent sometimes. You want to chase someone off, try bending their ear. Give them a good sob story. The more depressing, the faster they'll run. Where was I going? Right, what I'm trying to say is, no one's interested in us. We're not celebrities or wanted criminals, and we're certainly not doing or transporting anything illegal. At least, I'm pretty sure we're not."

At that last phrase, Ben straightened up from his sullen brooding.

"What are we transporting, sir?" he asked regarding the gray container strapped to the truck bed. It stood fifteen inches high, and was about two feet wide and four feet long, with rounded corners, plastic handles and latches that made Ben think of cooler boxes.

The container had been preloaded for them sometime before they had climbed into the truck and set off. On first seeing it, Grim glibly asked whether they were transporting a dead child. Ben may have rolled his eyes at the remark, but it evidently infected his thoughts, for just then he couldn't scrutinize the gray container without comparing its dimensions to that of a small casket.

"Whatever it is, it's classified," answered Grim. But as soon he said it, Ben sensed something working behind the silence that followed.

They were still parked at the gas station, and sure enough Grim switched off the engine and sat staring in the vague direction of the neon OPEN sign mounted on the window of the convenience store. Absent the sunglasses and impudent smile, and with his eyebrows slanting low over his narrowed eyes, he almost seemed a different person just then.

"What's wrong?" asked Ben, somewhat troubled by the sudden change that came over his partner. The moment was brief, and Grim's features mellowed as he turned to answer.

"Maybe we should take a peek back there—make sure everything's alright."

The suggestion was made in a light enough tone that Ben understood the meaning behind it. He never would have dreamt of looking through any classified material; but the fact that his senior did not know what the cargo was somewhat stoked Ben's curiosity.

Was it even possible to look inside? Surely it was locked or sealed in some way that to open it would incriminate them. What if it was rigged for that purpose, as a sort of test? What if this whole mission was a test to see if Grim would follow the simplest instructions and stick to regulations?

Ben shook his head: too convoluted. Besides, if they were going to go to all that trouble, why bother sending him at all? Unless it was to keep an eye on Grim's conduct and report any transgressions...

At that, Ben realized the man in question was still waiting for an answer. And with a glance over his shoulder that reassured him the container sat undisturbed, Ben hurriedly said: "Seems fine. Let's just go."

CHAPTER 3

The sun had disappeared behind a blanket of thick clouds, and the golden morning gave way to a murky overcast day as they drove through the town's thoroughfare, passed a small shack that served as the town's post office, and crossed a residential area, where condemned buildings and dilapidated houses loomed with boarded doors and black, gaping windows.

Meandering along a hillside road, the truck slowed down and came to a stop before a massive landslide blocking the road.

They tried checking the map on their phones, but it proved to be an exercise in futility once they discovered the lack of coverage in the area.

"Let's go back," said Grim, putting the truck in reverse. "I'm sure we can get a map or directions from someone in town."

They stopped at the post-office, which seemed open for business when they drove past it earlier. Now a sign that read "Back in a few minutes" was taped to the shuttered door.

Grim drove on to Main Street and parked in front of Caleb's Sporting Cabin, a bona fide log cabin converted into a store, with a large display window exhibiting hunting and fishing gear. But it was evident from the dark interior that the store was not yet open.

"They don't open until nine," said Ben, pointing to the wooden plaque that listed store hours.

"Let's try there," said Grim, striding over to Howard's Everything Store. There, too, the windows were dark.

"Same here—they open at nine a.m.," said Ben, catching up to Grim and reading the white decal on the window.

"Yeah, but they usually get in there before to set up shop," said Grim, shielding his eyes to peer through the window.

"It's only thirty minutes away," said Ben. "Let's wait in the truck."

Grim stepped back, his eyes tracing up the building before settling on the row of windows above the store.

"You think the owners live up there?" he asked; and without waiting for an answer, he began shouting at the high windows: "Hey! Anyone up there?"

Ben glanced anxiously from Grim to the windows, wanting to stop his senior on the one hand and yet knowing from past experience that it was a wasted effort. Grim meanwhile went on calling—"Could use some help here!"—his booming voice carrying across the empty thoroughfare.

"Yeah!" called a distant voice behind them, prompting both men to turn around.

Across the street was the Tea Room, and in the distance, they saw a woman's blonde head poking from behind the shop's front door.

"What do you want?" she called.

"We're just trying to get somewhere," shouted Grim in answer. "Except the road's blocked. Landslide."

"Outside where?" she asked.

"Landslide!" he repeated, molding his hands to form a megaphone.

"You better come here and tell me about it," she called back, opening the door and stepping out to meet them. She wore a brown, utilitarian apron over her plain t-shirt and dark pants, and held a broom in one hand.

"Can I help you?" she said in a regular voice, looking down on them from the front porch as they drew closer.

"We're trying to get to a house by Lake Penumbra. We were heading there, going by Westfield Drive, but there's a landslide and we were wondering if maybe you have a map or know a different route that would take us there."

"The lakeside cabin?" she asked after pausing to lift her gaze and stare into the distance, possibly in the direction of their destination. She appeared somewhere in her late twenties, her long, light blonde hair was parted in the middle, and her sparse eyebrows were almost invisible against her pale brow, lending her an enigmatic look. Something about her attitude, be it the upward tilt of her head, or the way she held the broom handle as though holding a grounded spear, reminded Ben of a Greek statue.

"Yes, ma'am," said Grim.

"Spider's cabin."

"Pardon?"

"Sorry, just a habit of labeling people," she said without any hint of embarrassment. "Radney Atwood lives there. Gangly fella—like daddy longlegs. Anyhow, what's your business with him?"

"Just making a delivery," answered Grim reverting to his polite smile.

"Is that your truck there?" She nodded at the black pick-up parked across the street.

"Yes, ma'am."

The woman brought her gaze back to Ben. "And who's that with you?"

Ben found the string of questions odd for a server who seemed to have begun her shift and should have been in a hurry to get back to work. Her interrogation was more wary than curious, like a guard at the gate examining visitors before letting them in.

Grim clapped Ben's shoulder, answering on his behalf: "That's my nephew, Ben. Poor boy's got a mountain of student debt to pay, so he's working for me until he can land himself a decent job. I'm John Grimaldi by the way," he added. "People just call me Grim."

"Not with that smile you're not," she murmured a little wryly before offering her own name in return: "Olivia. Which road did you say was blocked?"

"Westfield Drive."

Again, she squinted into the distance, perhaps drawing up a mental map of the area. "Yeah, I know another way. I could give you directions, but I think it's best if I showed you."

"You sure?" said Grim.

"I was planning on driving to the farmer's market in the next town over, anyhow," she said standing the broom by the door. "Might as well go now."

"What about your shift?" asked Ben.

She shrugged as she reached back to untie her apron. "No one comes by here at this hour."

"But what if your boss finds out?" Ben insisted, haunted by the idea.

"You're looking at her," she rejoined with a quick smile, folding the apron and tossing it on a nearby bench.

Some minutes later the three of them were traveling down a tree-lined gravel road, Olivia leading the way in her compact SUV, and the two men following behind her in their black pick-up truck. As the gravel path merged with a two-lane asphalt road, Olivia signaled them to pull over to the side. She then, disembarked, and walked over to their truck.

"Just continue down that road there," she said, pointing the way. "Go left at the fork, and keep going until you reach the cabin."

Grim bowed his head, and made a gesture as if touching the brim of an invisible hat. "You just saved us a boatload of trouble."

"If you feel that way," she began, placing her hands on her hips, "how about you pass by the Tea Room on your way back."

"What for?"

"I don't know." She shrugged. "Maybe get something to eat?"

"Ah!" cried Grim with a small laugh of understanding. "Well that's one way of bringing in customers."

Her answering smile was easy and indifferent. "I do what I can. So should I count you in?"

"Depends... What's on the menu?" said Grim, ignoring Ben who was clearing his throat and sending all manners of subtle signals to get his attention. And just as he was about to tug his senior's shirt, Grim shifted beyond his reach, leaning out the window and resting his forearms on the ledge in a neighborly fashion.

"How do you feel about pie?" said Olivia.

Grim waved his hand in a so-so gesture. "I'm more of a cake man."

"We have that too."

"And tea?"

"Naturally," she said; then looking past him at Ben, she added: "How about you?"

"Oh, I'm…" Ben stammered. "I'll just have what he's having," he said, hoping to end the conversation.

"You sure?" she asked. Both their eyes rested on him, as though there was something unusual in his response.

Ben dropped his gaze and slid back in his seat, then looked back up to feign self-assurance as he nodded and said: "yeah," all the while hoping they didn't notice the heat suffusing his face.

The conversation went on without Ben, leaving him mired in a sense of awkwardness that revisited him even as he slumped back and pretended to check his phone. Embarrassment soon gave way to resentment as he glanced sideways at his partner, wishing he would shut up already and move on. Now that they knew where they needed to go, there was no reason to carry on talking to Olivia, let alone make plans to see her again. But like the cashier at the gas station, Grim likely wanted to draw out the conversation for his own sake. And though Ben had washed his hand of guiding and correcting his senior, he was somewhat disgusted with his unseemly conduct: If he was keen on chatting someone up, he could have at least waited until he was off-duty.

Not that he had a chance with her, Ben reflected, looking from Olivia to this rib of a lumberjack sitting next to him. A man of his age and rank should know better. No wonder he was in hot water when he can't complete a simple mission without bending the rules—and how far can you bend something before it irrevocably breaks?

A sulky silence fell between the two men as they drove on, and while Ben had no intention of airing his grievances, he half-expected his senior to make small talk or try to conciliate him in some way. Instead, Grim kept the window lowered, and with one hand on the wheel he rested his other elbow on the ledge, letting the wind whip into the truck cabin to drown out the quiet.

CHAPTER 4

Finding himself unable to sleep on the eve of their mission, Ben had gone down to the organization's library, browsing the rows of books with no particular purpose in mind before deciding on a whim to look up the town they were heading to.

That afternoon's one-on-one briefing had offered little in the way of information beyond instructing him on his task, and that he and Grim were to deliver a container to a "specialist" named Radney Atwood, who resided in a lakeside cabin on the outskirts of Eidercrest; what this specialist did or specialized in was never brought up. But being a young bureaucrat of no account, Ben was used to these parsimonious briefings: no one told him anything, no one volunteered any information unless it was relevant to his assignment. What little he knew about the organization would fill a five-page report. Like most personnel, he knew its official name—the Mycelia Sterilia Society, or MSS—but fell into the habit of referring to it as 'the organization' to be able to allude to it in public without worrying about outsiders overhearing him. Not that its existence was a secret—the organization did not hide its presence; but much like its plain-sounding sobriquet, it relied on obscurity and abstraction to avert attention, carrying out its operations in secret, prevailing in a sort of nebulous network, with fingers in several pies, such as pharmaceuticals, research and development, and even charity.

What he found at the library (apart from reports on the town's water crisis) were a scant number of newspaper articles that chronicled the decline of tourism in the area, and subsequent selling of the closed down resort. Ben guessed it was bought by a dummy corporation belonging to the organization, and having acquired the condemned lakeside property, they proceeded to demolish all nearby cabins save one, which—compared to the old photos—was renovated and augmented. In all likelihood, a single cabin was all they required, and by leveling the other cabins, they gained a spacious property that served to distance the one remaining cabin from public grounds.

Something about it reminded Ben of the horticultural practice of pruning spent flowers to further enhance the beauty of the crowning blossom. Not that it did anything to improve the cabin's appearance he observed, as they stood in front of the stocky wooden building sheltered under interlacing branches of towering evergreens. It sat at the edge of a low plateau, overlooking the water from a modest height of ten or twelve feet, a solitary structure stark against a forest so dense it imbued the air with a verdant hue. Much like the faded photos, an eerie hush permeated the place: no breeze ruffled the reflected image on the lake's surface, nor susurrate through the green needles above. It was all very quiet.

Grim, his finger poised to ring the cabin's doorbell, turned to ask: "Was that you?"

"Was what me?" Ben asked in return.

"I thought I heard giggling," answered Grim, ringing the doorbell.

Ben had no intention of answering, but a moment later was compelled to say: "Why would I be giggling?"

"That's what I was wondering," said Grim, ringing the doorbell again.

"I told you to ignore it," yelled a surly female voice from somewhere inside the cabin. She sounded young, more so when she gave a sharp growl. "Ugh! It's just one of Jerris' stupid little pranks!"

Grim and Ben had time to glance at each other before the door was answered by a red-haired girl in a yellowing sleeveless dress. From her initial sullen expression, it was evident she had expected someone other than the two strangers, whom she now regarded with widening eyes before slamming the door shut.

"Sir—" spoke Ben over the fresh burst of giggles issuing from behind the closed door—"Sir, are you sure we have the right address?"

"Right address, wrong person," said Grim, opening the door and letting himself in.

The two men stepped into the pine-paneled foyer, finding no trace of the redhead. To their right, a narrow flight of stairs led up to the second floor; to their left, the entryway opened into a small living room, where sat a man on a large green sofa, watching them as they entered—not Mr. Atwood, but a stranger in a calico shirt, jeans and pointy boots.

"Can I help you gentlemen?" he said. The man, neither very young nor yet touched by middle age, spoke with wary courtesy, as though he was the owner of the house; indeed he eyed them with a look of latent challenge as he sat with one arm draped over the back of the sofa and one thin leg crossed over the other, resting his ankle on the opposite knee.

"Is Mr. Atwood here?" asked Grim with equal reserve.

The man continued to stare at them with an unfulfilled smile, seeming to have taken their measure and found them wanting.

Grim ignored him and was about to head upstairs only to hear footsteps that preceded a lanky bedraggled person tying his robe as he descended.

"Who are you? What do you want?" he demanded, firing both questions in quick succession.

"Radney Atwood?" asked Grim, if only to be sure.

Ben too had his doubts; having seen the specialist's profile, he found it difficult to match the well-groomed, bespectacled individual from the photo to this person, whose pink eyes matched his florid skin, and who seemed irritated by the question.

"Yes! What do you want?" he snapped back.

"Delivery for you, sir," answered Grim in a mollifying tone.

"I didn't order anything," Atwood grumbled, trying in vain to smooth back his wild hair, which obstinately sprang back into its disheveled state after each pass.

"It's a gift," said Grim after a pause of hesitation. "A gift from the company, to thank you for working with us," he emphasized, hoping to deliver a hint within his vague answer.

And just when a look of clarity dawned on Atwood's face, the man on the sofa bent forward.

"If it's a cheap trinket with a logo, tell them to keep it," he volunteered, as though the matter concerned him as well.

"Thane, please," said Atwood. "I can handle my own affairs."

"Yeah, far be it from me to handle your private affairs."

Thane smiled as he leaned back, spreading his arms over the back of the sofa.

Grim broke the awkward silence that followed, asking Atwood if there was a bathroom he could use.

"Upstairs... uh, first door to the left," Atwood replied, a little distracted.

"If you don't mind, sir, I'd rather you show me where it is," said Grim with a subtle look that instilled command into the polite request.

"Right, th-this way," stammered the other, leading Grim up the narrow stairs.

As soon as they were gone, Thane got up from the sofa and strolled through the front door to the truck parked outside.

Ben followed him with his eyes, but was too dazed by the scene that took place to realize what Thane intended to do until he heard the loud click of the truck's tailgate.

"Hey!" cried Ben, running after him. "Get away from there!"

"Is that your gift there?" Thane demanded, pointing at the gray container.

"That's private," answered Ben, only to be ignored by Thane, who went over to the passenger side of the truck, peering through the windows.

For a man not expecting much, he seemed eager to find the package, observed Ben as he anxiously shadowed Thane, expecting him to open the door and rummage through the glove compartment.

Instead, the odd man wheeled round suddenly. "Who's your master, boy?"

"Excuse me?" Ben stammered.

The other man uttered an exasperated sigh at resorting to using layman's terms. "The company you work for—the enterprise you sold your soul to—the faceless entity dangling a carrot in front of you."

"That's private," was Ben's invariable answer; he began to wish Grim was here with his knack for inventing things on the spot to deflect intrusive questions.

"*That's private*," mimicked Thane. "You know what else is private? This property you're standing on," he added, bewildering Ben, who failed to see his point.

Thane meanwhile had circled back, and the sound of the container being dragged across the corrugated truck bed brought Ben back to his immediate problem.

"Leave that alone!" he broke out, pushing back the container.

"What? I'm saving you the trouble of taking it in," said Thane, pulling the container out again.

Ben shoved it back in. "Our business is with Mr. Atwood. This doesn't concern you," he asserted, placing a hand on the container to keep Thane from pulling it out again.

To his surprise, Thane chuckled at this, reached over, and gently pinched Ben's cheek the way he would a child.

"How about you go chase that squirrel over there? There's a good boy," he said.

Ben pushed him away, but the shove did not do much apart from surprising Thane, who a moment later laughed and raised his hands in a "come at me" gesture. Ben obliged him another shove. This time the man fell back a step or two, granting Ben a measure of confidence. Again, he pushed Thane back with similar success, silencing the skeptical inner voice that warned Ben against starting a fight he couldn't finish. Then again, maybe Thane was all bluff—a smart-mouthed coward who couldn't fight back.

But just as Ben was congratulating himself on fending off this meddler without Grim's assistance, Thane grabbed Ben by the back of his neck and rammed the top of his head into Ben's face.

A blinding starburst sent Ben staggering back; and while he covered his face and fought back tears, he heard some scuffling, which he took for Thane's dragging the container across the truck bed.

He opened his eyes, and saw Grim's hazy form, standing with his back to him, staring down at Thane, who had fallen to the ground on his back and was scrabbling to get up.

"Mr. Atwood sends his regards," said Grim with surprising calm but not without sarcastic emphasis on the last word. "He said you'd better not show your face here again."

His vision being half blurred by the blow to his left eye, Ben could make out Thane as he rose to his feet, though he wasn't sure about the smile the retreating man seemed to cast up at Grim, whether it was a smile at all or a sneer of contempt.

"I'll just come back later," he said, and went on chuckling to himself, as if quitting a game with two boys who at some point grew cross and surly with him.

A couple of minutes later, Grim and Ben sat on the same sofa Thane had occupied, waiting for Atwood to fetch a bag of frozen peas for Ben's bruised face.

The latter looked around while he waited, his good eye skimming over pine walls with charts, tables, and abstract diagrams tacked onto them, trying in vain to decipher them or gain some hint on the specialist's line of work. Next to him sat Grim, his legs freely extended, using the precious cargo container as an ottoman on which he rested his crossed feet.

"You shouldn't have done that," Atwood dolefully cried out from the kitchen.

"You shouldn't have had him over in the first place," answered Grim, tipping his head back to let his voice carry through the door.

The specialist emerged with the bag of frozen peas, looking a little more like himself in his thick-rimmed glasses. "If I'd known you were coming, I'd have gotten rid of him."

"Like you did with the girl?" Grim pointedly asked.

"Oh she's…" Atwood trailed off, smiling down at the bag he held and began fumbling with it. "She's with Thane. They just come here sometimes, and she—you know, helps around the house—cooking, cleaning…"

"Uh-huh," said Grim, his half-closed eyes more eloquently skeptical than his reply.

"And Thane—Thane's a really nice guy! Oh sure, he can be a bit of a gadfly sometimes… And he might come across as abrasive, but he's harmless! Wouldn't hurt a fly."

"And people?" came the rejoinder from Ben.

Atwood said nothing but uttered a dismal grunt that might have been a laugh as he handed Ben the bag of peas.

"Why was he here in the first place?" Ben wanted to ask. But the question dissolved from his mind within seconds of placing the frosty bag onto his eye and cheek. The bag was wrapped in a threadbare dishtowel, and as the persistent ache grew numb under the seeping cold, Ben decided he would much rather sit back and listen with his eyes closed.

"You're going back to living like a hermit," said Grim, bringing feet down and planting them on the floor in a wide stance. "No friends, no rendezvous, not even a repairman to fix a faulty, broken, or leaking anything without checking with the organization first."

"Checking with the organization," echoed Atwood with

a snort as he eased himself into a chair. "I'm not even an employee of your organization!"

"No, but you're under direct contract," returned Grim, fixing him with a sharp look. "As long as you live under their roof, you live by their rules. The whole point of planting you in a remote lakeside cabin was to keep you away from prying eyes."

"Silly me, and here I thought the whole point was for the sake of my research."

"How so?"

"Oh, don't play dumb now. You know what type of research we're conducting here."

"You tell me," shrugged Grim, affecting disinterest to hide his ignorance.

The feign was ineffective: Atwood gave a delighted, "Aha!" clapping his hands together, as though to close the matter. "Above your pay grade, is it? Well, I guess that's that. Now, I don't mean to be rude, but if the two of you will kindly skedaddle, I'd like to start ASAP."

Back in the truck, Grim was on the phone with the director, updating him on the situation.

"Yes, sir. It's with him now. One thing though: He's been in contact with some of the locals."

Ben held his breath, trying to better hear or at least catch a few words from the other end. No such luck, especially when Grim shifted his phone to the other ear.

"No, it's more than that. There were two individuals on the premises: a female—white—maybe high school or college-aged—and a male—also white—maybe thirty-five or forty—a panderer from the looks of it... yeah, I suspect recreational drugs were involved. I chased them off, but I doubt they'll keep off for good."

You only chased one off, corrected Ben, though he kept the thought to himself.

Meanwhile the voice on the other end grew loud enough that Ben caught crackling blips of it in the quiet interior of the truck. Whether the director was outraged in general or taking his anger out on Grim, he maintained a neutral expression, though the longer Ben observed him, the more tired he looked.

"Well, I didn't want to risk blowing our cover, sir," continued Grim once the tirade died out. "Someone might come looking for them, and it'll look suspicious if they happen to disappear on the same day we drive into town. It's a small risk, granted, but it's your call, sir."

There was silence on the other end, then Grim shifted in his seat, lifting his head from its premeditative stoop.

"Sir?" he said, a note of surprise in his voice. "I—yes, sir. For how long? Yes, sir. In the same cabin? Oh. Of course. I'm not sure but—yes, of course, sir. I'm sure we'll manage. Will do, sir."

"What'd they say?" asked Ben after Grim hung up.

"I guess we're staying."

"Staying? For how long?"

"Apparently, until they're satisfied the research is progressing smoothly and our specialist friend keeps on the straight and narrow."

CHAPTER 5

Sunlight broke through the heavy clouds in canting shafts, and to sample that mild air with an outstretched hand, Grim drove with the windows down, his loose hair whipping about his face. Now and then, he would glance at Ben, showing signs of initiating a conversation which the young man dreaded.

Though the cargo had been delivered without incident, Ben was still embarrassed by his near failure in safeguarding it; whatever Grim was about to say promised to be something along the lines of "Nice job keeping watch!" or "Maybe next time you'll learn to keep your eyes open, dumbass!" or any similar flak he had grown accustomed to receiving from his colleagues or squadmates whenever they failed their tasks.

Regardless of the role Ben had or hadn't played in their failure (or occasional success), in the hierarchy of the group, he was the unhappy runt who took the blame for shortcomings beyond his control: If their equipment failed, it was because he didn't check it; if they didn't make time, it was because he slowed them down. Ben bore the brunt of it with varying degrees of frustration and indifference, knowing from experience the futility of arguing his case against a group more interested in finding a scapegoat than assuming responsibility; moreover, he was thankful most of their abuse was verbal, with only the occasional shove or whack upside the head thrown in.

This time, however, Ben knew whatever censure was coming his way was justified, though that did not make anticipating it any easier.

A light backhand to his arm startled Ben out of his thoughts.

"Why the gloomy face?" Grim broke out with candid energy. "We just got ourselves a mini-holiday. Enjoy it while you can!"

Ben stared in confusion at his grinning partner. "I thought we were supposed to keep an eye on Mr. Atwood."

"Enough to keep him out of trouble," amended Grim, "or keep trouble from knocking on his door. So we just check-in somewhere decent, and drop by now and then just to make sure he's working like he's supposed to without any distractions. Easy, right? Come on! When was the last time you got some time off?"

"This past spring," answered Ben in earnest, "I came down with the flu and took sick-leave."

He failed to see why Grim found this funny; still, Ben smiled a little, influenced by his partner's mood, and overall glad that, for once, no one was yelling at him.

A light shower began to fall by the time they reached Main Street, which was showing signs of life in the form of a few cars parked on the opposite side, and a few customers entering or leaving Howard's Everything Store.

"I thought we were going to check-in somewhere first," Ben pointed out as Grim parked in front of the Tea Room.

"We can ask our local guide about that," said Grim, taking

a moment to run his fingers through his mussed hair. "Besides, we said we'd stop by on our way back."

A small bell jingled as they stepped into the Tea Room. Inside, the atmosphere was dim from a combination of dark walls and subdued lighting. Both men hesitated at the sight of empty tables and chairs, thinking perhaps Olivia had not yet returned from her errand. Then a familiar voice faintly called, "Be right there!" from the back room or kitchen, and after glancing at each other, the two men settled on a nearby table next to a large window.

They looked about while they waited, admiring the grotto-like interior, offset by light wooden floor, varnished tables, and copper lights that gave off a warm, orange glow. Though the room boasted large windows, any sunlight streaming through them was absorbed or tempered by the black walls.

Ben thought the setting mysterious and elegant, but it was Grim who gave voice to his thoughts.

"Handsome place you have here," he said to Olivia as she approached their table. She appeared to have expected them, or at least betrayed no sign of surprise on seeing them.

"Thanks," she answered placidly, and was about to say something when her eyes fell on Ben. "What happened to your face?"

The question surprised Ben into touching his face before the ensuing throb reminded him of the darkening bruise.

"Oh, it's just the container—I mean package we were carrying—to be delivered," he stammered, caught off guard. While he had no intention of lying, he did not wish to relay the incident as it had happened.

"I was carrying it like this," he went on disjointedly, hoping Grim would intervene and invent something to save him, "and it just slipped from my hands and just... smacked me in the face."

Olivia looked to Grim, who raised his hands in a resigned shrug.

"I kept telling him he couldn't carry it on his own, but would he listen?"

She nodded, evidently not buying the story but deciding to leave it at that. "I'll get you some ice for it."

"Oh, you don't have to," protested Ben. "We've iced it already."

"You sure? Maybe some arnica for the inflammation."

Ben acquiesced without the slightest clue what arnica was.

"Remind me to never ask you to cover up for me," said Grim with a wry smile as soon as Olivia was out of earshot.

Ben swallowed back a choice retort, merely expressing a faint groan as he hid his face in his hands. But there was little time to wallow in embarrassment, and soon Grim kicked him under the table to alert him that Olivia was coming back.

"Let's have a look," she said, setting a first aid pouch on the table.

Ben tipped his face up for her to examine the bruise. As he did, he was struck again by her looks, and a certain radiance that emanated from her serene features; whether it came by trick of light, dark surroundings, or bestowed by his hazy, imperfect vision, he could not say. All he knew was that her proximity, and the whiff of sandalwood it carried, was unexpectedly agitating. Growing self-conscious, he dropped his gaze, neither hearing what Olivia said next, nor realizing that he had answered it, until she began applying ointment on his cheek using a cotton swab.

In a sidelong gaze, Ben caught Grim looking at him, but it was hard to tell from that angle whether his expression was neutral or hiding a faint smile.

"Let me know if your eyes start to sting," said Olivia, dabbing the ointment around his eyes.

"No, this is nice," said Ben; then realizing how weird that sounded, he hastened to add: "you have a light touch."

"Comes with the territory," she enigmatically rejoined. The brief procedure was over in a minute, and after reconfirming the gentlemen's orders, Olivia retreated into the kitchen, leaving Ben to stare after her in a light trance. Then embarrassment set in, and he avoided looking at Grim, expecting to find the other man regarding him with a mixture of amusement and pity— the type of look that made him feel naive and inexperienced. Which, to some extent, he was.

In an effort to discourage socializing with outsiders, the organization, though it publicly condemned fraternizing amongst its staff, tacitly condoned it as the lesser of two evils, going so far as to arrange social events before turning a blind eye to their on-going affairs. The result was a corporate in-breeding program that bred more contempt than produced happy couples. And while the arrangement delighted trainees and rookies—as well as some of the older staff who attended those evenings like bull sharks on the watch for fresh blood— the monotony of seeing the same faces and doing the same things wore down on Ben, who moreover found his shy and serious disposition a barrier that kept him from finding compatible partners, and began to fill his evenings with extra work in hopes of earning a promotion.

Ruminating on this, Ben now saw how starved his experience had been; and in a way he began to understand Grim's conducting himself like a furloughing soldier on the lookout for opportunities. It was true that though the organization preferred its staff to keep their affairs internal, it did not explicitly bar them from seeking romantic partners outside the inner circle—as long as they understood that any security breach or leaked information stemming from that union would result in their, and their partner's, immediate disposal. Or as someone aptly put it, their ties to the organization doubled as a noose.

The idea of that slip knot sliding closer on any perceived treason haunted Ben. Except now that concern was effaced by Olivia's presence as she set down their order of tea and cake. Grim murmured a word of thanks, and began to eat, prompting Ben to do the same.

The cake was excellent, plain but rich in texture, with a mild sweetness that complimented the tea. Ben usually preferred coffee, but the tea was fragrant and warming, and he decided that the change was pleasant. He looked up to say as much to his partner, but found him staring down at the empty space to his left with brooding, half-closed eyes and a vertical line pinched between his drawn eyebrows. An uneaten morsel of cake was still stuck to his fork, leading Ben to wonder whether Grim had not liked the taste or found it off.

"Something wrong?" asked Ben.

The look disappeared as soon as Grim glanced up at him, much like it did when they were parked in front of the gas station store.

"Hm?" he murmured.

"Nothing," said Ben. "You just seemed preoccupied."

Grim shook his head. "Good cake—delicious," he said, bolting down his bite. And perhaps aware of how forced he sounded, the senior added, by way of shifting the subject: "She's probably got a secret name for you like she did with Atwood—'Squinty' or something."

"Shut up." Ben smiled with downcast eyes, secretly giddy at the possibility Olivia would spare him that much thought.

"A nearby motel?" asked Olivia, echoing the last few words of Grim's inquiry. She was in the process of removing their empty plates and cups when he posed the question; and as she paused to consider, he qualified: "Anything within a five- or ten-minute drive from here would be ideal."

"The closest one I know is in the next town, about a twenty-minute drive from here," she said after a moment.

"Nothing in town? No guesthouse or rooms for rent?"

"Not many people stay here, unless they're staying with relatives. We used to get a handful of campers and homeless people, but they've been scarce ever since the commune moved here."

"They don't like outsiders?" said Grim, having heard of them from the cashier at the convenience store.

She shrugged. "They're not violent or anything. Just territorial. They'd sooner chase off outsiders than hurt them. I guess they're worried someone might come in to reclaim the property or drive them away. Can't imagine how: they used to descend on Main Street in large groups—quite a sight in a borderline ghost town like this. Howard would shake his head and say 'if only they were tourists instead of barefoot bums.' With their numbers they could have wreaked all sorts of havoc here and no one could have stopped them. But Thane keeps them in check."

"Thane?" asked Grim as both he and Ben looked at her.

"Nathaniel Moorhouse—though he prefers we call him Thane—or other titles like Alpha or Apex..." She shrugged again, though without any derision, as if allowing for a benign oddity. "He's their leader—maybe even spiritual leader. For a while you'd find members panhandling on Main Street, but he stopped all that. He doesn't like the idea of charity. Whatever we give, he makes them pay back through work—any work.

He sends some of the women over to clean and help around. I don't mind because it gives me a chance to feed them whenever I have something to spare—especially if they bring their children along... Anyhow—what were we saying?"

CHAPTER 6

"So, what do we do now, sir?" asked Ben once they were outside the Tea Room.

Grim twisted his mouth to one side, nodding his head as he thought the matter over.

"I guess we buy ourselves a couple of sleeping bags and camp outside his cabin."

Ben regarded him with a touch of apprehension. The light rain had stopped, but all the same he wasn't sure he liked the idea of camping out. "Why not the motel, sir? I know it's kind of far but if we get up early enough, we can still come by first thing."

"I don't know, Ben. The more I think of it, the more I prefer we keep close. A couple of nights, at least, just to keep any mischief at bay."

"You're worried about Thane, sir?"

Grim, his eyes fixed on the stores across the street, gave a slight smile calculated to diminish the subject in question. "Wouldn't be wise to ignore a clown who expects to be called

Alpha. Plus, he said he'd be back. Let's just get what we need and head there. I'll get some gear from the Sporting Cabin. You grab provisions from the Everything Store—food, basic toiletries, and as many water bottles as you can carry."

With that, they split up, each going his own way. Outside the store, Ben passed by a group of strident high schoolers, who stood talking and laughing in front of the plate glass windows. One girl amongst them struck Ben as familiar. The transient look he swept their way did not give him a chance to see much, yet the notion that he had seen her before kept nagging him, even as he grabbed a basket and began weaving about the narrow aisles of the Everything Store.

The name was something of an embellishment for an otherwise ordinary convenience store. Nevertheless, his basket soon got full and heavy, and he lined up at the cashier, where he read colorful, hand-printed signs that said: "We deliver!" and "Ask our staff if you can't find what you're looking for!" alongside a more recent-looking one that read: "Due to rising temperatures, we will not be accepting bra or sock money."

Howard himself manned the register, a portly fellow who asked if Ben found everything he needed and then went on making small talk, asking where he was from, and how he liked the town while he rang up all the items. Ben's monosyllabic answers would have poorly satisfied any real curiosity, but they seemed sufficient to Howard, who hemmed and nodded in conversation.

When it was time to pay, Ben found himself a quarter short, but the difference was overlooked by Howard, who told Ben not to worry and wished him a nice day as he handed him his bag and receipt.

As he stepped out, Ben caught the high notes of a laugh

that reminded him of the stifled giggles he had heard behind Mr. Atwood's closed door.

He stopped to survey the group, fixing his attention on the girl laughing alongside a blond boy with dark eyebrows, who had his arm around her shoulder and was leaning in for a kiss.

She wore her red hair up and had put on a light jacket, but without a doubt it was the same girl, petite and bird-like, with a slightly receding chin and prominent eyes screened under lowered lids.

As she playfully ducked and turned her face, presenting a cheek to the boy's advances, she caught Ben staring at her. Her smile faded into a cold expression. She half-pushed, half-patted the boy, who in turn noticed Ben. But instead of assuming a hostile stare for the intrusion, the boy grinned and wrapped his other arm around the girl.

"Likes to watch, does he?" the boy jeered. "Likes what he sees, too? Wants a taste of this?" he sniggered, and feigned biting into her cheek.

The girl's mean expression grew tense, pinched into mild discomfort as she tried in vain to push the boy away, or pull herself out of his yoking embrace. She did this without any real effort, as if afraid to exhibit any resistance or come across as losing her cool. None of their friends intervened as the boy carried on; a couple of them even had the detached smiles of spectators watching some mundane comedy.

Ben quickly lowered his gaze and strode across the street towards the pick-up truck.

"Aw, come back," cried the boy after him. "Don't be shy! We're all friendly here."

His tone was closer to proposition than a threatening taunt, and Ben almost wished it was the second.

"Creep!" called another from the group amid the raucous derision.

When he got into the truck, Ben was surprised to find Grim already in the driver's seat, loading a pump-action shotgun.

"Is that necessary, sir?" he asked, nervously eyeing the business end of the barrel.

Grim fed two more shells into the loading slot. "It's just for crowd-control purposes, in case he decides to bring a few friends from his commune. Can't hurt to be prepared."

"What about your sidearm?"

"Mine was taken. Why do you think I went and bought this? What about you? What'd you get?"

"I got water," said Ben, pulling out one of six bottles. "And I thought you might like some iced tea, sir, so I got a few cans."

"Good man," said Grim off-handedly, which somehow pleased Ben as he went on listing: "Graham crackers, marshmallows—"

"Marshmallows?"

Ben shrugged. "Never tried them before, sir, but I hear they taste good toasted over a campfire."

Grim considered him with an ill-concealed smile. "Anything else?"

He thinks I'm an idiot, thought Ben, rummaging through the bag. *He's the one treating this like a vacation, yet I'm the idiot.* "Let's see… I got some soup—"

"Takeout?"

"Canned."

"Take them back."

"What? Why?"

"We've got nothing to heat them with."

"But, sir, you said you'd take care of it."

"They're not well stocked in that department. It's mostly hunting and fishing gear. All I got were a couple of sleeping bags, and some protection," said Grim, patting the shotgun resting across his lap.

Ben did not appreciate the fact it sat with the barrel aimed at him.

"Sir, please, put it away."

"Relax, I got the safety on," said Grim; just the same, he obliged the nervous young man. "Take the soup cans back," he said, securing the firearm behind their seats. "Get some buns and a pack of hot dogs—condiments too."

Ben made a face. "Hot dogs, sir?"

"What's wrong with hot dogs now?"

"Do you have any idea what goes into them?"

Grim sighed, obviously not in the mood to argue. "Sit tight," he said, opening the truck door and jumping to the pavement.

"Where are you going, sir?"

"To get sandwiches from the Tea Room."

Half-an-hour later, Grim parked the pick-up truck just off the cabin's driveway, where he could get a clear view of the front door and some of the windows. He told Ben to stay inside while he disembarked and ran up to the front door. This time it was Mr. Atwood who answered it, and though he could not hear their conversation, Ben surmised from their pantomimes that Grim was letting Mr. Atwood know of their presence. The specialist nodded emphatically, blocking the doorway to keep Grim from entering—going so far as to almost push him away when Grim craned forward and tried to sneak a peek inside the cabin.

"It occurs to me, sir, that we could just ask Mr. Atwood if

we can stay with him," said Ben as soon as Grim returned, leaving Atwood to slam the front door shut.

"We could, 'cept the chief doesn't want us under the same roof. Whatever we delivered, it's still off limits to us—and by extension, so is the nature of his research."

"I noticed you were trying to look inside, sir."

Grim shrugged indifferently. "Just making sure he wasn't hiding any unwelcome guests."

"I saw the girl who was with him earlier."

"Where?" Grim turned to the cabin, bobbing and weaving as he scanned the windows for a glimpse of her.

"Back on Main Street, in front of the grocery store."

"Oh," said Grim, and he seemed to have lost interest in her as a subject until he asked: "Was she with someone?"

Ben considered the crowd she was with, struggling to categorize them. "I guess she was hanging out... with her friends."

Grim caught the note of uncertainty but said nothing.

Not our business, not our concern, thought Ben, invoking an off-shoot of the injunction that they were not to interact with anyone unless absolutely necessary.

As time wore on, the brown bag containing sandwiches from the Tea Room grew more conspicuous. The sun had shifted from its noon position and was weaving its shimmering light through a thick canopy of branches. Ben hesitated a few times, reaching for the bag before snatching his hand back for fear of taking liberties by eating ahead of his senior, who sat chewing gum in silence, his chair pushed back and one booted leg propped against the dash. The young man tried to cover his spasmodic act of reaching and retracting by pretending to shift in his seat, until Grim, without taking his eyes off the cabin, murmured: "Stop fidgeting and eat already."

Ben did as was told, taking his time unwrapping the crisp parchment paper (a far cry from the plastic wrapped vending machine fare!) admiring the neat cross-section of turkey, cheese, and an unknown red sauce which a moment later he identified as cranberry, and savoring the fact that Olivia prepared them with her own hands. In his mind, he traveled back to the Tea Room, with its easy elegance, its quiet atmosphere replete with mystery—

Just like its owner, concluded Ben with a wistful smile.

Grim soon followed suit, unwrapping a sandwich, taking big, distracted bites washed down with gulps of ice tea.

"What do you think it is?" he muttered, rousing Ben from a daydream.

The sandwich was gone but there was still some tea left in the can which Grim held aloft in one drooping hand.

"It's a kraken, that's what it is," he went on, answering his own question in a whisper so low that Ben hardly heard the response. "It's a kraken, I know it's a kraken. It's a damn kraken," he repeated, sounding more on edge with every varied reiteration.

"A kraken, sir?"

Grim, seeming to snap out of something, regarded Ben with mild surprise, as if he had forgotten the young man was sitting there.

"What about this kraken, sir?" asked Ben to cover the embarrassed silence.

The surprised look lingered a little, morphing into bafflement as Grim turned his vacant gaze towards the cabin again. Finally, he said: "You know what a kraken is?"

"It's a mythological creature, isn't it?" answered Ben with a vague suspicion that this wasn't the answer Grim was seeking.

"How about a globster?" said the senior, his eyes fixed

on Ben, searching for any involuntary sign of recognition. "Maybe that's what they call it in your circle. No? Come on—I'm sure someone brought it up—maybe friends from other departments."

"I don't have many friends, sir," said Ben. "I had some in training, but we all got assigned to different departments and—well, everyone is busy with their own thing."

"And before that?"

"I was in Tomia Academy."

"You're feral alum?" asked Grim with a hint of interest, or perhaps recognition.

"We prefer not to use that term, sir."

The senior shrugged. "No shame in that: ninety-five percent of kids attending there come from poor neighborhoods or foster care."

"I know we're sponsored," continued Ben, still following his own line of thought, "but we still pay our dues."

"By signing up, no less," interjected Grim.

"We're employed, we got a career and a future—"

"Everyone's a success story," the older man dismally concluded.

Ben was annoyed at that. "What did you expect, sir? I doubt you'll find many staff members who answered an ad and came in for an interview."

"No, they want their own breed of workers," Grim agreed, crossing his arms and leaning back in his seat. "And theirs is the most efficient way of going about it: start them young..."

"You don't approve, sir?"

The senior shot him a crooked grin, recognizing the trap question and deflecting it. "Would you rather have stayed in foster care?"

Ben dropped his gaze in a plaintive look. "I'm not sure why I was even in foster care. I was only seven back then, but I know my parents were alive at the time. I don't remember celebrating birthdays. Either we were too poor, or they might have been too out of it to remember. The only reason I know I was seven is because I've seen my birth certificate."

The remark impressed his senior, who regarded him with something like awe as he sat up. "Birth certificate? Where? How?"

"I knew this woman from the Archive Department. We went out for a while, and on my birthday she presented me with a copy of my birth certificate."

Grim gave a low whistle. "What did she want in return?"

"What?"

"You know, she must have called you later for something?"

Ben smiled uncertainly. "You mean like—"

"Like a service or favor—pull some strings here or there."

"Oh!" Ben gave a short laugh. "No, not at all! Why would she do that?"

"It's just SOP," answered Grim with a shrug. "A watch or tie clip is a gift. But a birth certificate? That's not easy to come by. She probably wanted something in return."

"I doubt it, sir," the young man rejoined, a touch resentful. "I'm just a floater—I don't have clout or anything worthwhile to offer in return."

Grim pondered over this, rapping his knuckles on the wheel before conceding with a nod. "Then she must have really liked you if she did that."

"She did... I mean, she's really nice. We're still on good terms, even if we don't see each other anymore."

"Is she available?"

Ben didn't like the look any more than the question that accompanied it. "I don't think she'd be interested, sir. When we last spoke, she said she had enough on her plate."

"Oh," said Grim, going back to watching the cabin, showing signs of falling into vigilant silence.

"Well?" asked Ben.

"Well what?" Grim asked in return.

"You didn't tell me your side of things, sir. Did they extricate you from foster care? Are you feral like us?"

There was a subtle shift in mood more tangible in Grim's answer.

"I don't remember."

"You don't remember?"

Grim's gaze roved across the dashboard, never fixing on one direction. "Maybe just snatches here and there—like leftovers from a dream—this boy I knew who had the same name…"

"Let me guess: Dogdaddy?" said Ben with a strained laugh, thinking he managed to beat his senior to the punchline.

Except Grim did not answer with a sheepish "you-got-me" smile, and instead appeared as if emerging from some murky shaft his mind had fallen into.

He fetched a deep breath and gave a resigned shrug. "Might as well be for all I remember."

CHAPTER 7

They passed the remainder of the day in the same spot, allowing short intervals for each to get out and stretch his legs or relieve himself. The latter was new to Ben, who was handed a small shovel for digging a six-inch deep hole and burying his business. Grim, catching the look of chagrin on the young man's face, smiled with a hint of malice.

"It's not all fireside stories and marshmallows, scout," he said, leaning out the window to pat Ben's head.

"I never said it was," weakly countered Ben as he turned and trudged into the woods.

"Leave a rock over your spot once you're done," called Grim out the window. "Don't get lost. And watch out for bears," he added, which Ben took for a joke. At least he hoped it was. The woods certainly sounded more alive than they did that morning. Now and then they heard a branch snap, or caught the reverberating echo of something in the distance, but when nothing came of it after the fifth or sixth time, they were less inclined to start up—or, in Grim's case, reach for his gun.

As afternoon crawled towards evening, and the weather

grew cold, they shifted their post and sat outside. Grim built a small campfire, found a couple of plastic chairs discarded near the lakeshore, and presently sat with booted feet extended freely towards the fire, whittling away at a stick.

Ben, on the other hand, was too nettled with minor bothers to appreciate the great outdoors. A dull, persistent headache radiated from his bruised eye; his feet remained cold, even after encasing himself in a sleeping bag as Grim had advised; the deceptively white chair had smudged his white shirt and khakis; and he was convinced wet-wipes and sanitizer were inadequate means of cleaning himself up. Much as he would have liked to air his grievances, he doubted Grim would offer a sympathetic ear. Instead, his senior kept whistling and whittling away at the same damn stick, now and then twirling it slowly between long, blackened fingers.

"Are we going to stay rooted to this spot?" grumbled Ben, trying to keep a shiver out of his voice as he held his hands to the fire. "You know if Thane had any intention of returning, he would have done that hours ago."

Grim said nothing and kept whittling.

"I'm sure Mr. Atwood is reasonable enough to keep his door and windows locked," Ben carried on. "He doesn't need us here guarding him like he's in witness protection."

Grim said nothing and kept whittling.

Ben glanced at the stick, shaved like a pencil with a long tapering point.

"Making arrows now, sir? Are we going to catch some wild game here? Is that what we're doing?" he went on, hoping to provoke an answer or even an angry outburst out of his senior partner.

Still keeping his head bent over his work, Grim finally spoke up.

"If you're unhappy with the arrangement, you can call HQ and tell them to pick you up. They could send a replacement. Better yet, they could just let me stay until they're satisfied. Here—" he stood up and handed Ben the sharpened twig— "stick it in your marshmallow."

Ben followed Grim with his eyes as he walked by, fighting the urge to hurl the stick after him. This was far from the holiday Grim made it out to be—unless he loathed the work environment to the extent that even this was preferable to him. Ben on the other hand would have traded this for a day of interminable meetings—at least meetings involved bathroom breaks with indoor plumbing.

He stared longingly at the cabin, with all the amenities it contained, and puzzled over the type of work taking place there, and the secrecy surrounding it. Already it was growing dark and the windows were not even lit. The more he deliberated on it, the stranger it all seemed.

His line of thought was interrupted by Grim handing him a wrapped half of turkey sandwich, manna from the Tea Room. Ben thanked him as he accepted it. The sandwich was cold but still fresh, and his mood lifted somewhat after eating, enough to attempt another conversation with Grim.

"What do you think he's up to in there?"

Grim did not answer, but followed Ben's gaze to stare up at the building they both were forbidden to enter, and it was evident his senior was just as clueless as he was.

Was he though, wondered Ben, remembering Grim's muttering about a kraken or something, with unaccountable vehemence. But growing tired of posing questions and getting ignored for them, Ben instead turned to his own thoughts, which inexorably carried him towards the owner of the Tea Room.

He tried to analyze what made her so compelling to him, wherein lay the points of attraction, and what made her plain and striking by turns? He could no more hope to answer it than capture light with his hands. Even as he tried to conjure an image of her, his mind could only recall faint impressions, the inadequacy of which made him yearn to see her next morning.

Perhaps he would too, if he could convince Grim to let him drive there to get breakfast. There was no reason why he wouldn't, recalcitrant as he was. But before that came the question of sleep, or rather who would sleep first while the other remained vigil.

"I'll stay up," volunteered Grim. "You go to sleep. I'll wake you up after midnight and then you can keep watch."

Ben opened his eyes to a pitch-black night. It took him a moment to remember where he was and recognize the person bending over him, shaking his shoulder to wake him up; but his memory soon returned when Grim threatened to roll him off the truck bed and shake him out of his sleeping bag.

More welcoming was the red coffee thermos, which sat by the glowing fire waiting for him.

"Where did you get that?" Ben suspiciously asked, thinking Grim might have abandoned his post to go back to the Tea Room.

"Mr. Atwood was kind enough to offer it a couple of hours ago. Go ahead, I already drank some to keep warm."

"That's very nice of him," said Ben as he began unscrewing the top; and after pausing to sigh appreciatively over after the rich, invigorating scent, he went on to say: "I guess he's thankful we're here to keep him safe."

"Well, it took some persuasion," said Grim, scratching his bristled jaw, "but he came to see it that way."

Ben noticed the shotgun Grim carried in one hand, and formed a clear enough idea of the stipulation involved. Not long after, he retired to the truck bed, leaving Ben with the injunction to feed the fire and keep it going.

Left to himself, Ben soon recalled his other duty: Logging his observations on his senior. It was odd that no one had called or texted to remind him about it—unless their extended stay was taken into consideration, and his supervisor had excused the delay on that account. At any rate, Ben thought it best to call as soon as possible and log an entry while his observations were still fresh in his mind.

He waited half-an-hour, allowing time for Grim to fall into a deep sleep while he mentally rehearsed his report. Then, using his phone's flashlight, Ben stole deep into the woods, making sure he was out of earshot before he called the number he was given, waited for the beep, and began recording.

"This is an assessment of Subject 6753-2, who had chosen for this mission to go by the handle Grim and shall henceforth be referred to by that name. Grim and I made our way…"

When he returned to the campsite, Ben thought it curious how dim his surroundings were, speculating that perhaps his temporary absence had recalibrated his vision. But as he soon discovered, the fire was dying out.

He rushed towards it, cursing himself for forgetting to feed it before he left, and began piling sticks onto the red embers. But in their damp state, they smothered the fire instead of rekindling it.

Knowing Grim would suspect something, Ben frantically searched for something to fan the embers. His eyes fell on the red thermos sitting by the dead fire, and seized by a desperate wish to cover his guilt, he unscrewed the top and doused the pile of twigs and ashes with coffee, making it seem like the thermos had accidentally overturned, spilling its contents onto the fire.

Having successfully covered his traces, Ben was left with the question of keeping himself warm for the next five hours. All he had was the pick-up truck, which on reflection offered a sensible shelter: too tight to comfortably sleep in, but dry and far better than shivering outdoors.

He managed to climb in and close the door without disturbing his sleeping partner—who unaccountably slept like a log on the hard truck bed—and sat facing Atwood's cabin.

The windows were dark, save for the occasional weak flare in the second story, which Ben took for bathroom lights, waxing and waning as the door opened and closed.

He heard a splash in the distance, frowned a little, and leaned forward, straining to see the patch of water beyond the cabin and surrounding trees. But under a moonless sky the lake was a pool of ink that gave up no secrets; and as he settled back, Ben soon saw the weak light flare again in the second story then disappear.

The sky was ashen pink by the time Ben's eyelids rolled back up again. He did not bolt up, but sat back, weighed by the sinking feeling that he had slept through the remainder of his watch. Then panic broke, and he stumbled bleary-eyed out of the truck and hurtled towards the lake to slap some water on his face. The commotion must have stirred his senior, who called for him in the bewildered accent of one jolted awake.

"I'm here, sir," Ben called over his shoulder, using the front of his shirt to wipe his face as he ran back.

Grim, expecting a crisis, had already kicked off his sleeping bag, and shotgun in hand hopped out of the truck bed in his black t-shirt and shorts.

"What happened?" he demanded as soon as he saw Ben.

"Nothing, nothing!" cried the latter. "Everything's fine, sir," he added, catching his breath as he surveyed the cabin. Touched by the rosy dawn, the pristine face with its closed windows seemed to attest to this.

"Where's Atwood?" asked Grim.

"In his house, I guess," stammered Ben. "I mean I'm sure he is, sir." He turned to follow his senior's gaze, and his heart gave a painful wrench when he saw the front door standing ajar.

Grim pushed past Ben, who stared after him in stunned silence. Panic and dread had so emptied his mind that it fixed on the trail of faint prints Grim's feet left on the moist dirt.

"Atwood!" called Grim, sounding distant to Ben, who looked up and realized that he had entered the cabin.

Ben followed him in, too distraught to have any qualms about trespassing.

The door must have been open for a while: outside air had penetrated the foyer; the smooth floorboards, gleaming with approaching daylight, were glacier cold to the touch. A dread, immaculate calm covered the entire house that neither of them thought to speak. What could they say? What was there to say when they found the house in perfect order with its sole inhabitant lying face down on the blood-soaked carpet of his living room?

CHAPTER 8

The sight of the body did not sicken Ben. Not right away. Guilt was what got him: the mounting consequences rising in his throat, and the truth which would inevitably come spilling out.

He took refuge in a nearby bush, fell to his hands and knees, and began to retch.

Feverish and freezing cold, he kneeled panting over his mess, too weak to swat away the feathery branches that caressed his cheek like crawling flies. The image induced another heave, though his hollowed stomach had already emptied itself.

Eventually he crawled backwards, leaned on a nearby tree trunk to raise himself to his feet, and somehow managed to trudge back to the cabin.

Grim seemed to have forgotten about him. Or else he may have disappeared to deal with his own bout of nausea. But no—from upstairs came a grinding groan of something heavy being dragged across the floor. This was followed by a loud clatter of several objects falling to the floor.

The noise stopped Ben partway up the stairs, wondering

whether his senior was throwing things in a fit of anger. To have never seen him lose his temper made it all the more terrible.

Seized with compunction, Ben held on to the banister as he lowered himself and sat on the narrow stairs. Something throbbed in his throat—not his knocking heart—not another bout of nausea, but something that produced a thin, wheezing sound with every intake of breath. He did not even react to the toes prodding his back until he heard Grim ordering him to get up.

"On your feet. We need to find it."

The tone surprised Ben: urging, but not quite angry.

"Find what, sir?" he asked in a dry, cracked voice that he himself could barely hear.

Grim gave him another push with his foot until Ben made room to let him pass.

"The cargo," answered the senior on his way down, jumping over the last few steps. In a few seconds, the ruckus started again in the kitchen, shot with Grim's occasional swearing.

Next to him, Ben felt like a snail, dragging his feet as he stepped into the living room only to stop short at the sight of Mr. Atwood's prone body.

Though face down, the head was partly turned to show a single eye, cloudy and fearfully round, forever fixed in its empty stare. Ben's mind balked at the notion that it was a body, a vacated thing that was no longer Mr. Atwood.

"The hell you staring at?" Grim yelled when he emerged from the kitchen and found Ben standing idle.

"Mr. Atwood..." Ben managed to say, his unblinking eyes screwed upon the bloodless hand.

Grim snatched a blanket off the couch and threw it over the body. "Now move. Search for it: Cargo, container—anything. Just look!"

And without waiting for a response, the senior pushed past him and attacked the living room. It wasn't twenty minutes before every conceivable storage and hiding space in the cabin was turned inside out.

Finally, Grim stepped away from a ransacked coat closet. He moved slowly, his hands clasped over his head, his face devoid of emotion.

"It's gone," he said with terrible calm that lay like a heavy slab over Ben, who a moment later visibly flinched when Grim bellowed his name.

In such small quarters, and with many overturned pieces of furniture, the young man had no chance of escaping his senior's wrath.

"How did this happen?" he demanded, seizing Ben's arm.

"Sir, I don't know, I swear! I didn't see anything!"

"The fire was out when I got up," said Grim, tightening his hold. "I told you to maintain it. Is there something you want to tell me?"

"I- I accidentally spilled coffee on it," Ben stammered, trying to control the erratic pitch of his voice.

"Don't you lie to me, Ben. You start keeping things from me and it's not gonna end well."

Ben managed to check a fluttering laugh, turning it into a tense smile as he floundered through a series of false starts, wildly wavering between giving up the truth and covering it.

"Sir, I swear, I didn't see Thane, or- or Mr. Atwood, or anyone at all!" he maintained. "I mean, we have to en- entertain other possibilities, like someone being in the house long before we came back. Or maybe he climbed in from the other side of the cabin."

As he spoke, he tried to wrest his arm free, and managed to

release it for a fraction of a second before Grim caught him by the shirt and slammed him against the wall.

"Bullshit, Ben. Bullshit!" the senior barked, rattling him with a repeated slam. "You're telling me someone managed to climb out the window, carrying a container that big, without making the slightest noise or drawing attention?"

"S- Sir, I just remembered!" Ben cried out, his voice thin and ragged. "I heard a splash sometime yesterday."

"A splash?" repeated Grim, slightly easing the arm he had lengthwise pressed to Ben's collar.

"Yes, sir. From the lake."

Grim searched his face. "How big of a splash?"

"It was... it was several yards away so I'm not sure. But that's gotta be significant if I was able to hear it all the way—"

There was no point in finishing his sentence when halfway through it, Grim left him and ran out to sweep the lakeshore.

And incapable of remaining on his feet, Ben staggered to the sofa, where he collapsed and sat with his head hovering between his knees, listening to the faint splashing outside as Grim waded through the shallow waters.

The senior returned about a minute later, tracking wet footprints across the wooden floor.

Ben sprang to his feet in time to avoid Grim's flipping the couch on him.

"Yes, sir, I'll go outside and search," he mumbled with downcast eyes, making for the door.

"Don't bother! Nothing out there but sunken trash."

"It sounded small, sir," Ben remarked, offering a detail he wouldn't have volunteered when the focus was on the container, or something approaching its size; and as Grim cast him a sidelong look signifying his awareness of this convenient lapse, Ben weakly added: "Might be important, sir. What if it's the murder weapon?"

"I doubt it. The man's throat was slashed and he bled to death."

"Oh," murmured Ben, rubbing his own throat with an agonized glance in the direction of Atwood. "What are we going to do now, sir?"

"I guess we roll him up in a carpet and keep him out of sight."

Ben turned to Grim, who stood regarding the shrouded body, and whose untied hair, modest attire of t-shirt and shorts, and absurd expression of mild inconvenience invested him with the quotidian air of a homeowner who came down one morning to discover the mess his dog had made.

"I think we'd better report it, sir, and await further instructions."

"We need to retrieve the cargo, first."

"But, sir, it's a security breach!"

"So, stick your finger in it!" Grim broke out. "It's bad enough Atwood was killed on our watch. If they find out their precious cargo's missing, we'll both be drawn and quartered."

The argument robbed Ben of any resistance. Throughout the morbid process of wrapping Atwood's body in the living room carpet and hiding it behind the rearranged furniture, Ben hung on the words "our" and "we", implying a shared blame and consequence, when Grim could have justifiably said "your" and "you". No doubt it was the pragmatic view of the situation: the one in command usually bore the majority of the responsibility; and yet Ben was so used to associates and seniors saving face by pinning the blame on him that it seemed almost incredible to work with one willing to shoulder some of the blame.

What if Grim said it to earn his cooperation in covering up the matter? But that made little sense when Ben was the negligent one who stood to lose more than his senior did. Then again, being on probation meant that Grim himself was on thin ice…

While Ben was turning the matter over in his mind, Grim had gone upstairs to wash up and found himself a flannel-lined shirt jacket, which he wore with the same jeans he had on yesterday.

He came downstairs and bade Ben to do the same, allowing him five minutes to wash his face and put on something clean.

On his way to the bathroom, Ben passed by Atwood's cramped bedroom, catching sight of the overturned mattress, strewn books and other personal items. Sunlight streamed through the window, irradiating the general disarray, and he felt an arbitrary sense of pity for the man to whom these small things had once been a source of comfort, and were now tossed aside.

Ben had never had an intimate brush with death, was never exposed to the rites involved. These matters were taken care of by the organization, covering everything from termination to aftermath; to him death was as abstract as birth, a private, mysterious affair taking place behind closed doors—a new being arrives unbidden just as a person abruptly departs. And perhaps it was this ignorance that bestowed the whole situation with a sense of unreality. Shock had given way to numbness, even as he assisted Grim in stowing the body, so that now he felt an urge to go downstairs, unroll the carpet, and look at the body again.

But five minutes could only be stretched so far, and instead of lingering, he headed to the bathroom, undressed and washed up, wishing he had time for a shower. Just the same, he was glad for a chance to freshen up, trading his wilted shirt for a clean one, and his stained khakis for brown corduroys. He did this with something like reverence, reflecting on himself and how he would have liked to have his personal belongings treated in his absence, picking up and putting back some of the scattered clothes, not out of any deep sentiment, but out of instinctive respect coupled with some inert guilt.

He found a Navy wool blazer which he thought would be useful to wear against the cold weather, and was trying it on when the cordless phone began to ring. Ben stared at the red blinking light, wondering who could be calling, and whether he should answer it or let it ring.

It stopped on the third ring, after which Ben heard Grim's muffled voice from the kitchen downstairs.

"Yeah, we ended up coming back here," said Grim, his voice rising in conversation as Ben came downstairs and stood in the kitchen doorway, pushing back the blazer's overlong sleeves.

"Mr. Atwood was kind enough to let us spend the night here," Grim went on, utilizing the cordial, workman tone he assumed whenever he spoke with strangers. "Oh, we just unrolled our sleeping bags and slept on the floor... Mr. Atwood? No, he's had a rough night and he's all bundled up now, dead to the world... What? Oh, we'll just swing by to pick it up for him... It's no trouble. Alright. See you in a bit."

"Who was it, sir?" Ben asked as soon as Grim replaced the handset.

"Olivia, from the Tea Room. She called to see if Atwood wanted his usual order for breakfast, and was offering to have it delivered. I told her we'd pick it up for him."

"Sir, what about the cargo?"

"What about it?" said Grim as he rose to leave.

"What do you mean, what about it? Sir!" Ben expostulated, starting after Grim, who stalked out of the cabin without answering and was getting into the truck.

CHAPTER 9

The early morning waxed fair, promising clear blue skies as they drove to town. No words were exchanged between the two, and on Ben's side, the silence was partly shamefaced, though he also felt that to listen to anything besides the hum of the pick-up's cabin would be too grating for his nerves. His eyes lit on the scenery that passed them by, from thin streams braiding through mossy rocks to scintillating outlines of sun-backed trees, fixating on all the fine details of grain and texture in hopes of drowning out the thoughts that made his feet restless, and his cold hands twitch between his knees.

Main Street, though never bustling, was once again deserted. Like yesterday, Olivia was busy sweeping the Tea Room floor when they arrived. She greeted them with her latent smile and general air of unbowed serenity as she handed them Atwood's breakfast in a medium-sized paper bag, asking if they wanted anything as well.

Grim, passing the bag to Ben, asked where they could find Thane. Their hurry was such that they remained in the pick-up with the engine running, ready to drive off as soon as they received directions.

"Got some business with Thane?" asked Olivia with detached curiosity.

"Just a private matter I need to take care of on Mr. Atwood's behalf." Grim smiled in return. "See, Thane's been to his house yesterday, and it seems he borrowed something that Mr. Atwood is anxious to get back."

Olivia looked from him to Ben, who slid back in his seat to hide his face from view.

"We would have asked Mr. Atwood for directions," Grim continued, sensing her doubt, "only we didn't want to disturb him."

"I can give you directions," she said after another pause, "but unless he invited you over, I doubt he'll let you in."

"That's fine. We just want to talk to him."

"No, you don't understand, I meant let you enter the compound."

"He owns the property?" asked Grim.

"About as much as your local delinquents own the junk yard," answered Olivia with a shrug. "Not that it keeps him from being territorial about it. Then again, no one came by to kick them out. I suppose it's not implausible that he bought it, even if he doesn't believe in cash commerce. At any rate, he won't let anyone in unless he invited them—or they offer him something."

"You mean like a service?"

"Or an offering in the literal sense."

Grim looked around, as though searching for something that would answer for an offering. "We're a little short on livestock," he concluded after his brief survey.

"So you are," agreed Olivia. "But what they're aching for is food, medicine, and clean water. They live by the lake, and I'm pretty sure that's their main water source, which can't be good since the lake's not fit for swimming in, let alone drinking. They forage and try to grow things, but I doubt they can thrive on that. Thane wants the commune to be self-sufficient; he disdains charity about as much as cash, but even he can't afford to turn away provisions. He'll probably let you in if you provide something in return."

"How do you know all this?"

"Sometimes a member or two come by to help around with some of the chores—didn't I tell you this? It's Thane's idea of paying me back for the food I give them—mostly items I can't sell because they're no longer fresh."

"You think you can spare a little something for us to take? The stores are closed, and we're a little short on time. Anything you have, we're willing to take—I mean buy—unless you frown on money too."

"I'm not enough of an idealist to shun cash," she answered with her approach to a jaunty smile.

After procuring a cardboard box containing a bag of flour, two dozen eggs, a bottle of cooking oil, and a few gallons of filtered water, the two men drove back, taking a diverging road that curved along the other side of the lake.

"What do we plan on doing, sir?"

"We find Thane. We make him think we've brought a peace offering. Then we grab him and make him cough up the cargo. After that, we call HQ, report the situation, and tell them we have the creep in custody. Best case scenario, we get away with a slap on the wrist."

"But what if he doesn't have it, sir? I mean, how can you be sure he's the one who took it?"

"Because he has the look of a kid who wants your shiny toy—or whatever shiny thing he's not privy to see. We don't know what the cargo is," Grim added, unclasping the steering wheel to straighten his fingers in a minute shrug. "Could be experimental drugs, or an advanced filtering system, or research documents he thinks he can sell—or barter for something…"

"Last night you said something about a kraken, sir."

"I say a lot of shit," said Grim. "Anyway, even if it's worthless to him, he could have taken it as a trophy. If he sees himself as a so-called 'Alpha', you can bet your career he's sore over the bum's rush he got yesterday. Wouldn't put it past him to get back at Atwood, thinking it was his idea."

"Poor Mr. Atwood," murmured Ben, visited by a fresh pang of guilt.

"Poor nothing!" snapped Grim. "The man was either trouble, or slouching towards trouble. Should've known better than to get involved with that prick. But never mind him—what's in the bag?"

"What's that, sir?"

"That bag you're clutching like it's full of bankrolls."

"Oh," said Ben, unrolling the top of the wide paper bag and peering inside. "There's a muffin, and coffee and uh—" removing the lid from a round container—"Eggs benedict."

"You can have the eggs. I'll take the muffin," said Grim.

The road terminated at an iron gate, where two bored-looking men stood guard, one shouldering a rifle, the other holding a shotgun which he leveled at the approaching vehicle.

Grim stopped the truck just a few feet short of the vine tangled spokes, lowered the window, and when asked to state his business told the guards he was delivering goods from Olivia.

The shotgun-wielding guard nodded to his friend to go back and check, keeping his weapon trained on the two as he ordered them to get out and place their hands on the vehicle.

"Didn't expect high security—you guys storing warheads in there?" Grim bantered as he was searched.

The guard ignored him, chewing a wad of something and working his jaw with bovine leisure before moving on to search Ben, who raised his hands and declared he was not carrying anything, hoping to get out of it.

"It's not an option, scout," vainly warned his senior, the point being driven home by the guard, who slammed Ben against the hood of the truck, kicking his legs apart to frisk him.

Having rummaged through the box of provisions, the rifleman reported back to his buddy that all was clear, after which the shotgun bearer said they could go in but had to leave the truck outside.

Grim tried to argue that it would be faster to drive in and deliver everything.

The guards refused, saying that they would be more than happy to take it off their hands if they couldn't carry it in.

Ben caught the slight jaw clench Grim made before conceding. He parked the pick-up to one side, making sure it was locked before taking the box of provisions. Ben walked by him, carrying a sloshing gallon of water in each hand.

Beyond the gates, they passed by a wooden sign on which the original welcome message was effaced with black-painted print that read: "Here I stay."

Ahead of it loomed the resort, a two-story neoclassical building. From a distance, one could see traces of its former grandeur, though the apparition soon vanished under dried weather stains weeping down a cracked facade, and clumps of ivy creeping through shattered windows.

Children roamed the overgrown lawn, never straying far from the adults, who were either sitting or manning small portable grills, where over live coals they grilled mushrooms, potatoes, small fish and ropes of meat or organs skewered with sharpened twigs. Smaller children gathered there too, some carried by their mothers in one arm or a sling, or held back from standing too close, drawn by the glowing heat and rising smoke, more interested in the process of preparing food than eating it. Though most of the adults were adequately dressed in frayed or faded clothes, their children wore either an oversized t-shirt or ill-fitting trousers, cinched at the waist with a cord and trimmed to accommodate their small stature. The discordant layers of talk, wails and household clanks of enamelware were sometimes pierced by shrill cries or laughter rising from a group of children surrounding a bathtub (somehow relocated outside) where they stood splashing a distressed piglet, either trying to give it a bath or drown it.

Dozens of eyes stared at the two strangers and the things they carried, a wave-like sequence of heads looking up from their various occupations to stare at the approaching pair, warily following them with their gaze as they walked past. No one stepped forward, much less charged at them to claim the provisions that fixed their interest, though that didn't stop a few individuals from standing at the ready, as though waiting for some signal to lunge forward and snatch the prize.

Ben furtively scanned the stony faces turned to him, seeking out the man they came to see. He bumped into Grim who had suddenly stopped in front of him.

"Any of you can tell me where I can find Mr. Moorhouse?" he shouted, looking around at the gathering crowd. "We've got a delivery here for him."

A woman with frizzy white hair in a simple cotton dress approached them.

"What's your business with ba'al?" she asked in a gruff voice, pretending not to glance at the contents of the box.

"We're looking for Mr. Moorhouse," Grim answered.

"That is what you call him. He has many names, my ba'al."

Grim, who stood a head taller, looked down at her through a brief frown before nodding slowly.

"The lady from the Tea Room sent these," he continued with a returning semblance of a smile. "She said some folks here were in the family way and could use the extra rations."

The woman scrutinized him, squinting in the sun, holding back her answer, perhaps trying to unnerve the truth out of him.

"Very kind of her," she finally said in a tone that was anything but grateful. "I'll take it from here."

"Oh, it's no trouble," said Grim, dipping the box out of her reach and taking a step back in one deft move. "We were told to hand it to Mr. Moorhouse himself if you could take us to him."

She glowered at him, evidently not appreciating the answer, and she made them wait outside while she entered the building to check if they could see him.

In the interval, the two men stood shifting the weight of their load from one arm to the other, and the crowd broke up, most of them returning to their respective occupation. Somewhere in their midst came a voice that hissed: "make it—make it bleed, oh, make it bleed! make it bleed, make it bleed, make it bleed…"

Ben felt a gentle tug on one of the gallon bottles, and looked down to find a child placing both hands on it, trying to claim it for herself. Thankfully her father stepped in to carry her off without so much as a glance at Ben. A minute later the white-haired woman came back and bade them follow her into the cavernous lobby, where a shattered chandelier formed a centerpiece amid green saplings, shooting through cracks in the floor, seeking sunlight that poured through tall French windows.

Behind them, other men and women came in, filing in and seating themselves on the floor. This confused the two men, who stood looking about at the gathering congregation. Soon the crowd formed a semi-circle or horseshoe curve, surrounding an empty chair set on a low platform before the tall French windows.

Grim glanced at Ben with a philosophical eyebrow raise that said: "Might as well..." before setting down the box and sitting cross-legged on the floor. As Ben did the same, a ripple of turning heads marked the entrance of the chief figure, who stepped amongst his seated people with arms spread low, letting his splayed fingers incidentally skim over heads and scalps as he passed them by.

Ben happened to sit along his path, and though he shrank away, Thane's fingertips still grazed through his hair, passing on an unaccountable shiver.

Thane shortly reached his elevated seat, where he sat leaning on his elbow, scanning the gathered mass, waiting for the last whispers of parents hushing their children to die out. His face was darkened by the sun blazing through the windows behind him, blending his outline with that of his makeshift throne. And when silence fell on the great hall, he straightened himself and spoke.

"We had a harsh winter and a rough spring. But we managed to pull through. Together with the surrounding green, we flourished under the summer sun. I promised you land fertile, free, and ripe for the taking. I delivered. I said that we were going to establish ourselves on the bones and ruins of others. And now look at us: Like mighty trees taking root, we will grow on these rich remains. We will rise and prosper. This spot used to draw pleasure-seeking hedonists, and because it no longer lives up to their standards, they have shunned it, just like they have shunned you. They are blind to its potential. Well! I see that potential. I see that potential in you, in us, in this land. Years from now they will want to come to our gardens, but they will be barred. They will be kept out. They will be kept out because they are poison. Their economy impoverished you. Their medicine sickened you and your children. Their system was rigged to serve the elite, and suck the life and resources away from the rest of us—to stupefy our children and thwart their potential. No more!"

Ben tuned out the polemic, surveying the room, the sea of faces, some smiling, some frowning in dull anger, until his eyes fell on the familiar heads of the blond boy and his girl, the same couple who stood outside Howard's store; only now it was she who was pressing her face to the boy, nuzzling the side of his neck, trying to draw his attention away from the sermon. All her efforts were in vain: the boy's gaze remained fixed on the central figure ahead as if she wasn't there; and after a while she gave up and settled her head on his shoulder.

After the sermon had ended, a few members of the dispersing congregation lingered with the intention of approaching Thane. Grim pushed past them, using the large box to clear the way.

"I need to speak to you," he said to Thane as soon as he

got close enough, interrupting his discussion with the blond young man, who had rushed ahead of them to say something to Thane. The blond kid, eyeing the pair, grinned once he recognized Ben. But before he had a chance to say anything, Grim had pushed the box of provisions onto him with the off-hand instruction to "Go and put these in fresh water or something."

Thane didn't seem in the least bothered by the intrusion, maintaining his smile as he nodded to the blond kid. "Go on, Jerris. Take it to the pantry," he said. Jerris' expression turned sullen before he trudged off.

"I had a feeling you were coming," said Thane, leisurely spreading his back against his chair.

"Good," Grim answered. "How about we skip the niceties and you just return what you took?"

Thane raised his eyebrows in surprise. "What I took?"

"Look, I'm not here to meddle with whatever arrangement you and Atwood had going. If you had some score to settle, that's your business. I'm just here to take back what was not his in the first place."

Thane, still seated, leaned to one side, propping his head on one hand. He remained in this position for some time, giving the impression he was considering something. The silence in the lobby was prevalent enough that they could hear the distant shrieks of children outside. Spot-lit by the sun, everything in the lobby not directly touched by its light was veiled in shadows.

Finally, Thane lifted one hand and scrunched his mouth in a curt shrug. "I haven't the slightest idea what you're talking about."

Grim stood with his thumbs hooked in the front pockets of his jeans. He tilted his head to one side, and under his lowered lids, his eyes caught the sun, acquiring a liquid amber hue as they fixed on Thane.

"Listen, pissant," he began with dead calm, "I didn't come all the way here just to watch you play holy man, or inspired leader, or whatever pseudo-ideological flimflam you're trying to sell. I'm here for the cargo, the cargo you saw us deliver, the same cargo you were sniffing like a dog begging for scraps, the very same cargo that's no longer with Mr. Atwood—"

"Cargo, cargo, cargo," mocked Thane in a flat tone.

"You know what I'm talking about," sharply interposed Grim as his adversary chuckled.

"The question is whether you know what you're talking about," Thane retorted, dropping his voice to a confidential register. "See—you can't go around accusing others of stealing your precious shit, when you haven't the foggiest idea what it is they stole."

Grim, who stepped forward to confront this, halted midstride as he felt a sharp poke at his back. Ben knew it was a sharp poke thanks to a similar jab that assailed him, though his was blunter, given the larger diameter of the shotgun muzzle.

In some mysterious way, the guards at the gate had been summoned—or perhaps had moved in to watch the lobby entrance during the sermon—and were now leveling their weapons at the outsiders.

Ben now understood the expression of bowels turning to liquid, though thankfully the term remained figurative in this case. He looked to Grim and copied him as the latter half-raised his hands, bending his arms at the elbows which he kept at his side. The sight of his senior preserving his composure—eyes lowered not with abject defeat, but with the pragmatic air of trying somehow, without turning his head all the way, to get a look at the narrow barrel pressed against him, so close that the tip of the barrel dug into the back of his shirt, disappearing under a fold of fabric; the sight of him keeping calm reassured Ben, even if he felt a numbing weakness stealing up his legs. The wool blazer was thick enough to insulate the temperature of the shotgun barrel, yet it was hard to ignore the pressure of its round mouth held flush against the small of his back, as though a giant leech had latched onto him.

Thane meanwhile lifted both hands up in an upward sweep, as though presenting something with a flourish, letting daylight filter through the gaps between his fingers. The chair's wooden joints creaked in the semi-dark, vacant lobby as Thane leaned back, crossing the gaunt ankle of his left foot over his right knee.

"I say we're done here," he said. "These two gentlemen will show you out. Give my *regards* to Olivia," he added, mimicking Grim's previous send-off.

CHAPTER 10

Outside the compound, Grim and Ben sat in the pick-up, each mired in his own form of self-abasing silence. Ben's came with sickening heart-thuds that did funny things to his stomach. Grim, meanwhile, occupied himself with checking his shotgun, making sure it was still loaded and nothing was tampered with or stolen. It was his way of keeping his mind from racing like it did with Ben, who waited until he had put the gun away before hazarding to say: "Sir, I think we should call HQ. It's just going to get worse if we don't report it now."

Grim took a few seconds before turning to him, raising his eyebrows with a glint of mischief. "Should have taken a peek when we had the chance."

To which Ben expressed a soft wheeze meant to be a laugh. "An hour ago, you said we'd be walking out with both the cargo and culprit."

Grim gave a small shrug. "An hour ago, I imagined we'd be barging into a ramshackle house, the security detail of which is a handful of thugs armed with nail bats."

"That's why we need to call HQ, sir. We can't deal with the situation on our own."

"There's still time to salvage the situation. As far as the organization's concerned everything's still hunky-dory."

"Except we're in deep trouble," said Ben, staring ahead as he sank down in his seat.

"Can't get deeper than one cargo missing, one specialist dead, and the culprit still at large," agreed Grim with a sage nod.

The young man gaped at him with impotent outrage. "How can you be so calm? We're talking dereliction of duty and a whole other list of offenses! That's more than docked payment or demotion—we're talking interment—I mean internment!"

"All the more reason to salvage what we can. You don't tell someone you've knocked over their fishbowl while Goldie and Skipper are still flopping on the carpet. First things first: we need to know what we're after."

Ben leaned over, burying his face in his hands. "I can't do this," he groaned. "My head hurts. I'm gonna be sick. I'm gonna throw up. I'm gonna end up in a cell—" his head shot up—"No, I need to calm myself. I need to take a few breaths. I need to calm myself... I need..." he kept muttering, lowering his head until it fell again into his hands. "Oh, I need a drink!"

While Ben went through the motions of collapse, Grim found a toothpick, and leaned back in his seat with one foot propped against the dash.

"Take up smoking," he indifferently suggested, biting down on the wooden pick without so much as a glance away from the skies he was contemplating. "At least it keeps your head clear."

"Like I need a tumor in my life," Ben shot back, dropping his hands to glare at his senior.

"As opposed to a fatty-liver?" the senior needled.

Ben jumped a little, slapping away the finger poking his side. "Well, at least it won't send me towards an early grave!"

"Yeah—death as a retirement plan," said Grim, returning to chewing his toothpick with an almost wistful smile. "What a concept!"

Ben turned from him with an eye-roll; and just as he began contemplating calling HQ in secret, Grim snapped his fingers.

"That lady you went out with," he said, wagging a finger at Ben, "the one who gave you the birth certificate... Where did you say she worked?"

"Archives Department," answered Ben after an uncertain pause.

"Got her number?"

"I guess I do. I'll have to check my contacts."

"You do that."

"Why? What for?"

Grim started the truck and was pulling away from the gate. "Just find her number and let me worry about the rest."

It took but a minute for Ben to find the name he was searching for: Harper, Archive Department. If she knew her last name, she probably kept it to herself. Everyone in the organization was on a first name basis with everyone; the practice was common enough that few preferred being called by their surname, something usually borrowed from an alias and tacked on like a nickname. The only other form of distinction were titles, and those came with rank. If the practice served any purpose, it was to cut off any affinity with outsiders and keep members from seeking their biological parents or family members. And while it wasn't outwardly taboo to find out one's birth-assigned family name, the elaborate and knotty procedure often discouraged individuals from trying; even if they bore through it, the answer they got was never accompanied by any official document; moreover, any individual looking into personal records was often discreetly tabbed and monitored for suspect activity. All the more reason why Ben's copy of his birth certificate seemed a fine and rare thing.

"Found it," he said, holding up his phone.

"Good," said Grim. "What did you say her name was?"

"Harper."

"Harper," repeated Grim to himself, turning the wheel to make a sharp turn.

"Why do you need her number anyway?" asked Ben.

"We still need to find what's in the container."

"You mean the cargo? But, sir, she's in Archives. They don't keep information like that in her department."

"Perfect. They won't suspect her of passing on information."

"Not if she can't access it in the first place," Ben pointed out.

"She got your birth certificate, didn't she? That's not something they'd store in Archives. I'm sure she has her private channels."

"If you say so," Ben replied, if just to settle the argument without conceding. "Want me to call her now, sir?"

"Not yet. We still need to find a phone."

"Why? What's wrong with using our phones?"

"I'd rather we use something not tied to HQ, just to be safe."

They began at the post office, where two payphones were mounted on the side of the building—or rather one payphone that was out of order and a hollowed-out booth covered with graffiti and strewn with empty bottles and crushed beer cans.

Ben, his hands stuffed in the blazer pockets, raised his shoulders in an indifferent shrug. "We could use the phone at Mr. Atwood's."

Grim stared at the defunct unit while he considered this. "We could, but… can't guarantee it won't be tapped." He remained standing with his arms folded, thoughtfully eyeing the weak pendulum swing of the broken receiver dangling from a frayed cable before opting to try the gas station.

As they went down Main Street, Grim brought the truck to a jolting halt, then backed it a few yards until his window aligned with that of the Tea Room.

The front porch was crowded with boxes surmounted with mismatched table lamps, a double-deck cassette player, and other miscellaneous sundries often found buried in attics; but what had caught his attention was a white sign placed in one corner of the window that read: "Room For Rent."

As soon as they got out of the truck, Olivia emerged with a wooden crate bearing books and an old clock radio with the cord wrapped around it.

"What's all this?" asked Grim as she set the crate down next to a box of creased paperbacks.

"Just thought I'd put the upper floor to better use," she answered. "It kind of occurred to me yesterday, when you were asking for accommodations. My uncle used to live up there until he passed on. After that, the place more or less turned into a storage unit."

"So you're putting it up for rent?"

"Well, it's fitted with all the amenities: bathrooms with running water, working electricity, a small—"

"Is it ready?"

"I guess—as soon as I clear out a few items."

"We'll take it."

She chuckled. "You know, you two are quickly turning into my favorite customers." Her lingering smile fell a little on seeing them regard her expectantly and understood the offer was in earnest. "What? Really?"

Grim lifted his arms in a shrug. "If it's short-term accommodations, then sure."

"How short is short-term?" she asked.

"Do you rent by the hour?"

She shook her head with a tight smile. "I'm not running a motel here. Has to be a minimum of two nights."

"Fine by me," was Grim's prompt answer.

Olivia considered him, still unable to tell whether or not he was serious. "I thought Radney the spi—sorry, Mr. Atwood—I thought you were staying with him."

"It was just for the night. Does the room have its own phone line?"

The owner of the Tea Room squinted up at the upper floor. "Most people would ask if the running water's clean, or whether I got cable TV, or..." she placed her hands on her hips, "... yeah, it comes with its own phone line. It receives calls, but you can't use it to make outgoing calls. I've been paying—"

"No problem. We'll take it," Grim interposed.

She uttered a sound that might have been surprise or protest; even Ben, who liked this accommodation for his own reasons, worried his senior's unwavering interest might backfire.

"Don't you want to know the price first?" asked Olivia.

"Sure, what is it?"

"It's..." she paused for a quick mental calculation, "... seventy-five a night."

"Sixty?" he countered.

She smiled, having at last found the limit of his enthusiasm. "Seventy-five," she insisted, crossing her arms.

"Sixty and we'll help you move your stuff."

"Seventy-five. It's not up for negotiation."

"How about fifty? I'll throw in the boy to do your dishes, and you kick us out at the end of the day."

She turned aside to attenuate an irrepressible laugh of disbelief. "What happened to staying two or three nights?"

To which Grim raised his arms in a hapless shrug. "Can't afford it if you bleed me dry upfront. Look, I know business isn't exactly booming, I can see why you want to squeeze every... sorry, make the most out of every opportunity. But it's not like you're expecting a tourist bus to come trundling along at any moment. We're the only out-of-towners looking for lodging. So how about this: sixty a night, and we have all our meals in your fine establishment? I guarantee it'll add up to more than just rent alone."

"Fine," said Olivia, throwing up her hands in a lighthearted show of reluctance. "But only if you agree to pay upfront and help me stash all this junk in the shed."

Within an hour, the last box was stashed in the shed. And after paying up front, stating that they didn't mind that the room wasn't in pristine condition, Grim quietly closed the door behind Olivia's descending figure before making a beeline for the phone.

The airy studio apartment was bright with white walls and pale floorboards, modestly furnished with two army cots as temporary beds, a simple desk pushed against the wall, where south-facing picture windows offered a clear view of Main Street.

While Grim ducked under the desk to plug in the phone,

Ben stood nearby, staring out the window. If he were to take three steps back, the back of his knees would touch the edge of his cot.

"Alright," said Grim, brushing back his loose hair as he rose from under the desk. "Copy this number down and forward it to Harper. Tell her to…" he paused, trying to think of how best to convey his message, inducing her to call a strange number without rousing suspicion.

"I'll tell her to call," began Ben, thinking out loud, "and make a reservation at the Tea Room—for lunch. And I'll tell her to try the Raskovnik salad from their secret menu."

Grim considered him with slack-jawed humor. "Scout, we want her to call back, not block your number."

"No, you don't get it, sir. In Slavic lore, Raskovnik is a magic herb that can unlock or uncover anything that is locked or closed. The secret menu thing is code for calling incognito. And lunch is, you know, her lunch break."

"Hunh." Grim nodded. "And how can you be sure she'll get all that?"

"I'm pretty sure she'll look up Raskovnik, find out it doesn't exist, and from there she'll probably understand the message is in code."

Grim's reaction was odd enough to startle Ben: he stepped forward, held Ben's head in both hands, then pressed his forehead to Ben's, closing his eyes as if concentrating while Ben nervously looked about in confusion.

"What's that for, sir?" he asked as soon as Grim pulled back.

"Just wanted to see if I could absorb some of your smarts," said the senior, releasing Ben's head with a playful shove.

The confused frown remained on Ben's face as he smoothed back his hair, surreptitiously feeling his forehead for a welt.

CHAPTER 11

The next couple of hours dragged on while they waited for the phone to ring. If Harper had received or even read the message, she gave no indication of doing so.

"Did she text you back?" asked Grim, who went from sitting on the edge of his cot to stretching out on his back, keeping his feet planted on the ground.

From the depths of his cot, Ben answered, "No," in an equally colorless voice.

"Should have told her to call for brunch," Grim opined after an uneventful minute had passed.

Ben frowned. "Who goes out for brunch?"

At that, Grim suddenly rose up and headed to the door. "To get brunch," he explained when Ben asked where he was going.

The apartment had two doors: a kitchen door leading outside to an external stairway, and a connecting door that opened to a set of stairs leading down to the Tea Room. Olivia said she would leave the latter unlocked up until closing time, and through it Grim descended to order his meal.

After a minute, Ben decided to follow—not to go down after him, but to sit on top of the stairs and listen in on them. Part of it was the young man's adherence to his task of keeping eyes and ears on his subject; even if he couldn't see him, the fact that the stairs were almost adjacent to the counter made it easy to catch the conversation floating up through the banisters.

Grim must have placed his order already, as their colloquy had moved past small talk regarding their accommodation.

"How's the business with Moorhouse?" asked Olivia.

"Oh, it turned out to be a big misunderstanding," he eluded.

"I thought it might be. I'm no expert on character, but Thane doesn't strike me as the type who'd steal things."

"How so?"

"I don't know. I guess it's a point of pride for him that he never admitted to wanting or needing anything."

"Why want when you can take?" Grim asked. Olivia must have regarded him a certain way for him to elaborate: "I mean he took over that property, didn't he?"

To which she answered with a touch of impatience: "Look, I'm not his advocate. I'm just saying stealing just doesn't seem to be one of his proclivities. He even joked about how his father had beat it out of him—left him with these big scars to remind him to keep his hands to himself…"

The remainder of the statement was lost to a series of shrill beeps as the phone in their apartment began to ring.

Ben scrambled to answer it, and before he said, "Hello?" he heard Grim bounding up the stairs.

"I don't have time, so you better make this quick," said Harper as soon as Ben answered. Between the urgency of the remark and Grim motioning Ben to do something that he did not quite understand, the junior stood motionless until Grim snatched the receiver and told him to shut the apartment door.

"Harper," said Grim, putting the call on speakerphone.

Her response crackled through the small speakers. "Who is this?"

"A friend of Ben's. We need your help with something."

A siren began howling somewhere in Harper's vicinity.

"Where are you?" Grim asked.

"Never mind that," she said, raising her voice to be heard over the siren's crescendo, which swiftly faded out. "I'm supposed to be on my lunch break. I only have five minutes to spare, so get to the point."

"We need you to dig something up for us—something classified."

"Do you have clearance—" she began before cutting herself off with a derisive snort, dropping her voice to a soliloquized mumble. "What am I saying, of course you don't or you wouldn't have called."

"Look, I'm under probation—" he began, when suddenly she hissed: "Go away!"

"Excuse me?" said Grim.

"Not you! This guy keeps bothering me about something––I said go away!" she broke out, thoughtfully muffling the receiver. "You bother me one more time and I'm gonna break your nose and won't stop till I break all ten fingers and toes! Yeah, that's right! You try me again, fella! I've got a crowbar here for creeps like you!"

After a long pause during which Grim and Ben stared at each other, and the latter stifled a nervous laugh, Harper returned to them.

"Okay, he's gone now."

"You carry a crowbar with you?" Grim asked.

"Don't get smart with me…!"

"Yeah, alright—back to our topic. We were assigned to deliver some classified cargo to a specialist: one Radney Atwood of Lake Penumbra. We want to know what the contents are."

"Why?" she asked suspiciously.

"Because they're missing."

"So call someone else. That's not my department."

"I can't," said Grim. "I'm under probation, you know."

"No, I don't," she shot back. "I don't even know who you're supposed to be."

"My ID is 6753-2. You can look me up when you get back. Anyone associated with me is probably under surveillance too. Look, the cargo's missing, and we're in deep shit. That's why we called you: no one will suspect you.

"It's not my department," she painstakingly emphasized.

"I know what you're capable of. Ben told me about that gift."

"What gift?" she asked, feigning ignorance.

"His birth certificate."

"That little—!" she spluttered through an astonished laugh that swallowed up the crucial epithet; not that it mattered when the words preceding it conveyed its sentiment. Ben felt like announcing his presence to her, but Grim went on to say: "We're not trying to blackmail you. We just need your help."

She gave a long, tired sigh. "I don't need any of this."

"Come on. I'll make it worth your while."

"With what? Money?" she gave a derisive chuckle. "That's all I need: people coming in and asking me who sent a big, fat transfer to my account."

"I'm nothing if not discreet," Grim reassured her. "I keep a stash for emergencies like this. Ben will send you the location.

Help yourself to it. Or don't—if you'd rather hold it against me as a deterrent."

A stretch of silence preceded a crisp click. Ben stared at the phone speaker, his jaw slack with the realization that Harper had hung up on them.

"What just happened?" he said, somehow unable to speak above a whisper.

Grim ignored him and began writing something on a pad of notepaper.

"Here," he said a moment later, handing Ben a scrawled note. "Copy that into a message and send it to her."

Ben held the piece of paper but felt too stupid to read it. "Sir, she hung up on us."

"Rise and shine, sweetheart," said Grim, briskly patting Ben's face as though to wake him up. "We need to send her the location, stat."

"But she—"

"She has our number," the senior finished for him. "She might even have time to check on that stash if we send her the location now."

In the middle of copying down the note, Ben noticed Grim taking his wallet, phone and key fob before heading towards the kitchen door.

"Sir?"

"I'll just swing by the cabin. I want to see if we overlooked anything. Plus we left our clothes there. You stay put in case Harper calls back."

After he left, Ben stared at the kitchen door in dazed silence until he heard a knock on the other door.

"Hey," said Olivia as soon as he opened the connecting

door. "I saw your uncle leave without picking up his lunch, so I thought I'd bring it up."

Ben glanced down at the tray she carried before stepping aside to let her in and as she began setting down cups and plates on the desk, he stammered, "It- it's fine if you want to just leave the tray."

"It's no trouble," she said. "Besides, I only have two trays. Can't afford to keep this one here."

"Right." Ben laughed, sweeping the notepad and scrawled paper out of her way. Sunlight touched her bare forearms, and for a moment he fixated on the silken yellow glint of downy hair that he never had noticed before.

"How's your injury?" she asked, her green eyes on his.

"Better," he said, lifting his hand to feel the largely forgotten bruise until it gave a faint throb of pain under his touch.

"Remind me later to bring you some arnica," she said, making the offer with the detached solicitude of a physician; and while Ben thanked her, he couldn't help wondering whether she was moved by general concern, or whether her care went a little deeper than that. It may have injured his vanity to recall that she lavished members of the commune with equal attention. Then again, he never flattered himself that she harbored any special feelings for him; yet on the other side of that sobering view was a wild hope that he tried to ignore, even as it obstinately beat about like a trapped bird.

The lunch she set down included mugs of hot coffee, the aromatic steam of which curled and beckoned. The air, the setting, the company—all was perfect balm to his frayed nerves. He wanted to close his eyes and savor this fleeting moment; he even considered asking her to sit with him for a minute, weighing the possible sting of rejection against the scant likelihood of her accepting. Meanwhile, she remained standing in the middle of the room, surveying every corner.

"We had a twin bed here," she said, glancing at the cots, "but it was in shambles, and I wasn't sure about the condition of the mattress…"

He didn't know what to say, except to spout something about the cots seeming comfortable enough. Seeing her stand there reminded Ben of her air of easy elegance, from the crisp white shirt she wore under a brown apron, to the way she twisted her long, bleached hair into something like a loose braid and wore it pinned to the back of her head; and when she carried her scrutiny to the large windows, it took but a moment to imprint in his mind the uninterrupted curve that began at the tip of her lifted chin and sloped down her neck.

"Do you have everything you need?" she asked. "I noticed you didn't bring any overnight bags or anything."

"Oh, we did. We just—" he vaguely gestured with his hand––"left them at Mr. Atwood's. Grim's gone to fetch them."

She smiled quietly at him. "He lets you call him Grim?"

"Well, sure," Ben replied, forgetting the uncle-nephew cover story for a moment, until Olivia remarked with a slight shrug: "I guess I'm traditional like that. I'd feel odd calling my uncle by his name alone."

"Right—right!" Ben laughed, his heart dipping into his stomach as he realized his blunder. A minute or two ago he hardly believed his luck in having her to talk to without Grim being there to overshadow him; now he worried he might say something that would compromise their cover.

"I think I hear customers coming in," he fibbed, glancing at the connecting door, as if providing her with an excuse to leave.

"No, I think that's just some folks standing outside," she said. "Besides, if anyone comes in, I'm sure Madlyn can take care of them."

"Who's Madlyn?"

"A high-school student—well, soon to be dropout if she doesn't get her act together."

Ben gave her a tentative smile. "I don't follow…"

"She and a few of her peers have taken to spending more time at the commune than in a classroom—especially that boy, Jerris," Olivia explained, glancing out the window as she spoke, as though expecting to find him standing somewhere on Main Street. Or perhaps it was more the memory of them standing there that drew her gaze—as was the case with Ben, who recalled the crowd of delinquents he had encountered outside Howard's store. He knew Jerris was the blond, having heard Thane call him that, and guessed that Madlyn was the redheaded girl at his side.

"Aren't they part of the commune?" Ben asked.

Olivia continued to look outside as she answered: "No, just some local kids looking to replace their strict families or dysfunctional homes by joining another."

"I thought Thane didn't welcome outsiders."

"He makes allowances for young, impressionable members," she said, regarding him with a half-formed scathing smile, "especially if he can put them to work."

Her remark recalled yesterday's episode of Madlyn answering Atwood's door, and Thane sitting there like a middleman overseeing a transaction. A slight shudder ran through Ben, and his mind reeled with a series of questions: whether anyone knew about the illicit arrangement; whether Mr. Atwood paid for such services, and whether the whole sordid business had something to do with his murder. But for fear of bringing up Atwood's affairs, the young man kept his questions to himself.

The conversation dwindled after that, focusing on generalities like the town, and what decided them to spend a few days here, to which again Ben essayed ignorance, play-acting the nephew subject to his eccentric uncle's whims. And perhaps finding nothing illuminating in his vague answers, Olivia soon excused herself to return to work and went downstairs.

Not long after Ben closed the door with a sigh of relief, Grim barged through the other door, carrying a bundle of clothes under one arm.

"Did someone call?" he breathlessly asked approaching the desk, as though he heard the phone ringing.

Ben answered with a tacit shake of his head, following Grim with his eyes as the latter carelessly flung the bundle of clothes to one corner, shut the kitchen door, then paced back and forth a few times, punching the palm of his hand.

"Did something happen, sir?" Ben asked, agitated by his senior's behavior.

Grim stopped punching his hand and looked up.

"Atwood's body is gone."

CHAPTER 12

Grim began to laugh.

The sound was so strange, so extraordinary, that at first, Ben could only stand and listen to it, forgetting the terrible news that preceded it. Then the shock wore off, and an unprecedented heat mantled his head.

"Stop laughing!" he shouted, just short of lunging forward to seize his senior, who now collapsed into sitting at the edge of the bed.

"I'm sorry—I'm sorry," repeated Grim through residual mirth. "It just sounded so fantastic when I said it out loud. I mean, imagine a dead body just... *fft*!" he whistled with a flick of his hand.

He seemed about to succumb to fresh peals, but in the end the few stray giggles died out as he leaned forward, cradling his head in his hands. He stayed that way for a few moments; and just when Ben was moved to say something, Grim raised his head, letting his hands drop between his knees.

"You know that carpet we rolled him up in?" he said quietly, without a trace of levity in his eyes aside from a sparkle of residual tears. "It's gone too. It's like he just up and vanished."

His unfocused gaze dropped a little under gathered brows as he stared into the empty space beyond his knees. Then slowly, his forehead grew smooth with dawning realization.

"Up and vanished," he nodded, finding new meaning in the words. "This is good."

Ben caught the grave whisper of each syllable, but failed to fathom their import, thinking perhaps his senior meant to say, "This is bad," but in his distressed state had mixed-up the two.

"This is good," Grim repeated, as if he sought confirmation from Ben, who up until that point had been floating somewhere between incredulity and denial; but the reiteration sent him grabbing for the table or chair before he collapsed to his knees.

He's lost it, thought Ben; aloud he said: "We're screwed."

"No, scout. Think!" said Grim as he stood up, inclining his head to bring it into Ben's line of vision; the latter's eyes were wide open, but they could not focus on his senior's face.

"Think about it!" Grim insisted, clasping Ben's shoulders. "They can't punish us for what they can't hold against us. A dead body is incriminating. A missing body is an open case."

The wheels began to turn in Ben's mind, but they moved so slowly that it took him half a minute to answer.

"He's gone, sir. Missing or dead, he's still gone. And we're still responsible."

"I know, scout, but look at it this way: where was Atwood when he disappeared?"

So absurd was the question that Ben was compelled to look at his senior, who gave him an encouraging nod.

"In his house," came the obvious answer—so obvious that Ben had time to doubt whether it was the right answer.

"Right," said Grim. "Which is strictly off-limits to us. So

how would we know what the hell happened to him if we never went inside."

"But we did go inside."

"They don't know that, scout."

On the surface, this made perfect sense. Yet something was missing, some crucial detail...

"The cargo," said Ben.

"What about it?"

"What do you mean 'what about it', sir? It's gone!"

"So? How would we know it's gone if we never went inside?"

"No, no, no!" the young man moaned. "This is insane! You're not suggesting we report this? The whole idea of keeping us here was to keep an eye on things! How will we even explain his disappearance? It's negligence, it's... unacceptable!"

"It's just one of those things," answered Grim with an elaborate shrug.

Ben's frustration was beyond expression: he looked away with a grin of disgust, hid his face in his cupped hands, then took a deep breath before dropping them.

"Okay, okay. Walk me through this, sir. An adult man, and a large container—full of classified material, mind you—simply vanish. And our excuse is: they just did." He began to laugh, his mirthful voice rising to a high-pitch as he spoke. "Oh, this is great! This will go well in the report!"

Having recently spent his hilarity, the senior did not laugh along, but turned away and stood looking out the window. His reaction was not calculated to slight or ignore his subordinate, yet in the uncomfortable silence that followed, Ben read it as such and resented it. He was tired of being jerked around by the other man's caprice.

The young man went on doggedly staring at the back of Grim's head, gray eyes turned steely behind their wet film, allowing him time to turn around and admit his schemes were all madness and no method. And after the allocated period had passed without result or reaction, Ben lifted his arms and let them fall, clapping his sides in a show of exasperation.

"First he kills Atwood, now he hides the body. He's messing with us, sir. You know he's messing with us. We can't ignore this. We have to do something!"

It almost surprised Ben to hear himself raring for payback, though he couldn't deny his outpour of anger and frustration had an exhilarating taste. Oftentimes, such negative emotions were counteracted with a sense of guilt, or the notion that one should rise above the need to act on their volatile humors. But this was different, since the target of his enmity proved to be amoral, and had moreover brought it on himself; plus, the young man's outrage wasn't for himself, but on behalf of the organization. In his intrinsic classification, Radney Atwood, however distant, was affiliated to the organization; whereas Thane and his followers were the small-minded and superstitious other, whose cankerous nature manifested in a violent retaliation against a perceived insult. And while Thane was the apparent perpetrator, in Ben's mind there was no separating leader from followers, since no doubt they would champion his actions. They might think they're above the law, but the organization will not roll over and play dead to their transgression.

So certain was Ben of his senior's shared view, that it startled him to hear the veteran say: "Atwood's expendable. Now that he's dead, he's lost his value in the eyes of the organization. It's the cargo they care about."

He kept his face averted as he spoke, and from where he stood Ben could only see the highlighted outline of brow and cheek, and between them a downward slant of lashes.

"That's what they care about, so that's what we're after," Grim repeated with a soft rap of his knuckles against the desk. "We'll stay here, wait for Harper's call, and proceed from there," he concluded, accompanying each point with a dull knock on the desk.

"That's it?" Ben all but shouted in response. "That's your plan? Sit here and wait for a call that's never gonna come?"

"I said I'll go after him once I know what's in that box," the other man calmly answered, raising his head without turning. "There's no point in rushing in blind like we did this morning. We had a decent look at the place, we know where it is. Might need some recon, but I'm sure I could figure out a way to bypass those guards. We just have to be patient—treat this like a hostage situation. Thane so much as suspects we're coming for him, and we can kiss that cargo goodbye."

The explanation was wasted on Ben, who could not afford to be patient—not when he had a report to make by the end of the day—any more than fathom why his partner chose to be passive about the whole matter.

"That's your excuse, then?" he impetuously goaded. "I thought for sure a gunman like you would be able to take down those two guards. Why'd you get a shotgun when you're not going to use it?"

Grim turned on him. "What do you want me to do?" he challenged in an undertone. "Get you a rifle? Go back there, storm the compound? Kick down doors? Mow everyone in the way—men, women, children. Is that what you want? Shooting our way into the compound? Clean and simple."

He kept his voice just above a whisper, stepping forward as he spoke, closing the distance between him and Ben, who fell back a few steps till the back of his knees bumped against one of the cots.

"Only they'll shoot back," Grim went on with a baleful grin. "Oh, you bet your peach fuzz they will. You might have missed the shell casings and bullet holes, but I saw them. We'll all be firing at each other till we're out of ammo—never mind the ones wasted because you can't hit the target under those circumstances. What does that get us, Ben? Empty clicks and nowhere near our target. With survivors closing in on us. You want that, Ben?"

Somehow, his quiet tone was more intimidating than any leap of anger, which nevertheless was there albeit smoldering behind a calm front. To draw him from the brink of that outburst, Ben said: "You're right, sir—you're right. Going after them on our own won't solve anything. That's why we need to call for back-up," he added, as if all along this was the point he was trying to make. "And I know what you're going to say—it's far from an ideal solution—but hopefully there won't be that many casualties. After all, the situation isn't as bad as it was with Duncastor—"

"The hell you know about it?!" Grim demanded in seething anger, all but lunging at Ben who fell back onto the cot and cowered with one hand raised.

The question was more of a challenge than inquiry—not that Ben had any intention of answering, except he knew it was due to some negligence or failure on Grim's behalf that the chain of command questioned his competence, and decided them to send Ben to keep a close watch on Grim. The generalities of the incident were freely exchanged as commonplace gossip, which was perhaps why Grim did not suspect Ben knew anything more than he should. Yet, evidently, the subject rankled with him, as he seemed unsatisfied with subduing his subordinate into silence.

"Here…" he snatched Ben's phone out of the blazer's pocket and flung it at him, "… you wanted to contact HQ, why don't you call them now? Tell them how this whole mess started—who slept on the job when it was his turn to keep watch."

And having vented his scorn, Grim went and sat at the desk with his back turned, propping his crossed ankles on one corner.

Ben remained where he sat, staring into space, transfixed by an inward turmoil of emotions, chief amongst which were anger and a vague sense of betrayal. He maintained an outward appearance of indifference, though the corners of his mouth twitched and strained under the effort. All at once he felt himself too drained and exhausted to get up, weighed down with troubling thoughts, which he struggled to put into order. The last thing he wanted to do was sleep, but as he remained where he lay, the cot cradling his tired body, he soon began to drift off.

When he opened his eyes again, Ben found the room empty. The noon blaze had long subsided, deepening the sky's blue. His phone lay inches from his face, and when he turned it over to check the time, estimating an hour had passed, he saw it was actually five past three.

He sat up, pressing a hand to his heavy head, and wondering where his senior had gone, though not without a measure of gratitude for his absence. Whether Grim was still angry, remorseful, or indifferent, the ensuing awkwardness would be too much to bear.

Ben noted Grim's empty plate and cup when he approached the table for his own share, and hoped the other had left on some errand to allow him to eat in peace.

The coffee was cold yet flavorful, as was his sandwich. He surveyed Main Street while he drank and ate, taking several small hungry bites.

Besides the occasional car driving by, most activities took

place outside Howard's store, where Ben spotted Madlyn leaning against the wall as she had the day before. Only now she was talking to Grim.

It was Grim, and no doubt—even if he stood with his back turned, there was no mistaking the dark, shoulder-length hair, the army green shirt jacket and dark blue jeans. Ben watched him lean closer still, his head almost floating over hers. Then he stood back, turned his head to blow smoke, holding a lighted cigarette in his half-lifted hand.

"What is he up to now?" Ben wondered, then decided he would rather not know. From day one, it was evident that Grim saw this whole mission as some sort of paid holiday, and he was not about to let minor inconveniences, like Atwood's death, or the cargo's disappearance, ruin his fun. Or perhaps in his mind he was rectifying the situation, albeit at his own, leisurely pace, making the most out of this grace period.

"As far as the organization's concerned, everything's still hunky-dory."

Maybe it was for him: After all, he wasn't the one responsible for the whole debacle.

A close-mouthed sneer soured Ben's boyish face. Just when he thought he could rely on his senior, the man showed where his own priorities lay.

So much for looking after each other, thought Ben, glancing down at the laughing pair, diminished by their distance.

The worst part was he, Ben, did not know what exactly awaited them in terms of punishment. At best it was a black spot on his record that might stunt his career, much like the aged office boys fetching coffee and running errands for their juvenile seniors; at worst, he might firsthand see the nethermost blocks of the organization, and gain a better understanding why former staff members, with their sensitive information and vital secrets, disappear down there, never to emerge again. Many a rumor was exchanged over drinks concerning condemned members who still had their good health, which they unwillingly gave up in the service of medical experiments. (Oh, to go back to a time when he could enjoy such horror stories with the same amused detachment Olympians afforded to the ordeals of mortals!) Even if those scaremongers colored their stories with gruesome details, Ben knew there was a kernel of truth to them, having once heard a scientist from the organization's pharmaceutical branch grumble about a shortage of human test subjects, which he claimed were more efficacious than rodents.

The same youth and good health he enjoyed to the point of taking it for granted now seemed to mark him for an unimaginably cruel fate. And with a foreboding shudder, he now understood the wistful smile behind Grim's: "Death as a retirement plan. What a concept!"

Perhaps that's what he'd been doing: living on borrowed time and denying the inevitable, like a delirious prisoner raving and laughing by turns as his captors dragged him to some unknown fate.

CHAPTER 13

Grim stared up at the rising ring of smoke, watched it dilate into a wreath before it dissipated into the blue.

"Cute," murmured Madlyn in a dull tone, promptly looking away as if repenting showing a grain of interest.

But she had shown interest, which to Grim was an encouraging sign.

He had no intention of breaking his smoking hiatus, but seeing her take a smoke break, he decided he may as well join her. The strategy was calculated to be indirect: he just happened to walk out of the Everything Store intent on enjoying a cigarette in peace, and the lighter in his pocket just happened to be empty, its true purpose was drawing sympathetic attention from nearby smokers who, more often than not, would step in to offer a light.

As expected, Madlyn produced a lighter and held it to him while he brushed back his hair and leaned in with his cigarette. And having rendered him that small service, and a minute later remarked on his modest smoke trick, she went back to leaning against the white brick wall, pretending he wasn't there while she took a drag of her own cigarette. Like a lot of teenagers, she blew hot and cold, oscillating between seeking attention and detachment; and having established contact, she now retreated into the relative safety of detachment, squinting her large eyes, more to produce a guarded scowl than against the mild sunlight.

But if she expected him to approach her now, he disappointed her by mirroring her disinterest. He had a hunch they both wanted something from each other. Whether or not Madlyn knew Atwood was dead, the man provided her with something she sought, be it material gains, a diversion, or some means of rebellion—depending on whether she came on to him or was talked into it. Thane's presence at the cabin pointed towards the latter, though it did not rule out the possibility of his arranging their meeting under the guise of spontaneity before letting matters take their course.

At any rate, it was likely she was on the lookout for a replacement, which was why Grim placed himself in her line of vision—well, near its edge, if he was to take a measured approach and let her approach him rather than spook her with his advances. He suspected Thane had warned her about him, and decided that to subvert her expectations was to rouse her curiosity. And curiosity, in her case, was more compelling than any stern warning.

Still, it was challenging to stand idle without the option of reaching for his phone, figuring it would make him look preoccupied and unapproachable. Already he was halfway through his cigarette, while Madlyn stalled finishing hers by checking her phone. And yet, out of the corner of his eye, he noticed the black puffer jacket she wore had slipped off her right shoulder, something that was hardly accidental given the make of her jacket. Moreover, as she lowered her phone, she continued looking to one side, raising the cigarette holding hand from elbow level to over her bare shoulder in an attitude of airy indifference. The oversized jacket had all but swallowed her small frame—and perhaps that was the point: to exaggerate her waif and bird-like appearance.

Grim refused to take the bait, and just when he was on the verge of tossing his cigarette, Madlyn asked with a derisive sniff: "So what do you think of our little town?"

Her tone implied that she didn't think much of it and invited him to agree.

He glanced back at her with a subtle eyebrow raise as though he had not expected her to talk to him.

"Oh, it's not so bad," he murmured. "There's a certain rustic quality about it."

"Yeah, we're just lousy with rust and mold," she snorted, taking another drag.

"I'm sure it has its points of charm," he said, turning to survey Main Street.

"Like what?"

"Nice friendly folks, for one."

"You mean the local yokels," Madlyn rejoined.

Grim smiled at her. "Sounds like you're ready to pack up and leave."

"And leave all this behind?" she laughed acerbically. "Slaving away, waiting tables in this shithole. I'll say this much: at least I'm earning my keep. My mom used to constantly bitch about how I'd never amount to anything if I dropped out. As if I'm not old enough to take care of myself."

"How old are you anyway?"

Her smile took on a patronizing slant in the manner of one deigning to answer a stupid question. "Old enough," she answered, giving him a quick once-over with her eyes, perhaps musing on the true motive behind his question. "Anyway, what's sitting on my ass for eight hours going to get me? That's what Poppa used to say."

"Poppa?"

"Thane, I mean. He says the system is set up to make us stupid—that all that sitting makes us stupid—turns our brain into mush and makes us receptive to their programming. He says the only way to beat the system is to unplug and live your life. Imagine wasting the prime of your life being spoon-fed facts you'll never use. But if you raise a point like that, they fail you or send you to the counselor, saying you got behavioral issues. That's how they turn you into workplace zombies. That's how they got our parents, and look at them! They don't call them white or blue 'collar' workers for nothing. It's the truth, if only you stop and think about it."

"Truth with a capital T?" returned Grim. "Or the truth you want to hear?"

Madlyn rolled her eyes. "Yeah—that's what my mom wants to know," she said, perhaps implying Grim was dangerously close to sounding like her. But in the next moment she brightened as she continued: "Poppa—I mean Thane—Thane says there's potential in me. That's why he picked me."

"Potential for what?"

"We're still searching, but he felt I have this raw energy that was just going to waste!"

Grim refrained from remarking on that. The conversation was hovering close to an area of interest for him, chiefly Atwood's final days and her role in the affair. No doubt Thane told her to keep her mouth shut on the subject, and for fear of revealing his true motive, Grim feigned waning interest.

He blew out his last puff, ground his spent cigarette, and tapped out a fresh one, turning to Madlyn for a light. She obliged him, this time using the smoldering tip of her own cigarette.

"You have nice eyes," she said irrelevantly.

"Well... thank you," he faltered, somewhat caught off-guard. "Yours are nice too."

She smiled up at him, maintaining her close proximity. "What do you do anyway?"

"Oh, I'm just a simple courier," he answered, affecting world-weariness as he fiddled with the pack of cigarettes.

Madlyn nodded, looking away as though contemplating something potentially profound. "Like a deliveryman?"

He shrugged. "Something like that. Except I'm more specialized in a way."

"Oh," she said, losing interest.

"You know how some things courier companies won't touch or deliver? I deliver those."

Again he gave a vague answer, letting her fill in the details.

Her smile returned, and she was unable to keep her round eyes from bulging a little. "Like what? Like illegal shit?"

He made a slight grimace meant to downplay the severity of the matter. "It's all relative."

"Relative how?" she echoed. "Are we talking drugs? Weapons? What?"

"Oh, it's not so much weapons as parts; not so much narcotics as, say... ingredients?" He paused for effect. "I'm sure you've seen the goods we delivered to Radney."

She shook her head, frowning a little. "N- no?"

He nodded mysteriously, blowing out a thin plume of smoke.

"So you're good at smuggling things?" she asked when it became apparent that he wasn't going to say anything.

"I'm no mule, but I do pretty well," he said, unable to hold back a self-assured smile, thinking he had her eating out of the palm of his hand; but her next remark showed him she was thinking the same thing.

"How about you tell me all about it over a drink, then?"

He laughed at that. "I thought this was a dry county."

"Who told you that?"

"I don't know. I just haven't seen any bars or liquor stores here. Does Thane provide? Or did Radney keep a still in his garage?"

Madlyn rolled her eyes. "Free booze on tap. Wouldn't that be a barrel of laughs? No, we just get it from Howard's."

"I was in just now," said Grim, nodding at the large window. "Couldn't find anything there harder than energy drinks."

"That's because Jerris and the others used to break in and run out with a six-pack in each hand. So now Howard keeps them stored in the basement. The only way in there is through a trap door behind the counter."

"That's a lot of work going up and down a dingy basement just to get a cold one."

"I know, right! But that's how he does it. And they're not even cold. Radney bought them by the case and they'd be piss warm. With all that space, you'd think he could—I don't know—stick a fridge or ten down there."

Once again, their talk had drifted towards an area of interest, and Grim was poised to ask about Atwood's final day. But something in her last sentence caught his attention.

"All that space down where?" he asked.

"The basement warehouse. That's where he stores most things that aren't on display."

Grim surveyed the small building. Somehow, the "Everything Store" claim seemed less like an empty boast now.

"How big is it?"

She shrugged. "I don't know—like as big as a basement warehouse or something?"

Something occurred to Grim, and occupied him so that he kept staring at her until she snapped her fingers at him. He blinked and fixed his unseeing gaze on her lifted hand, or rather the delicate fingers poking through the puffed sleeve.

"Did Radney have a basement in his house?" he asked, still beguiled by the overstuffed sleeve and its resemblance to an engorged worm in the final stages of devouring her arm.

"Huh?" she confusedly sneered at the sudden shift in subject. "How should I know?"

But Grim had already ground his cigarette, and as he strode back to the Tea Room, he heard her cry after him: "Hey! What about the beer?"

He took the stairs two steps at a time, barging through the apartment's kitchen door, just to grab the truck keys off the counter.

"It's just me," he called out. "Going back to Atwood's. I might be onto something. Stay by the phone."

He slammed the door behind, thinking that if Ben was still asleep, the racket should wake him up. Far beneath his clipped tenor was a blend of shame and guilt that he found easier to push down than admit.

A basement, he kept thinking over and over like a prayer as the truck bumped and sped through tree-lined roads. At some point he was aware of absently rummaging through his pockets for something, then noticed the cigarette dangling from his lips, and realized he was searching for a lighter. He snatched the unlit cigarette and tossed it out the window with the rest of the pack.

The cabin was still in the same sorry state they had left it in, so that it took him longer to sweep the floors in search of an access hatch. Twice he swept the living room, foyer and coat closet with no results. The kitchen with its tiled floor seemed the least likely place to find anything—and yet, he noticed a walk-in pantry with relatively new wooden floorboards mostly covered with a large, woven rug. He threw the rug aside, and, sure enough, there in the floor was a flush handle surrounded by an inconspicuous rectangular outline.

The hatchway opened to a set of concrete steps that descended into a dark basement. Before heading down, Grim paused to call Ben and update him. But the phone kept ringing, with Grim silently then hissingly urging his subordinate to pick up.

CHAPTER 14

The phone buzzed in Ben's pocket.

He pulled the bicycle over to the side of the road, scraping his shod feet against dirt and asphalt. A breeze sprang up, cooling his perspired skin while he checked his phone to see who was calling.

Half-an-hour ago, he had made up his mind to take matters into his own hands, and knew where he had to go. The question was how to get there without alerting his senior. Grim was still in conference with Madlyn, but who knew when he'd be back, or whether he would hear the truck starting all the way across the street? Then the young man remembered a bicycle he had glimpsed while they were storing boxes in the shed behind the Tea Room. The bike was a forlorn thing, touched with rust and tucked so deep in a dusty corner, that Ben worried it might be defunct or require some attendance. But as soon as he wheeled it out, checked the chain and tires, he found it was in fair shape, and was able to pedal off without being discovered.

That is, until now.

Then again, it was only a matter of time before Grim realized he was neither in the bathroom, nor in bed, despite having arranged the pillows and blanket to prolong the illusion. Still, it was better than receiving a call from a higher-up checking in on the situation here. A call like that would be tricky to answer and a mistake to ignore.

Ben removed his blazer, the collar of which trapped prickly heat at the back of his neck, stuffed the still-buzzing phone into its inner pocket, and draped it over the handlebars. The breeze had stopped, but a cooling draft soon billowed his shirt as the bike rattlingly sped down the road.

Five minutes later, he stopped a few yards from the iron gates, where two different men stood guard.

Asked what his business was, Ben answered: "I'm here to join the commune."

The guards exchanged humorous glances, then told him to leave.

"Look, you can search me," offered Ben, lifting up his arms. "I don't have anything on me. Just please let me in."

"Get out of here!" cried one of them with an upward sweep of his arm. "Alpha's not looking for initiates at this time."

"Where's Thane? Let me talk to him," the young man entreated. He made the mistake of stepping forward and was answered with two individual gun barrels pointing at him.

"Make tracks, boy, before you find your insides on that tree," said a guard with prominent glaring eyes.

Ben complied and retreated without a word, wondering whether he should have come with some sort of offering like they had this morning. It then occurred to him to try to pay them off with some of the cash he had on hand; he doubted Thane's elevated principles had trickled deep enough to inoculate his flock against bribes. But such had been his hurry to leave before Grim returned that, as he checked his pockets, Ben realized he had left his wallet back in the apartment. He despondently went on wheeling his bike down a path that curved around a clump of trees till he disappeared behind them. From there, he peeled off the road, trampling through the tall grass towards the eight-foot wall surrounding the compound, and walked alongside it, searching for a way in—a collapsed segment or a large tree that grew near the wall and threw a sturdy branch over the wrought iron spikes. This begat the idea of standing the bike against the wall and using it to help him climb up.

The idea worked well-enough as he reached and grabbed one spike shaft in each hand, planted his feet against the wall, and slowly walked them up. After that, he struggled to pull himself up, stuck in an ungainly position before his feet slipped and slid down the wall. It took a few failed tries before muscle memory from his training days kicked in, and he threw one leg over the top of the wall, taking care to avoid the spikes, braced his foot against the base of the shaft, and managed to hoist himself up. He paused for a breathless chuckle of triumph before rearranging himself to clear the rails without getting impaled, and landed hard on the other side, the ground receiving him with surprising rigidity. But he made it nonetheless, and for fear of being discovered, he kept his head down and skittered through the tall grass.

A dense orchard of unkempt trees soon received him, and expecting to find children roaming about, Ben dug into his trouser pockets for a couple of peppermint rounds that Olivia had left with his lunch, hoping the candy would purchase their silence. Yet so far, not a soul was met or heard; compared to the populated grounds they observed this morning, the shady groves appeared deserted, with little more than fingers of light sloping through the trees.

Just when Ben began to suspect he may have landed in an adjacent property, he reached a clearing that overlooked the lake, and traced the shoreline with his eyes till he spotted the looming resort building and started towards it.

The sprawling lawns appeared just as empty, save for a comatose pig lying next to an overturned table, and a couple of mangy chickens, fretfully chirping as they hopped off the pig's round flank to scratch and peck the brown earth.

But the closer he got to the building, the more he began to hear melodious traces of a song meandering through the grand double doors. Thrown wide open, they showed men and women crowding the entrance: some stood or leaned against walls, cradling their babies; others sat on the floor with toddlers in their laps as they continued to sing over them.

For fear the two guards might come this way, Ben squeezed himself into the crowd and entered the building. None seemed to mind him as he pressed past them, though none made way for him either. The air was close, pregnant with the living odor of breath and exertion, and hung with acrid smoke made visible by filtering sunlight and suspended in ghostly ribbons over their jolly heads. Ben passed over a seated man, who whooped over some part of the song, punching the air and almost inadvertently delivering a painful strike to the young man, who shrank back in time to avoid it. Finally, he reached the lobby with its high ceiling, and was able to lower the fist he had closed over his nose.

He expected to find Thane at his throne-cum-pulpit, but it was a white-haired woman who had the stage and was leading the assembly in their lively song. Her role was brief, concluded by her flapping her hands to hush the crowd. And as a reverent silence seized the room, Thane stepped out of the vine-covered wings.

He did not take his seat, but stood eyeing the faces surrounding him in a semi-circle. The weight of his unblinking gaze was magnified by the stillness it inspired: even small children and infants were not heard in those seconds that seemed to stretch to minutes. Ben was nowhere near the front row, yet even as he stood in the half-dark, away from any shaft of light, he couldn't help wondering if Thane's hawkish stare would pick him out of a crowd. But the man in question went on scrutinizing the assembly without any perceptible interruption in his survey. And having established his presence so, the severity of his expression mellowed into something like affection.

"My people!" he thundered. "My kindred! The sweet notes of rapture had fed me to satiety! These are not the sounds of empty bellies and weak constitutions. These hardy, hearty voices shake the very vaults of the skies. Let them hear us, for we are made for a greater purpose! Never will we pine and beg and put collars around our necks for meager rewards. We have transcended these hideous wants. Exult in the freedom we have traded for that miserable life. But lest we forget where we came from—lest we take these heights for granted—let us look back on where we began. Let us look back on those black days when we measured our worth by false standards. Mark me! For I stand before you as an example." He went on as he began unbuttoning his calico shirt, "I present to you the stigmas of that life."

The shirt dropped to his feet while he stood with his sinewy arms laterally extended, palms out, displaying the ragged scars—scars in various shades of white and livid pink—scars encircling his arms and stretched over his pasty chest and tufted stomach. His head was slightly bowed but with the eyes looking ahead, almost challenging the room.

"Like you I was weaned on capitalism, on worshipping these icons, man-made and false. Such was my fervor that I sold my body for a canvas: one by one, I had them tattooed on my skin. These symbols bound me fast to the ideas of others. No more! My eyes were open to the truth. And once I saw them for what they were, they became so vile that I took a razor, and then and there began shedding my old skin." He broke off, allowing time for that image to sink in before continuing. "The scars you see are but reminders of shackles that once were and now are no more."

The arms came down, and he went on pacing the stage without bothering to put his shirt back on. "A parasite that bears its true form and makes evident its intentions, is a known enemy. More insidious are the institutions that come to you in the benign guise of health and education. Young Bobbie there—" he pointed at some unseen person in the crowd, where presumably Bobbie sat—"was a number in their system. A child who struggled to express himself, to communicate with his parents. They took Bobbie to so-called experts, desperate to get him talking. And what did their experts do? Two—three different doctors put him on the same medication which made him worse. He lashed out at everyone. So-called therapists charged a king's ransom alleging help and got nowhere. Not only was he not talking, he was miserable and upset. You all know him—but look at him, now! Come my boy, come forward."

A boy of about seven stood up at his parents' behest and made his way to the front, guided by the hands of other members that encouraged him along the way. When he reached Thane, the man clasped the boy's shoulders with benign gravity and turned him to face the audience.

"Now look at him," Thane repeated, smoothing the boy's silky brown hair with fatherly pride and tenderness—the unexpectedness of which Ben found almost touching. "This sweet child—a son to us all—calm, focused, and most importantly happy with his life. Tell me, Bobbie—and tell everyone—do you miss your old home? Hm? Do you want to go back to it?"

Bobbie shook his head vigorously in answer to both questions.

"And what would you say to anyone who promised you gifts to go back with them?"

Again Bobbie shook his head.

"What if they said you can leave for a new life in a new place?"

Bobbie glanced at the audience before whispering something with downcast eyes.

"Speak up, son, let them hear you."

"Here I stay," the boy mechanically repeated.

"Louder, Bobbie! Let them hear your—" and before Thane could finish his sentence, Bobbie burst out with a ringing reiteration, to which Thane threw back his head and laughed as the audience broke out with equal delight. The boy, somewhat overwhelmed at the applause and attention, lowered his head with a shy, gap-toothed smile.

With the sermon ending on that happy note, Ben made for the stage, moving against the dispersing crowd. So convivial was the atmosphere, so full of the familial spirit, that no one shoved past him, but let him pass unimpeded. That is, until a rude clap on Ben's shoulder jolted him out of this perception, and he promptly discovered that one of the guards had seized him and was about to throw him out. Resisting his arrest, the young man lurched forward, arguing that he just wished to have a word with Thane.

His loud protests reached the ears of the man in question, who at that moment was speaking with a few members of the commune, and who glanced up to see what the commotion was about. Without interrupting his conference, Thane raised his hand beckoned the guard to bring the boy.

"Be not inhospitable to strangers lest they be angels in disguise," he benevolently edified as the guard approached him; to Ben he simply said: "What's your business, boy?"

"I want to join the commune."

Some of the members surrounding Thane thought this warranted chuckles and exchanged glances, while Thane himself remained unmoved by this.

"Where's your friend at?" he asked.

"I ran off, sir. He doesn't know I'm... here," said Ben, faltering at the end when he perceived a subtle reaction all around.

"We don't use titles like 'sir' amongst us," Thane informed him without further explanation, leaving Ben to conclude the word had either been banished for its ties to their former life, or because Thane preferred his own choice of titles.

"Yes, of course..." said Ben, pausing to omit the fatal word.

Thane smiled at him. "And what decided you to join us?"

"I was inspired—by the sermon I heard this morning—and just now. It opened my eyes to what you said yesterday—when we met at Mr. Atwood—"

"You sure it wasn't from getting smacked in the eye?"

"Oh," Ben smiled sheepishly, stopping himself halfway from touching his blackened eye. "That might be it too," he owned. "See, I was never taught the important things in life. Everything with the old man was just work, work, work—"

"Is he your pop?" Thane asked.

"No. Well, he's an uncle—of sorts. I'm adopted, you see, so he's not really my uncle—just a legal guardian of sorts—or was, since I'm an adult now and can make my own decisions."

The more he struggled to explain, the wider Thane's smile seemed to grow, though his tone was stern when he next spoke.

"This isn't some pleasure island, boy. We may not answer to anyone, but we still put in our share of work."

"But it's in the service of something grand and noble," Ben hastily qualified. "I want to be a part of it. To feel like I earned my place here."

Thane gave a faint sniff of a laugh then turned away and began to walk. His pace was slow and leisurely, like a man strolling through a botanical garden, perhaps inviting Ben to follow him.

Ben did follow, almost asking if he could stay; yet an inner voice warned him against speaking without being addressed. Their stroll carried them through the tall French windows and out into a wild garden. Now and then, Thane would come to a halt, keeping his back to Ben, seeming on the verge of saying something before moving on without uttering a word. He was barefoot, and though not a man of large or heavy stature, he could not stand long without worming his long toes into the rich soil, as if trying to root himself to that very spot.

"Our numbers are large," he finally said, still with his back turned and his hands clasped behind. "With many mouths to feed. What can you contribute to the commune?"

"Whatever you need, I'm willing to do," asserted Ben.

Thane bent his eye on a thicket of barren trees. "Can you craft? Can you hunt, fish, or forage?"

"I can learn," the young man professed, hoping his enthusiasm would make up for his inadequacy.

Thane received this in silence; and finding his own answer paltry, Ben was on the verge of saying more when the other man spoke.

"We don't just welcome anyone with open arms. We need to be sure they can withstand a tough life—that they're not parasites looking to live at the expense of others."

The words themselves did not give Ben pause so much as warn him of what was to come. He hardly withstood half-a-day of camping outside Atwood's house, and now he had to consider going days without regular meals and proper hygiene, to say nothing of hard, thankless labor...

But no—he couldn't afford to dwell on it; he knew he would chicken out if he did. Besides, that was the old, useless Ben—an inconsequential agent who only had to tag along, observe and report. This Ben was irrevocably tied to the mission by his own blunder. And he knew he could be resourceful: if he managed to get in, he would find a way to locate the cargo and sneak out. It might not even take more than a couple of days. And then imagine the look on Grim's face when he, Ben, returned, starving and dirt-crusted, but beaming with triumph over the missing cargo, which he would be carrying—or transporting—back in some way...

"Whatever it takes, I'll do it," Ben agreed. "I'm tired of not getting anywhere in life. One chance to prove myself, that's all I ask."

The words seemed to satisfy Thane, who finally turned to face him. He led Ben back to the building, where he called for someone to fetch them a drink.

"For the initiate," he stipulated, and in a matter of minutes, a tray bearing two glasses of some opaque, umber liquid was brought to them.

"Whatever it takes," said Thane, raising a glass to toast the occasion.

"Whatever it takes," said Ben, raising a glass to down his drink in one go.

The frothy liquid smelled like the inside of a well; he saw it had a thick consistency though he did not expect it to be pulpy—at least not to the extent of feeling something slimy slide down his throat. He gave a choked, involuntary cry, issuing more from his nose than mouth; but lest any sign of disgust injure his chances, Ben screwed his eyes shut and drained his glass.

At that instant, he extraneously recalled the famous toast, "Here's mud in your eye!" and thought the expression apt—if ill-timed—as he swayed blurry-eyed, heaving a few breaths, and fighting to keep his stomach from doing the same. If he began to have doubts or second thoughts about his plan, they winked out as soon as his eyes rolled back in their sockets.

CHAPTER 15

The first returning sensation was that of a gritty surface pressed against Ben's temple and cheek. He lay on his side with a head so heavy it strained his neck and shoulder. And though he expected a dizzy spell agitating him as soon as he sat up, that was not why he remained down.

When he tried to raise himself, Ben discovered his hands were tied behind his back, while his feet were bound together. Soon followed the realization that he was blindfolded too, which came last thanks to a lingering numbness that made him somewhat insensible to the band placed over his eyes.

He took an unsteady deep breath to calm himself. After all, he was an initiate, and the situation showed symptoms of hazing, a rite he was familiar with thanks to his training days. This certainly explained why Thane's interview was not quite as rigorous as Ben had expected. Actions trump words, and what better way to test his mettle than to subject him to a test.

His cheeks puffed up with the breath he blew out, releasing it nice and slow. This was a test, after all, one which he couldn't afford to fail. No doubt this was a test—in spite of his reluctance, Thane had looked pleased at gaining a new member—maybe even flattered. Why would he suspect anything? Meanwhile, it was hard to breathe. Either he was overheated, or the room itself was too warm and humid: The damp blindfold wilted over his eyes, and his sweat-sodden shirt clove to his back. He began to shift uncomfortably, trying to unstick the fabric, then froze when he heard something.

Either the sound had been elicited by his squirming, or caused by another presence in the room. Ben raised his head to listen, and hearing nothing surreptitiously sniffed the moist air, which bore hints of a sweet, grimy scent, like hay or straw laced with rot. The prevalent hush soon began to unnerve him, and he fell back on regulating his breathing to calm himself, telling himself that apart from being bound and blindfolded, there were no signs of immediate danger. So he kept inwardly repeating as he slowly released one long exhale before drawing in another. But the second breath stalled a moment when he heard someone speak over him.

"Oh, lily boy—white lily boy," a raspy voice intoned. "What are we to do with you?"

The words crept cold, and the breath Ben caught vanished through parted lips. All thoughts of hazing and tests abandoned him as he wrestled between a panicked need to struggle free and an abating wariness to keep still lest his fearful writhing encouraged the man hovering over him.

Half-expecting—indeed dreading the subsequent touch that might follow, and which grew more formidable when nothing seemed to happen, Ben remained motionless, transfixed by fear and listening for signs of the man's movement. Surely, he had to shift or shuffle his feet, or do something other than remain hunched all gargoyle-like over him. But seconds piled on seconds without sign or sound, without even an odd laugh to relieve the cruel silence. Unable to bear it, Ben began to move, essaying to sit up, when a hand was laid over his head.

"Oh, he's a twitchy one he is," spoke the gravelly voice with a lilt of humor, the hand smoothing back Ben's hair in long, loving sweeps. "There's a good lamb. Now you just keep nice and still and it'll all be over soon."

Ben could not answer. Every response seemed to disintegrate into fine powder before it was uttered, more so when the calloused hand cupped his chin to lift it, as though the person attached to it was trying to get a good look at him.

The young man clenched his teeth to keep his lips from trembling, swallowing back a lump and feeling it bob down his throat. Do as he would to bolster his resolve, he could not settle whether this creep was even part of the initiation—let alone what that rite entailed. The older boys from his training days may have been cruel when it came to hazing, but rules and retributions kept them from crossing certain lines. No such boundaries applied here.

On the brink of calling out for help, Ben obstinately pressed his lips together, stifling all the small involuntary sounds, which nonetheless issued softly through his nose in a string of hitched exhales. He then felt the thin edge of a knife or machete along the side of his neck with the hilt grazing his clavicle.

"You make a sound," warned the voice, "and I'll gut you like a fish and make you eat your insides."

The sharp edge seamed down his throat and was lost to the numbing cold as a dead calm settled over him. Like a rooted tree in the face of an avalanche, whatever terrible thing that was to come, he could not hope to ward it off. And the final vestige—the last illusion of control was to lie still and let whatever horrible thing that was to happen take its course.

All at once his body seemed a separate thing, as though he had been expelled from it. There was no comfort, no solace in such thoughts. It was a reduction in the service of survival, of preserving a part of him against the worst of what was to come, or containing as much of his parts that were to be shattered in the coming blow, so that afterwards he may try and piece them back together.

So he remained in that catatonic state, marginally aware of the unseen creep, who was doing something to the ropes binding his ankles, failing even to register the sensation of being lifted and carried outside; only after he had been laid down on a bed of wooden slats did his shock-addled mind begin to thaw and perceive the strange chanting surrounding him.

The song concluded in due course, after which Thane spoke, the crackle of fire in his voice.

"We chosen few have shunned the outer world—a diseased world, rampant with greed. We have shunned its society and built our nest here, over these ruins, to lead our lives in peace. But instead of respecting our wishes—instead of leaving us in peace, the outer world came looking for us: enamored with owning every living soul, its arm like a greedy snake winding through every nook and crevice. And what does a hive do when an arm dares disturbs it? It fights back. Before you is an agent of that enemy—a finger of the very arm that tipped the vat, and poisoned our waters. Why? Because they want to sicken us, they want to eradicate us! They think we're not wise to their plan. They believe we'll come running back, begging them to cure our ailments. But here's my answer: I say we give them a taste of their own poison. I say we make an example of this agent and others like him!"

Still enmeshed in his trance, Ben understood what this was leading to. It was the same old story: someone was angry, and he was selected as a sacrifice to appease them. From what he gathered, their grievance was over the polluted lake, and the fact that he was in no way responsible for it mattered little when he answered their idea of a corporate type—an effigy turned scapegoat, on which they focused all their anger and exasperation. No one saw the absurdity in all this; or if they did, Thane smoothed over those cracks in reason with strong strokes and deft words. Nothing will change for them come tomorrow, except the fleeting satisfaction that they have struck back and insulted their foes in some way.

But comprehending all this in the strange, omniscient way one gains an encompassing understanding of events in a dream, such as knowing what's beyond a closed door without having to open it—comprehending all this did little to rouse Ben out of his trance. The preceding sensation of a knife's edge sliding down his throat seemed to have severed him from his reality. His body lurched as the bed of slats was hoisted up and carried forward, and a musty odor foreshadowed the faint splash as two-by-two the men stepped into the water, and there lowered the slats, which Ben now understood served as some form of a raft. Cold water seeped through, soaking his side; at its touch, his trance broke.

Panic-stricken, Ben started with a frantic squirm and kicked his bound feet. He must have pushed against something, as with a pitch forward the raft began to move. The hands holding him fell back with loud splashes, almost capsizing the raft; but soon it settled and continued to drift.

Whoever bound his feet had been careless—unless the creep with the knife had tried to undo the ropes for his own purpose; either way, Ben felt the ropes slacken enough for him to separate his ankles a trifle, and after a series of wrenching and twisting, and scraping the heel of his shoe to pry it off, he succeeded in pulling one leg free. His hands remained bound behind him, and just as he tried to figure how to deal with them, he felt the raft jolt again and heard vexed plashes before wet hands brushed against him to grab him. He shrank back, but they seemed to come from all directions, as did their angry shouts and cries. Again, the cold water washed over the wooden boards, reminding him how easily he could sink down.

Suddenly, a hand that had caught the edge of his pant leg seemed to jerk back, as if its owner had slipped, or stumbled, and fell into the semi-deep waters. Then another pair of hands likewise yanked back, their surprised yelp cut-off by a splash.

Things grew quiet, and all Ben could hear as he raised his head was water gently lapping the wooden raft. Even the crowd lining the shore could not be heard. In the eerie stillness, and in his temporary blind state, the odor of slimy water was all he could perceive.

Then, something struck the raft from below, sending it and its passenger flying into the air. In that briefest of brief moments in which Ben still hung suspended in the air before gravity forced his plummet, he had a moment to wonder whether he would hit land or water, and if the latter whether he could still make it to shore with his hands bound. Too soon the answer came: his head broke the surface of water, and the rest of him followed as he plunged deep down.

The feeble kicks that had begun in air now grew furious. He tumbled and twisted, desperate to orient himself. Not being far from shore, his body soon reached the lakebed; and having located firm ground, he pushed his feet against it and surged upwards, trailing behind a cluster of minute bubbles till he broke through the surface, open-mouthed and gasping.

Ben coughed and spat the foul, metallic taste, clenching his teeth against the swelling ripples and craning his neck to keep his mouth and nose above water. The blindfold, now plastered over his eyes, seemed to further smother him, and it was all he could do to keep panic from boiling back up as he struggled to stay afloat. Which direction to swim for seemed irrelevant just then, so long as beneath him his legs swung and kicked and kept him from sinking.

But all at once, something lashed around one of his ankles, and the living rope constricted as it pulled, dragging him down. The precious air he had toiled for now rushed out of him, his sunken cry not so much sound as a foamy wake. Another tendril stole over his shoulder and wrapped around his neck, towing him back. Then, something more substantial than water enfolded him, like jaws of a Venus flytrap that snapped him up in blind haste, leaving one leg still jutting out. Not granting him a chance to twist and thrash, a needle jabbed Ben's side; and within seconds, he fell still.

CHAPTER 16

Ben felt tightly packed. Not physically: his conscious, or soul, or some intangible part of him seemed wedged somewhere in the center of his body under a weight so tremendous that nothing moved—not even a breath was drawn.

Then an outer pressure was applied, and he had the sense of being pushed down—or rather pumped—again and again, in a quick, steady rhythm, until all at once a wet rushing force alleviated the pressure, letting him expand out into his body in aching, lung bruising coughs.

He was turned over and his hands were subsequently freed. But the chest pain was still fresh when he felt another discomfort: that of being carried, his body slung against something hard and unyielding, a surface covered with raised slabs that dug into his middle. He gave a pained groan, caught a fleeting glimpse of the shifting ground, complained inwardly of his awkward position, was almost certain he was going to slip and fall; but whoever it was that carried him little heeded his involuntary pained groans and coughing spasms.

All the aches and pains did little to fix the reality of the episode in his mind; and when he next opened his eyes, it was to the bright ceiling of their rented room, with the comforting texture of a fleece blanket over his chest. The washer-dryer unit churned soft in the kitchen, and a lingering aura of coffee added the last touch of sunlit, domestic calm. Everything, in short, was incongruous with the preceding events that Ben almost fancied the whole harrowing incident was nothing more than a fever-induced nightmare.

Except he swallowed now, and winced at the raw, barbed feeling it inflicted. The hand he lifted to rub his throat smelled like rust; both it and its counterpart were coated with a dried glaze of dirt.

Ben turned his head at the sound of the bathroom door opening and saw Grim emerge, sleek-headed with a bath towel around his waist. He paused a little as he stepped out, as if surprised at finding his subordinate already awake.

If there was a hint of relief in his eyes, Ben didn't get a chance to see it: his attention was taken up by the angry bruises covering Grim's arms and torso. Something about it harkened back to the scars Thane had shown during his sermon, but while his were old and ragged, the marks covering Grim were fresh and geometric in pattern, almost like panels had been pressed to his skin.

Grim's face clouded over, his brief surprise hardening into stern indifference as he headed into the kitchen without saying a word.

Ben meanwhile had dropped his gaze, trying to muster some defense for his actions; yet as his senior took his time in the kitchen—whence the dryer's churning terminated with a click of its door—the young man saw little use in trying to explain his motives. Only results would have excused his foolhardy action.

Grim reemerged, now dressed in his accustomed black t-shirt and shorts, his black hair smoothed back, the damp tips of which feathered out behind his ears.

"How you feeling?" he asked, dragging a chair to Ben's bedside.

The neutral tone surprised his subordinate into lifting his head from its penitent bend.

"I- guess I'm okay, sir," he faltered, meeting the sharp gaze with a look of uncertainty.

"Any weird sensations?" Grim pursued. "Any auditory or visual hallucinations? Phantoms? Dizziness, giddiness—vertigo?"

"I guess I'm a little light-headed."

"You be sure and tell me if you start to feel anything out of the ordinary, you hear?"

"Yes, sir."

"Good. Care to explain how the hell you ended up playing virgin sacrifice with the rat king and his merry commune?" Grim demanded, switching suddenly from calm concern to cold acrimony.

"Actually, I..." Ben was about to correct his senior on a technicality, but a look warned him against attempting any smart comebacks. He cleared his throat and began again. "I don't think he's that picky, sir. He wants us both gone."

Grim looked away with a caustic smile, folding his arms as he leaned back in his chair. He had the clean aura of one fresh out of a shower, but like Ben's hands, there was something dim about his complexion that made the whites of his eyes brilliant and his teeth glisten by contrast. "So you went all the way there just to check if we're still on a want-to-kill-each-other basis."

Ben contrived to meet his gaze, then dropped back to staring at his own balled up fists. "He tricked me, sir."

"Tricked you into what? Into playing lamb for the slaughter?"

"No, he…" Ben paused to get a fresh start. "I told him I wanted to join the commune. I did it to get the cargo back. It all seemed to go well, until—well—until it didn't."

"I see," dryly said Grim, folding his arms.

The lack of sympathy galled the young man. "Why are you mad at me for?" he broke out in a flare of temper. "I was trying to fix my mistake. I didn't go there just to mess around with Thane and his commune. I assure you it was the other way round! They're the ones who seemed to get a kick out of doing—whatever the hell they were trying to do!"

For a moment, Grim didn't say anything, leaving Ben to wallow in self-pity. Then he leaned forward, and delivered a sharp flick to Ben's left temple.

"I don't give a damn about your good intentions," said the senior with underlying anger. "That's no excuse for going off half-cocked. The situation could have easily sailed past deep shit and into FUBAR territory. He could have had you tortured or killed—not that you need me to point it out to you," he concluded with a sniff.

Ben hid his wounded look, pretending to rub his left temple. He remained unsure of what next to say, whether he was expected to agree or apologize—not that he could trust himself to say anything without his voice trembling. A meek nod and a "Yes, sir," was what came easiest to him, though somehow he guessed a mollifying answer was not what his senior was after. In fact, he didn't seem interested in any answer as he slumped back in his seat and fell into pensive silence.

"How'd you manage to find me, sir?" the young man faltered out once the quiet grew unbearable.

"I traced your phone."

At the mention of his phone, Ben made a convulsive gesture, clutching his bare chest as if reaching for his breast pocket.

"Relax, it's over here," said his senior, getting up to fetch the phone out of the desk drawer. From there, he held it up for his subordinate to see, and much to the latter's relief, the screen was black but otherwise appeared intact. Besides losing his phone, Ben dreaded the possibility of Grim finding or reading messages concerning his secret task; he somewhat wished it was broken, if just to absolve him of that responsibility now that he was falling behind on his report.

Grim tossed the phone back into the drawer and slid it shut.

"We're not calling HQ, so you can forget about it," he muttered as he returned to his bedside seat, moving with a slight limp. "I'll be holding on to it just to make sure you don't run off on your own again. I'd tan your hide if I had the energy. Then again, I'm pretty sure at some point you were kicking yourself and thinking 'Oh, if only I'd listened and stayed by the phone like I was told to!' But no—no you had to do things your way because: 'we're not getting anywhere doing things your way, sir!' but ah—see, that's the rub, scout, because I was getting somewhere," he grumbled, grimacing a little as he sat down.

"You heard back from Harper, sir?" Ben asked, sweeping a downward glance in Grim's general direction and noting the same faded grid-like indentations covering the senior's legs.

"If she called, no one was around to answer," Grim pointed out, absently scratching a raw-looking patch of skin on his arm. "No, I went back to Atwood's. Found a trapdoor in the kitchen leading to a subterranean lab of sorts: equipment— aquariums—some sort of cell room with clear polycarbonate walls—I think you see where I'm going with this."

Ben did not, but hazarded a guess. "You found the cargo?"

A corner of Grim's mouth hitched up in a half-smile—less derisive and more surprised at his subordinate's lack of awareness. "You know that thing that grabbed you in the lake? That's the cargo."

His subordinate stared at him, perplexity passing through slow understanding and into incredulity. In trying to explain to himself what had happened, Ben had presumed his leg got tangled with some stray rope; or more likely, a floundering member of the commune had grabbed his ankle and dragged him down to drown him, stabbing his side as an added measure. But these presumptions were provisional at best, filling a gap where explanation was wanting; neither theory satisfied why the second arm that closed around his neck was vine-thin, or explained the mass that enveloped him like a hand closing over a moth.

"But the cargo container couldn't have been wider than three feet, and that thing was…" Ben paused, struggling to get an estimate of its size.

"Must have been a nymph when we brought it in," said Grim, as though that clarified matters.

"What was it, sir?"

"A kraken."

"You said that before."

"I know it, scout."

"No, I mean—afterwards you said you were full of crap, sir. But you were right."

The senior looked away with cool diffidence. "Yeah, well, there's a world of difference between being right and expecting the worst. I guess in some stupid way I was hoping to prove myself wrong just by saying it out loud. Not that it's a shot in the dark given the setting, the secrecy—the 'specialist'—it's been one the organization's pet project for the past couple of years."

"Pet project for what, sir?"

"Oh, anything and everything, I imagine."

"Well, what type of creature is it?"

Grim sat hunched over, elbows on his thighs, and hands loosely clasped between his knees. As he spoke he began to move slightly in a gentle rocking motion that he seemed unaware of.

"I know about it as much as any grunt hired to guard the facility that houses it," he said offhandedly. "I know it's living—it's sentient: it eats, it thinks—it breeds…"

The last was a stilted postscript, after which he trailed off and grew still for a moment, staring into the distance.

"So what do we do now, sir?"

Somehow the words reached Grim through his thousand-yard stare. "I don't know. I don't even want to think about how the hell we're going to catch it."

"You said you guarded these things—"

"I said I guarded a facility that housed them," Grim irritably corrected.

"Then, what's the usual procedure for an escaped kraken?"

"Locate it and coerce it back into its cage," answered Grim, accompanying each step with an emphatic, almost sarcastic nod to illustrate the oversimplification of the process. "But that requires a whole team armed with weapons, equipment—"

"You have your shotgun, sir."

Grim chuckled at that. "Against a kraken? Pfft! Haven't got a prayer, son." His smile disappeared as soon as he said it, dropping his gaze to stare past his right knee. "You know, I went out to look for it. Found some tracks and followed them

into the woods. Almost got close to it. I know I was. That's
when I realized I wasn't sure what to do next. Or maybe I
did—I just..."

It might have been a restless foot that vibrated Grim's
knee; it was hard to say: just when Ben noticed it, his senior
trailed off, bent forward and pressed his forehead against his
clasped hands.

"Did you check the underground lab, sir?" the young man
chipped in, buoyed by the idea. "Maybe there's something
there that could help. After all, if Mr. Atwood was supposed
to look after the kraken himself, I'm sure the organization
provided him with adequate tools and equipment in case of an
emergency like this."

A lengthy minute passed without response, and just when
Ben's heart sank, thinking that the other man had already
scoured the lab and found nothing of use, Grim lifted his
head back up.

CHAPTER 17

"How long have I been out?" Ben asked as he passed by the window and saw the world outside steeped in amber light.

"About eighteen hours," answered Grim, who had stepped into his jeans and was shrugging on the same plaid shirt he wore when they first arrived.

Ben likewise retrieved his original attire of white shirt and khakis, all rumpled up from the dryer. But when he went to put on his shoes, he found only one had survived the incident, the other having been kicked off in his struggle to peel away the ankle ropes. He sadly pondered the bachelor shoe before casting it aside, removed his socks, and stuffed them into his trouser pockets, hoping Atwood's wardrobe would offer something in his size.

As they drove back to the cabin, Ben kept scratching a spot over his left hip, lifting the side of his untucked shirt to re-examine the swollen welt there.

"Leave it alone. You're just making it worse," warned Grim, fishing something out of his shirt pocket. "Might as well start taking these, given what we're dealing with."

"What for?" Ben asked, regarding the semi-opaque brown bottle Grim had pulled out.

"Think of them as an extra layer of protection against—" the senior thoughtfully wagged the bottle while he searched for an apt phrase—"Well, let's just say it makes you less desirable as prey and leave it at that."

Ben, seizing upon the word "Prey", and at the same instant catching the steering wheel Grim had momentarily released to shake out a pill, nervously asked: "You mean it's man-eating?"

"It's more what you might call a carrion eater," Grim answered, swallowing his pill dry before passing the bottle on to his subordinate.

"So it's not deadly," Ben surmised, reflecting on how things played out—how the kraken had caught him, thinking perhaps he was a corpse, and then released him when it discovered he was not.

"I said it prefers carrions—I didn't say it's incapable of making them," Grim sharply corrected. "You'd be a bloated corpse if I hadn't made it to you in time."

"Thank you, sir," muttered the young man, stung by the response. "I know I'm more trouble than I'm worth," he added with an air of self-castigation.

Grim glanced at him with a sneer. "Don't drag your hang-ups into this. I know I spout a lot of crap, but I mean it when I say we look out for each other. And also stop nursing that bottle and take one, already. You'll need it to keep your head on a swivel. Especially when it comes to krakens. Remember: the best practice is 'keep your distance and do not engage.'"

He seemed about to elaborate, then closed his mouth in a grimace, scratching the back of his head in agitation. "Not that we have a choice—there's no avoiding engaging with it. So, let's just try to keep our distance and stay protected."

"By taking these?" Ben asked, holding a red pill up to the setting sun to examine it.

Grim shook his head, well-aware of the weakness of his plan. "Well, maybe you should keep a distance."

"What about you, sir?"

"I got my own rig, I'm covered."

"Rig?"

"Protective gear. 'Tegmen' we call it."

"Like hazmat suits?"

"Not exactly, no," answered the senior without further elaboration.

Down in the underground lab, Grim switched on the fluorescent grid lamps suspended from the exposed ceiling; one by one they flickered, like blinking sentinels waking from a drugged sleep. Unlike the homey cabin above, the white-walled lab waxed neat and untouched, and to Ben's dazzled eyes, every surface sparkled as if seen through a film of splintered glass; the bubbling aquatic tanks, the console unit, the shiny lines of instruments, trays, and glass dishes—once ready and now bereft of purpose—all bespoke a lonely preoccupation like that of an expectant parent prepping a nursery for their infant.

In secret, Ben entertained the possibility that Atwood might have slit his own throat; it remained secret because he lacked evidence to support his theory: No knife or other sharp instrument was found near the body; then again, it might have been there, albeit lost in the disarray when Grim turned the place upside down. But above all, Ben wished this was the case because it altogether cleared him of any responsibility, since it would have happened regardless of whether or not he kept his watch. And yet, the immaculate state of the secret lab alone was a testimony to Atwood's eager devotion; moreover, the man seemed anxious to start working, and was indeed working till late on that fateful night.

On that account, Ben kept his thoughts to himself as he moved alongside Grim, who headed straight towards the lab's main feature.

"There," he said, pointing out a transparent polycarbonate wall that divided a spacious cell from the rest of the lab. "I've seen a setup like this before. That pipe though—" leaning to one side to get a better view of the wide-mouthed pipe extending from one of the cell walls—"that's very unusual. The whole idea of keeping the kraken contained is to minimize holes it might escape through." He surveyed the interior of the cell, the floor of which dipped several feet below, as if the enclosure itself was an inground pool. "Those drain holes there are covered with grates. Krakens would often pry them out and poke inside, like they're trying to squeeze through."

"Can they?" Ben asked, watching the senior gnaw his thumb out of the corner of his eye.

"Ever heard of a six-hundred-pound octopus squeezing through a one-inch diameter hole?" said Grim. "I've never seen it, but imagine it's something like that. Maybe it's not to the same extent as an octopus, but it's enough to make you sleep with one eye open. We've had a few cases where kraken broke those grates, not to escape so much as to get some of the maintenance guys in. Oh, they loved to mess with us, they did! They'd do it a couple of times and behave themselves while the guy who drew the shortest straw went in to fix the grate or whatever else they broke. I was on shift when they were sending one of them in. The scientists kept reassuring him that this specimen was a docile one, and that other repairmen went in before and came out unharmed. You should hear the smug tone they had while explaining it, like they understood that specimen's personality or behavioral pattern. Not ten seconds after the maintenance guy walked in, we heard screams as the same docile kraken that kept to its corner tore into him."

Ben stared at Grim, who in turn stared at the empty enclosure, with traces of the same faraway look he had when first describing what the kraken was.

"What happened to the maintenance guy?" asked Ben.

"You know the worst part was that none of it was necessary," Grim continued, seeming not to have heard the question. "The grates were irrelevant. Even if they were taken off, the kraken couldn't go anywhere. But no, they just had to send someone in…"

He trailed off, and instead of repeating his question, Ben inquired on how the maintenance crew managed to enter and leave the enclosure without the kraken breaking out.

Again, Grim seemed to not have heard the question; but a second later he said: "See that corridor there?" first pointing to and then leading Ben towards an L-shaped corridor adjacent to the kraken's enclosure. Two doors stood on either end of the corridor, each with its own keypad. "You need to enter a security code to open either door," Grim went on. "It activates the electrified floor in that corridor. The voltage is high enough to deter the kraken without killing it. It also turns on all these lights above." He indicated the recessed spotlights in the ceiling that were presently flooding the enclosure with white light. "Krakens like it dark, and usually that's how they're kept until someone has to come in. The lights act like a flash grenade—it stuns them for ten to fifteen seconds. Not enough time to do anything—then again, it's never a good idea to go in at all."

"So, what if we draw it here," Ben began, "get it into the enclosure and then activate the floor?"

Grim shook his head. "Each enclosure has its unique security code and we don't have that. Besides, the doors are open now, which means the system is not even set up. The lights are on but the electric floor is not. Could be malfunctioned. Or maybe they meant to send others after us to take care of all that."

"Perhaps Mr. Atwood was meant to set it up," suggested Ben, nervous at the thought of staff members encroaching on them at this stage, even if they were a maintenance crew. "Otherwise he wouldn't have been able to handle a creature this size."

"He doesn't have to," said Grim. "I'm sure the container it came in had enough liquid to keep it viable for days without substantial growth."

They both stood quiet for a moment, then Grim headed for the console unit installed between the enclosure and small aquatic tanks. It featured a control panel of gauges, dials and switches, which so far did little besides turn the aquarium lights and filters on and off. Ben's eyes skimmed over labels with codes, numbers, and others less obscure like "Flood," "Pump" and "Drain"; none however seemed relevant to the electrified floor, which no doubt Grim was trying to activate, given the sideway glances he cast in that direction each time he flipped a switch.

When nothing fruitful came of it, he abandoned the console, turning his attention back to the pipe that first roused his curiosity, this time entering the enclosure for a closer look.

A set of crude steps carried them with reverberating footfalls down the sloping concrete floor and towards the pipe's mouth, laterally projecting three feet above ground. Grim stooped to look inside, and his phone's flashlight revealed a thin, wet trail glistening down the bottom curve of the pipe. He traced it with his fingers, sniffed them, and frowned.

"Lake water," he murmured, wiping his fingers as he scanned the ceiling, estimating their position.

Ben, following his gaze, noticed the semi-invisible white letters that read: "lake level", indicating a thin line that ran along the walls of the cell; the line ostensibly marked the water limit, which would fill the cell without flooding the rest of the lab.

"You think the kraken got out through here?" asked Ben, returning to the pipe.

"If it did, we'd be swimming here instead of standing," answered Grim, sticking his head into the pipe's maw. "Probably got valves in there to control the water flow," said his faintly echoing voice. He withdrew, absently sweeping his hand along the rim of the pipe, as if still puzzling over its purpose.

"Maybe they're trying to see how the kraken fares in contaminated waters," Ben suggested. "I mean, they raise them in controlled environments, maybe they want to see how they handle being exposed to toxins and water-borne pathogens."

The senior glanced at him as though the possibility hadn't occurred to him, then fixed his gaze back on the pipe. "Well, if that's the case, they've got their answer now."

"Why? What else would they use the pipe for?" asked Ben, somewhat nettled by the lack of conviction.

"Oh, I was going to say it might be a feeding tube of sorts, seeing how a whole person can fit in," Grim answered. "You dump a corpse into it and…" he made a sliding motion with his hand.

"You mean a carcass," Ben amended.

"Corpse," Grim insisted.

The young man swallowed back something, trying to regain the ability to speak without worrying about losing the contents of his stomach—not that there were any contents to speak of. All of a sudden, he felt light-headed, though he was certain it was from faintness and not due to the morbid turn the conversation took.

"Not that I've seen them deliver bodies to the enclosure—too messy," Grim went on, answering a question Ben couldn't bring himself to ask. "I guess they process them into pellets—"

"We're talking about humans!" Ben cut in and almost felt like shouting.

Grim shrugged. "Scientifically speaking, what's a dead body, human or otherwise?"

"Is that how you see it, sir?"

"That's how they see it," was the evasive answer.

CHAPTER 18

The sun had dipped behind the trees by the time they quit the basement, emerging to a parlor incarnadined with remnant light.

Ben was glad to come up to cooler, clearer air; easier to breathe, and by that virtue alleviating to a persistent queasiness stirring in him. Perhaps it was faintness that brought it on, or perhaps it was the onset of some waterborne disease, contracted when he fell into the lake. Whatever the case was, it was certainly not due to Grim's disturbing report, which Ben deemed to be little more than a tall tale guards invented to while away the long hours, adding gruesome details with each retelling; even if Grim was shrewd enough to spot an inflated story, Ben reckoned the man was not above repeating it to enjoy its effect. It was true that some of the organization's practices fell into morally gray areas, but there were lines that even they did not cross. Grim, by his own admittance, had never seen a corpse delivered into a kraken's enclosure; and the pellets they fed them might have easily been of animal origin, or lab grown as opposed to processed cadavers. The young man would have argued as much, only he did not wish to dwell on the subject, especially when they walked past the same spot where they first discovered Atwood's body. Drained of color, Ben fled upstairs to find the bathroom.

A few minutes later, he left the cabin, pale yet buoyed by a mild euphoria, stepping out into a twilight cacophony of crickets calling to one another. He found Grim standing near the base of the plateau, shining his phone light onto something circular like a manhole cover, submerged two feet below the rippling surface.

"I bet that's the other end of that big pipe we saw," Grim began, and went on to say something that was lost his subordinate, who suddenly wheeled round to scan the surrounding woods.

"What?" asked Grim.

"Did you hear that, sir?" Ben inquired, concerning a distant cry he heard.

Before the other man could answer, the sound repeated: a long cry, so harsh and ragged, it cut across red skies and tore through the crickets' clamor. Grim must have heard it too, judging by his starting eyes and the way his posture stiffened as if dashed with cold water; even the crickets fell silent to this sole cry trailing the wind's hollow moan in its wake.

Something about its unidentifiable nature reminded Ben of vivid accounts he read on nineteenth century battles—how, when cavalries clashed with canons, and wounded horses fell alongside or onto maimed men, their shrill cries were wedded with anguished wails of dying men. And while he could not settle its origin—whether human or animal—more confusing, perhaps, was the effect it had on him, by turns drawing him in and driving him off, like rolling waves tossing whatever was caught in their ebbing tide.

Without warning, Grim seized Ben by the arm and lead him back to the truck. The forceful reaction was odd, since Ben would have followed him without question; and yet, he almost resisted, not quite ready to quit the spot.

After they climbed in, and Grim made sure both doors were locked, he sat back and almost appeared at a loss for what to do next; somewhere about his eyes was a touch of breathless dread as he surveyed his surroundings.

Meanwhile Ben peered out from the passenger seat window, through which came faint strains of the strange cry. Too soon it died out, leaving him with an aching forlornness that nearly drove him to unlock the door and step out. He could not explain why the sound compelled him so, knowing only that it did.

So that when Grim finally decided to investigate the source, nervously muttering to himself: "Alright… okay… I need to get out there…" it was all his subordinate could do to keep himself from heartily assenting. He retained enough self-awareness to feel alarmed at his enthusiasm—this sudden infatuation with cries one could only describe as distressed. But the impulse sprang from a deep source, a part of him that superseded such reservations, akin to being plagued with a maddening itch in the presence of polite company, so that everything seemed secondary to stealing a private moment for a furtive scratch.

"Stay here," ordered Grim as he disembarked.

Ben jumped down from the passenger's side.

"I'm coming with you, sir," he announced when Grim regarded him with surprise and annoyance.

"I said stay put," firmly bade the senior, making for the back of the truck.

"Why?"

"I'm going after it."

"It?"

"The kraken."

"The kraken?" echoed Ben; and seeing him hesitate, Grim again ordered him to stay behind. But as soon as he withdrew, the young man moved to follow.

"Scout—" warned Grim.

"I want to help, sir."

"You've done more than your fair share," rejoined the other in a dry note while retrieving something from the truck bed.

Ben's own response tarried a moment while his attention was arrested by the black bundle Grim extracted from a hidden compartment. Whatever it was, it smelled of the lake, a metallic odor which now and then gave way to a more ichthyic stench.

"You're staying behind like we agreed," Grim added.

"But I took the pill, sir. You yourself said it provided an extra layer of protection. I know I may not have much to offer," he pleaded, "but I can be an extra set of eyes, or ears—I can cover your blind-spots. I'm still responsible for this mess, sir. Be it five feet or fifty, I intend to follow."

For a minute, Grim tried to stare him into backing down; when that didn't work, he shook his head but gave signs of a reluctant assent.

"I don't have time to argue," he said, stepping to the side of the truck for partial cover as he began to undress. "Stay behind me when we go in. And if anything happens, run and don't look back."

The black bundle, now unrolled and laid over the truck bed's rim, turned out to be a garment that more or less resembled a padded wetsuit. It had a bias zipper running from one shoulder to the opposite hip, and panels vaguely homologous with the torso's muscular structure; yet as a chitinous luster invested it, and the black stuff gave off a mottled sheen like a fine mist of sweat, it simultaneously resembled the segmented underside of an insect or lobster. For all that, the opaque material boasted an elastic quality, allowing it to stretch and give a little as Grim stepped into it and pushed his arms through its narrow sleeves.

More remarkable, perhaps, was the gradual change that came over Grim, from brows gathered in grave concentration over his half-hooded eyes, to the lofty bearing of his head: gone was the hoodlum slouch, and semi-bowlegged stance, replaced by the straight-backed carriage of an officer.

All this Ben observed in the brief moments it took Grim to sweep up his long hair and tie it in a small knot at the back of his head with practiced dexterity unhindered by gloved hands—all this had him wondering whether he was glimpsing the real Grim—the man who presumably braved polluted, kraken-inhabited waters to save him from drowning—or whether this was just one facet of many, as varied as his multiple names. Grim, Pale Horse, Dolon, Octavo—and, of course, Dogdaddy—none of them were real names, regardless of their owner's claim. If Ben could get a copy of his senior's birth certificate, what name would he find there? Not that he had any way of procuring it. Then again it made no difference, Ben concluded with a pensive smile. Grim is Grim, just as Grim can't quite cure himself of calling Ben "scout".

"Just so we're clear," said Grim as he balled up his discarded clothes, tossing them in the driver's seat, "I don't want you running off until we have an idea on its position. The woods distort sound, so we can't rely on that. The Tegmen's our canary in the mine."

"How, sir?"

"It reacts to the kraken's presence," answered Grim, strapping on a shiny black helmet with an opaque face shield that entirely covered his face, giving his voice a canned quality.

"I mean how can it tell when one's there?"

The senior heaved a weary sigh. "I don't know, scout—pheromones or something?"

"Bringing the shotgun, sir?" Ben asked when Grim picked up the weapon; and though he could not see the countenance behind the shield, Ben had a clear-enough impression of it when, instead of answering, his senior looked at him for a moment and wordlessly activated the small light mounted on the shotgun's barrel.

They started along the shore, treading the sandy soil in silence. A purple evening permeated the area, and the trees, casting dense shadows, greedily ate up what little light remained. Now and then, Grim would swivel his head to survey the line of trees, compelling his subordinate to do the same. The young man, fancying the kraken as some form of cephalopod, nervously wondered how fast or far the creature could travel on land. And just as he began to question his decision of following Grim, the man himself stopped before a shallow valley cutting through the shore, as if a row-boat had been dragged out of the water. It continued into the forest, slicking a wet trail against the trees, and leaving a clear wake of flattened grass and broken shrubs.

Their steps grew fainter as they walked in its tracks, traveling deeper into the forest, where visibility grew worse: more than once Ben started at the touch of low branches brushing his head or shoulder, and with no conversation to distract him, his unoccupied mind replayed the strange cries over and over, almost anticipating them until the memory of it began to disintegrate. Then he heard it: a heart-rending wail that poured glacial water over his heart and sent him shrinking back, covering his ears.

"She seeks her children!" exclaimed Ben to Grim, who

stood ahead of him, and who at that instant leveled the shotgun at the thicket ahead. Whether or not the senior heard him was uncertain—even Ben couldn't hear himself. The shrill cry rang clear in spite of his hands, thrilling through every nerve until his very fingertips seemed to crackle.

Mercifully, it died out, and in the brief respite, Grim glanced back and raised his fingers, motioning Ben to keep quiet.

"It spoke, sir," the latter whispered. "Did you hear it, sir? It was saying something," he reiterated, even as his senior kept his weapon aimed ahead without any indication that he heard him. Indeed, beyond the shrieking clamor, was a meridian of chatter through which Ben caught snatches of something like words. But he momentarily forgot about his discovery when in the half-dark he saw Grim seize up and stagger forward, as if struck from behind. The lapse was brief, and in a second or two the shotgun barrel went back up.

"It's close!" hissed the senior, keeping his gun trained ahead as he took a step back, obliging Ben to likewise retreat.

"Sir?"

"Shh! I'm drawing it out—"

He continued to withdraw, almost backing into Ben, who in that brief bump marked the changed texture of the Tegmen, and instinctively placed his hand on the back of Grim's shoulder. Instead of padded leather, he found raised slabs of sturdier stuff—like armor plates. They had to be: in his strung up state, Grim would have twitched off Ben's light touch, but clad in a dense shell, the senior seemed unaware of it; so the young man kept his hand there to better read Grim's movements and follow his lead.

In the meantime, if the kraken was close, it did not make its presence known—did not so much as stir the dry grass or snap a low-hanging branch. Ben could not hear it any more than catch a glimpse of it over Grim's shoulder. Then again, neither could he hear Grim's deliberate step as the senior continued his methodical retreat, hesitating now and then, as though he too was uncertain whether the creature was moving with them.

The kraken's shrieks rose once more, only now they sounded closer, filling Ben's skull and running electric currents under his skin. Yet the flinching subordinate endured, moving in synchrony with the man ahead of him. Before long, and without trying to, he began to hear something amidst the noise.

"We cannot thrall it," Ben murmured, repeating fragments of speech he caught, as though rescuing them from the swirling tumult. "A stench of death overhangs it..."

"Quiet!" whispered Grim.

"No, sir, listen," said Ben, and again paused, trying again to separate noise from speech, or its equivalent. "It is not fit. Sour blood, flesh sweet with rot. Familiar and not, it shares the blood, like once before..."

Grim was about to tell him once more to shut up when a loud crack broke through. The circle of illumination darted to one side in time to catch a tree starting to list. Then, from the impenetrable dark, something shot towards them. Grim held the shotgun diagonally in front of him in time to intercept it.

The flashlight was now pointed upward, and the peripheral light it threw touched the long black arm wrapped around the shotgun. Not an arm, but a hand—large and shimmering black, with rows on rows of opposing fingers—skeletal, dirt-crusted fingers, closing spider-like over the barrel, almost covering its entire length, and seeming capable of snapping it in half.

Ben fell back, hands flying to cover his mouth from which issued a string of uneven cries.

Two bony fingers of the large black hand slowly uncurled

and closed again, the kraken contemplating what it held and perhaps realizing this was not what it wanted. If they had uncurled again, those two fingers might have brushed up against Grim's face shield. And perhaps they did.

He drew a shuddering breath and in a low voice said: "Move." Then, in the next instant, he shouted: "Go!" and let go of the shotgun, turning to run, and giving Ben a good shove to get him started, all but carrying him off in the process.

The tall trees furnished hurdles to impede their swift escape. And after jolting their way through the woodlands, well-nigh ricocheting off the corrugated trunks, the two men tore out of the thickets, and brought up skidding across the broad gravel road, where they slowed down and checked for signs of pursuit.

In Grim's eyes perhaps they reached the road at the same time, but Ben knew he fell behind thanks to a fallen branch or root that almost tripped him. Presently a side stitch had him panting and hobbling up to Grim, who was undoing his chin strap, and seemed incapable of removing his helmet fast enough. It dropped to his feet, and one gloved hand blindly sought and found a nearby tree, against which Grim steadied himself. The first breath issued in a white vapor, yet his face was pallid, untouched by any color of heat or exertion; his stare was glassy, and as his hand slipped against the rough bark, he almost collapsed had his shoulder not struck the broad trunk and kept him propped.

But just when Ben was about to voice his concern, the moment passed—there for a blink, gone in a heartbeat, as if all the senior needed was a touch of air to regain color and return some light and steadiness back into his gaze. The look was gone, but the brevity of it made Ben stare at his senior, who now merely looked out of breath as opposed to—what? Fearful? Fear was part of it, yet not the whole. If it were mere cowardice, he would likely be giddy with relief and apt to expel the lingering nervous energy through laughter, more so since the danger had passed.

Ben knew it had passed, drawing his conclusion from the distant, despondent wails, full of languid dejection, as though the kraken had grown weary or dispirited in its pursuit and gave up the chase.

"It won't follow," asserted the subordinate with enough conviction to make his senior regard him curiously. "It sounds tired," he elaborated, wondering why Grim had not reached the same conclusion.

"Tired," Grim repeated, sounding unsure of what that meant but without questioning it.

"Sickly," Ben almost added, stopping short at the insufficiency of the word. Though certainly the bilious quality of the faraway moans made the kraken sound ill in some way. "You hear it too, don't you, sir?" he asked instead, fixing his eyes on Grim, who was still scrutinizing the dark gaps between the trees as though trying to pierce out the black bulk of kraken.

"There's gotta be a better way," he said, stepping back from his survey with more pragmatism than apprehension. "Let's go back to Atwood's. I want to have another look at that basement."

He remained quiet for some time after they had started down the gravel road—so much so that Ben feared his senior was angry with him for not keeping his mouth shut, or some similar infraction that compromised their expedition.

"You never told me it could speak," Ben began, coming across as oddly chipper when he meant to sound light and casual.

"They don't speak," Grim shortly replied. "They mimic. They use it to lure unsuspecting victims."

"If you mean the screaming, sir, then I agree—it sounded

so eerie and human. But I meant the other part—the things it said—it called you familiar. And something about shared blood."

At once, Grim halted his steps and stood with his back to Ben.

"Shared blood?"

"Yes, sir."

Moonlight touched Grim's profile as he turned his head. "Familiar how?"

For a confused moment Ben wondered whether the question was a challenge or genuine inquiry. Erring on the second, he tried to repeat what he could remember but found the words had flowed out of him like drained water.

"I don't know," was all he could stammer.

"You don't know?" Grim asked, turning to face him; and when Ben shrugged in answer, he urged: "Just now you said it called me familiar—how did you know? What else did it say?"

"Sir, I thought you said it can't speak—"

"I still want to hear it," Grim interposed, clasping both Ben's shoulders as if he suspected the young man would run off with his secret knowledge. "Alright, look—maybe I'm wrong—maybe it can communicate in some way that we don't understand and I was just repeating some baseless bullshit. Doesn't matter. I just want to know what you heard." The statement was uttered in a gentle enough tone, though there was no mistaking the underlying fervor—or the effort it took to keep it in check, as though the senior feared losing something vital in its wake.

This confused Ben as much as it touched him with pity: What possessed Grim to take sudden interest in what the creature had to say?

"I- I'm sorry, sir. But I promise you, I never got a chance to hear much. Just the few words I could make out—like picking up radio chatter buried in static."

Grim held him a moment longer, searching his face as if not entirely convinced.

CHAPTER 19

With no more to be said, the subject was dropped and a heavy silence descended on them while they walked back to the truck.

In due time they reached it, and just when each of them opened the door on his side, a band of five or six men materialized out of the dark and ambushed the two, pinning them to the ground as they bound their hands and feet. The process was more prompt with Ben, and after the two thugs left him pinioned on the ground, inches away from the front tires, they rushed over to aid their associates, who struggled to subdue Grim.

Ben couldn't see much, but heard a body crash over the hood of the truck, and heard another cry out before falling into the shallow waters. Not long after, the shout-studded scuffle died out, and he was hauled up and tossed into the back of the truck. The side of his head slammed down against the hard bed and ached, so that for some seconds he winced and kept his eyes shut tight, failing to notice that Grim was there alongside him. Soon after, the faceless men crowded into the back of the truck as it vibrated into life and rumbled onto the dirt path.

The men sitting in the back bantered with self-congratulating cheer, and if Ben needed a sign that Grim was alive and alert, it came in the form of his struggling to raise himself before one of the men bore down on him, placing his knee on the man's chest, and threatening to blow his brains out if he tried anything.

After an immeasurable time, the truck jolted to a halt, and Ben was dragged out feet first and made to kneel in the dirt. They were in the commune's compound, that much he guessed from the crowd circling them: men and women, young and old and very young. The engine roar still echoed in his ears, dampening the din of jeering, twisted faces, faces gaunt with shouts, amongst which outstretched hands pointed or clawed the air, reaching for them yet held back by an invisible line, so that they formed a pit around the kneeling pair.

Ben could hardly peel his eyes away from the seething mob, but eventually his circling gaze fell on Grim, who kneeled beside him with an impassive expression, in spite of the gash over his left brow bleeding down his face. Then, like a dog licking its chops, Grim tasted his own blood and found something agreeable in it, his tongue retracting below flaring eyes and between teeth that glistened in a thin, crooked sneer.

There was nothing reassuring in that expression, which Ben took for misplaced insolence, the last vestige of defiance before the sea of outstretched hands broke through the unseen barrier and swept forth to swallow them.

The young man's empty stomach turned, but the bile he spewed did little to clear his head or troubled vision.

Then a gradual hush fell over the crowd, the hands drooped, and the dozens of heads grudgingly turned towards one far-off voice that rose in sermon. It took no guessing to know whose it was; and while Thane spoke to his people, two armed men

came over and cut the ropes binding their feet before standing
them up to march forwards. One of the thugs must have led the
way to part the semi-distracted crowd. All Ben saw was Grim
trudging ahead, flanked by two guards who now and then gave
him a redundant shove. Ben himself was given a push or two,
though the clinging stench of sickness must have kept them
from harrying him too often. Someone from the crowd spat
on the procession, unintentionally hitting one of the guards
instead of the intended targets, which perhaps discouraged any
further attempts.

Unlike the previous gatherings, this one took place outdoors,
at a corner of the property Ben had yet to see. Drum barrels,
repurposed as fire pits, studded the open field. The air was thick
with a pungent animal stench, more so as they passed a high
corral fence, the wooden boards of which afforded glimpses of
reposing hogs, their round sides straining the boards.

"Visions trouble my sight with images of a wasteland.
Surely some revelation is at hand," shouted Thane, now less
than twenty feet ahead.

The light did strange things to his shadowed form, granting
him six arms instead of two. Try as he would, Ben could
not blink or strain his eyes enough to correct his vision and
make the extra arms disappear. And yet, was it a trick of light
and shadow when each hand gestured independently? One
pointing, one raised in supplication, one held up ready to strike
down, one held palm down, one making a fist, and one hanging
limp at the end of a lifted arm.

At Thane's feet lay a line of three bodies—or rather the
bodies of three men—and before them, Ben and his companion
were forced to kneel down, allowing the young man a better
chance to see the row of closed eyes and slightly parted lips,
the corners of which were upturned in something like awe and
gentle delight. Two seemed closer in age, while the third was

evidently the youngest; yet, as sleep anointed the sleeper with temporary youth, so now did a look of quiet rapture radiate through their reposing countenances.

Regarding the three men, Grim remarked with a raised eyebrow: "Well, someone took a good huff of ether."

Thane ignored his temerity and simply said: "They're not waking up."

"Mercy me," the senior flatly murmured. "Who would have thought contact with polluted waters made you sick?"

"Two seasons we lived by this lake. This never happened before," was Thane's even-tempered answer. He spoke with the forbearance of an interrogator letting a prisoner spend his bluster while taking his measure, calmly dismantling his argument.

"So?" Grim shrugged. "TB could take anywhere from two to twelve weeks before you start to—"

"Your boy fell in the lake with the rest of them," Thane pointed out. "Compared to them, he seems in good health."

Grim scoffed. "I don't know about your standards, but I doubt projectile vomiting counts as a sign of good health. He's been sick as a dog, all day. In fact, I wouldn't stand too close if I were you."

None of this seemed to have reached Thane's ears. "I want you to tell me what's wrong with them, why are they like this, and how do I cure them."

"You can't cure them without medical intervention. But since you got a thing against doctors and hospitals, you may as well just kill them and burn the bodies."

"I don't need a doctor when I have you here. You medicated the boy, now you'll help me treat my men."

"I got to him on time," Grim savagely asserted, fixing his dark eyes on Thane, who now stood a foot away from him.

"It's too late for those men." Unable to turn and face the crowd, Grim twisted his thorax and raised his voice to include them in his answer as he went on: "It's too late for those men. I wasn't kidding when I said burn the bodies—they'll soon be contagious. Those men are how you'll all end up if you don't pick up and leave. It's too late for them, but you all can save yourselves. This isn't some promised land. This hole—this piece of Gehenna—is not some lost paradise. The lake's contaminated—you can't grow anything here, let alone drink. You're barely getting by—getting by on charity, no less. The charity will run out, and if starvation won't get you, the infested water will—"

A forceful kick to his chest cut off Grim's portents as he doubled over and began to cough.

"The outsiders reveal themselves," said Thane, moving away from him and addressing his people with arms lifted as if to rally them. "They sow the seeds of dissent. They want us gone—uprooted. There is value in this land, this spot of earth so dear to us. We came here to shun the world. We came here to live by our own rules and conditions. We came here to establish ourselves as sovereign. I have proved to you that you need not beg for your repast. And you, in turn, proved that you are of hardy stock—hale and hearty! Not one here is like the soft-bellied hedonists—the epicureans strapped to their feed bags. Who amongst you thought this possible before you came here? And now the outsiders have seen it too: Are we not terrible? Are we not capable of thriving and multiplying? They fear it—they fear the coming generation that will topple them. Why else would they poison us? They see our potential and they fear it. What do you say to that?"

The humming crowd cried out in response, individual answers lost in the clamor of indignation. Singular voices began calling to kill the outsiders, spearheading a chant that repeated the same demand in a refrain. The guards, swept in the general wrath, poked the prisoners' heads with the business end of their rifles. The show of sympathetic anger was pleasing to Thane, though not having sanctioned any slaughtering, he stepped in to lower the leveled barrels by hand.

"Your anger is righteous," he said, once again addressing the mob, "it is born out of concern for these men," pointing at the laid out three. "To some they are brothers, or husbands, or sons. Yet we all value them. We all care for their well-being. The outsiders will talk yet. If they don't, I throw them to you to do with as you wish."

With that, Thane circled round the kneeling men, granting them a few moments to appreciate their situation. Then he came up behind them, almost insinuating himself between the two as he crouched down laid a hand on either of their shoulders.

"Their patience is thinner than mine," he said. "So, I'll ask again: what's wrong with those men and how do we help them?"

"Ask your patron saint for handouts," grumbled Grim, avoiding Thane's leer.

Thane seized a handful of Grim's hair and yanked his head back. "This is not something you can cure with over-the-counter medicine."

"Try Atwood, then," suggested Grim, flinching but without letting it transmit in his voice. "I'm sure there's a lot more he can offer."

Thane saw the trap, smiled, and gently released him before rising to his feet. "Sit tight. Pray we find something of use in your vehicle. I doubt either of you want to be torn apart by an angry mob."

Grim, too, rose to his feet, but was deterred by the trained rifles from taking a step in any direction. Not that he intended to go anywhere when all he did was face the crowd to warn them.

"Your leader just signed a death warrant for everyone involved here! You don't know who you're dealing with. If you think no one's going to come for us, you're in over your head. They know where we are and they'll come for us. They won't hesitate to scorch this land, steal your children, and gather all the warm bodies for their purpose. A bullet to the head is the best you can hope for, then. The solution I've offered you is the only one that would save you. I'll say again: Kill those men. Burn their bodies, and leave."

A profound hush met this, during which members of the crowd exchanged hesitant glances, seeking answering looks of skepticism or concern. Thane too held a lengthy pause of consideration, waiting for the undercurrent of confusion to settle before confronting it.

"I'm sure we all know the answer to that, don't we?" he reassured them with a conspiratorial chuckle. "Better yet, let's show them what we have to say to that. Do you know what omnivores are, boy?" he said, stepping in front of Ben and coercing him into answering.

"They eat plants and food of animal origin," said Ben after an uncertain glance at his senior.

His answer was disregarded by Thane, who preferred a more fleshed out version. "Hunters, predators—they go for the kill. It's not mercy, it's just more economic: saves them the energy of holding down their prey while they feast on it. Omnivores on the other hand? They don't care. They're opportunistic feeders. They're happy to take a bite out of whatever's in their way, and they're not picky. Food is food, and flesh—" he clapped his hands together as if to swiftly conclude the matter. "But why talk when we can demonstrate?"

While he spoke, two guards lifted Ben like a rolled-up

carpet and carried him to the hog pen, where they kept him suspended over the fence.

"What they can't eat, we burn," Thane elaborated with a growling rasp. "And what we can't burn, they eat. Your vehicle will be thrown in some ditch miles from here. Your so-called friends are welcome to try looking for you. Two, maybe three days from now there won't be a trace of either of you left. If you're lucky, you won't live to witness how slow the process is."

Ben cried out as one of the men holding him feigned letting go, further riling the hogs, some of which leaned their front hooves against the fence, wriggling their lifted snouts and squealing in anticipation.

"Last chance for parting words," announced Thane, turning to Grim. "Anything you want to say before your friend there takes a dip?"

Ben's raised head inarticulately besought Grim to say something, for God's sake! Just invent any of your damn lies to satisfy them!

Instead Grim's arms unexpectedly snapped up as the rope binding his wrists broke or fell. Instantly one of the guards fired his shotgun and sent Grim sprawling back. It was the last thing Ben saw before the men holding him over the pen let go, dropping him on the wrong side of the fence.

More hogs trotted over, snouts nudging Ben's side and stomach, snuffling for tender organs. They turned him over to better dig through the thin layer of shirt. Then, one of the pigs gave a sharp squeal and sprang back, as if stung by an electric shock. The same reaction repeated with another hog; soon the whole passel scampered back, leaving Ben kicking and cowering with panicked cries, insensible to the pandemonium outside of shouts and shots being fired, till at length something flew over the fence and landed inches away from his head. A thin splash of mud splattered Ben's eyes, blinding from seeing the figure who hauled him up and stood him against the fence. The next sensation was the welcome release of his hands, which flew up to wipe the mud off his eyes.

"I got you, you're alright, you're alright," came the phrase, frantically repeated, to which Ben could only echo, "Yeah, I'm okay, I'm okay," giving a few nods before his heated face puckered under an overwhelming rush of relief. The inarticulate horror of having seen Grim shot at, witness him fall, and lose any hope of rescue before being dropped into a pit to be eaten alive—it made Ben all the more glad for the reassuring arm that enveloped the back of his head, stealing a fugitive moment of privacy while he reigned in his sobs. Still, even after Grim lowered his arm, Ben struggled to let go, still pressing his face against the bony shoulder—or rather the Tegmen's spaulder.

"We need to move before they come back," exhorted Grim with a reassuring pat.

Goaded more by embarrassment than reassurance, Ben lowered his arms and drew back. His lingering shame soon took a backseat to surprise once he climbed over the fence and saw the now empty fields. The majority of the crowd had fled, though some remained, taking cover behind trees.

At his side, Grim kept a rifle leveled against any oncoming threat, making a few semi-circular sweeps with his aim while he retreated. Someone fired at them from a distance. Grim answered it with three shots, fired in quick succession, unhindered by the repeated task of pulling the bolt after each shot, performed with machine-like efficiency that sent each spent shell spiraling into the air.

That done, he urged Ben to his feet, letting him run some

distance ahead while he retreated with his rifle trained in the general direction of the first shot. Finally, they reached the truck, which had its doors wide open, the men neither bothering to close them, nor remove the keys from the ignition. In less than a minute, the truck tore past guards who were attempting to close the gates only to dive out of the way of the flying vehicle.

After putting some distance between them and the commune grounds, Grim pulled over to the side of the road. He got out, taking the rifle with him, and began dismantling it, flinging the parts into the lake. When he returned to the truck, he found Ben seated in the back of the truck.

"Let's go, Ben," said Grim, sounding utterly weary.

"I wanna sit in the back."

"Look," said Grim, drawing a long breath, "if you need a moment, we can wait a moment."

"I don't want a moment. I just want to sit in the back. I don't see what the issue is, it's not like I'm going to jump off while the car's moving or anything," stammered Ben in a strained tone that said more than he wished to say.

Grim studied him a moment, head tipped slightly back and brows furrowed in uncertainty. Without a word, he opened the door to the driver's side, grabbing the clothes he had on earlier.

"Here," he said in a mild tone, passing them on to Ben. "Go behind the trees there and put these on. You can chuck your soiled things into the lake."

Ben looked from him to the bundle of plaid and denim Grim held in his outstretched hand without making a move to take it.

"So you took a spill in the mud," said the senior with an indifferent shrug, taking the matter lightly. "So what? Just change into this and that'll be that."

The euphemism was not lost on Ben. Again his eyes darted from Grim to the clothes, smarting with shame before accepting them. He began to retreat, then half-turned, and without lifting his eyes murmured: "It never happened before."

Grim brushed this off with a dismissive gesture. "Happens to all of us at some point. No shame in that. Off you go now."

CHAPTER 20

It was almost nine o'clock by the time they pulled up behind the Tea Room. The hour seemed incongruously early to Ben, who, without the aid of a clock, would have guessed it to be closer to midnight. The back of the building had no windows to display the interior of the Tea Room, hence no way of telling whether the establishment was still open or closed for the day.

Ben would have liked to see what Olivia was up to, to be absorbed in the lamplit hush of sweeping floors, wiping tables and arranging chairs; to ground himself in a moment of order and stability, which seemed worlds away from the strident turmoil of the past forty-eight hours. Stare as he would at the solid wall, all he had was the tempered glow of kitchen lights radiating behind a small exhaust fan to tell him that some quiet occupation was taking place there. Just the same, he remained lost in that reverie, absently mounting the steps to their room while his eyes stared in imagination at the empty Tea Room—its sable walls and softly shaded corners, and the sylph-like figure of Olivia going about her business. So that it came to him as something of a surprise when a minute after they had entered their room, they heard a knock on the door connected to the Tea Room.

"What now?" muttered Grim, fetching a tea towel from the kitchenette and pressing it to the bleeding cut over his brow. He closed his eyes and sat down as soon as he did, as if overcome with dizziness, motioning his subordinate to answer the door.

"Hello, Ben," said Olivia. "Is your uncle here?"

Ben opened and shut his mouth a few times, struggling to answer the unexpected question. He had assumed Olivia came up to ask them if they wanted anything before she closed for the night. "He's a little indisposed right now," Ben finally answered, keeping the door ajar to obscure the rest of the room. "Is there something you want me to tell him?"

"Well, this concerns Radney," she said, or rather called, raising her voice as if she knew Grim was somewhere in the room and wanted him to hear her. "I'm a little worried about him."

"Why would you worry about him?" called Grim before Ben had a chance to say anything.

"He hasn't called in a while," she continued in the same capacity. "He calls at least once a day or every other day to order a meal or something."

"The man's going through a honeymoon period with his work," answered Grim from his corner, having moved his chair to the side of the desk to stay out of view.

"That's the problem: he tends to get wrapped up in whatever he's doing that he sometimes forgets to feed himself."

"Do you want to come in?" asked Ben, tired of standing in the middle of a borderline shouting match.

"I stopped by his house today," she said, stepping past Ben. "I saw your truck there, but no one answered the door."

Grim cast Ben a black look for letting Olivia in before he had a chance to change out of the Tegmen. "We were out," he answered, sinking a little in his seat, as if trying to hide his black garb from view. "We took Mr. Atwood for a walk in the woods."

"And ran into some trouble, from the looks of it." She nodded, crossing her arms.

"What, this?" Grim scoffed at the soaked towel. "Just had to chase off an ornery badger."

"I didn't know there were badgers in the area."

"Might have been a small bear, then. All I know was that it was small, furry, ambushed us then ran for cover. Probably thought we were coming after it or maybe trying to move in on its turf."

Olivia seemed to consider this. "Were you carrying a gun?"

"A gun?"

"The other day, Curtis said you bought one from the Sporting Cabin. Thought maybe you were out game hunting. The area has a history of animal violence against guns."

"Like I said," Grim began after staring at her for a moment, "we were out for a walk. We took Atwood with us to make sure he gets some exercise and fresh air before he works himself to death. That's all."

"Well, that's—very nice of you," remarked Olivia, lowering her crossed arms a little. "I'm glad someone's looking after him."

"Oh, psh. Atwood and I go way back," answered Grim with a self-deprecating shrug.

"Really?"

"Sure. I know all his vices, and he knows where the bodies are buried."

"Speaking of which," she began, causing Ben's heart to stall a moment, "I know I should have said this before but I don't allow smoking in here or in the Tea Room."

Grim gave a single nod and was perhaps capable of only one. "Yes, ma'am," he said, almost sounding faint.

"Also you might wanna get that looked at," she said, approaching Grim, who pressed the towel to the bleeding cut as if to hide it from her.

"I'll do that in the morning," he said, glancing up at her before turning away.

"Or you could let me take a look at it. I have a suture kit— won't take long."

Grim chuckled at that. "Running some back-alley practice in your spare time?"

"That's how we got Mystery Meat Mondays," she rejoined; and in the face of credulous stares, she added with a small shrug: "We're just talking First-Aid here. My dad was an army surgeon, taught me a few things…"

While she spoke, she rolled up her sleeve to show a long white scar that ran the length of her forearm. "Stitched this when I was nine. He supervised, of course—even showed me how to drain it. But the handiwork is mine," she said with pardonable pride.

Ben moved in for a close look before uttering a few words of sincere admiration, in part to make up for his partner's reticence; and when Grim still said nothing, Ben felt prevailed upon to add: "You know my eye feels a lot better too, since you treated it!"

Seeing she wasn't making any progress, Olivia offered an alternative. "There's a small clinic about twenty minutes away. They're closed now, but I know the doctor there. I could try calling him—"

"You don't have to do that," muttered Grim. The hand holding the towel was propped on the table, and he leaned into it as he closed his eyes, as if his last reserve of energy had been used up in that phrase.

"The longer the wound remains open, the longer the risk of infection," said Olivia.

The warning did not move Grim any closer to conviction; whether or not he even heard her was hard to tell while his eyes remained shut. But just as Olivia was about to leave, he lowered the towel.

"Doesn't look that bad, does it?" he asked. "Maybe a couple of butterfly bandages?"

She came back for a close look. "You mind needles?"

He made a sheepish grimace. "I can bear it, I don't have to like it," he said, hesitating a moment before adding: "just a fair warning that I might grab your hand at some point to make it stop. I don't mean anything, I just might need a breather."

"Yeah, sure," she answered in a soft voice.

When she fetched her first aid pouch, Olivia brought along a tray of unsold sandwiches.

"Just don't go expecting a free dinner every night," she scolded. "I set these aside for commune members. They usually stop by at this hour, only they didn't show up this evening—or even last night, now that I think of it," she pondered out loud as she took a seat next to Grim and began swabbing his brow, wiping off a brown layer of crusted blood or dirt.

Grim furtively shot Ben a look to keep quiet lest he nervously started bantering on the subject. But the latter was occupied with unwrapping a sandwich from the tray. They were cold but comforting. And while he ate, Ben watched as Olivia's deft fingers threaded a curved needle.

Grim sat still. His eyes were either closed or downcast, hidden beneath a conniving line of black lashes, and he might have looked meditative were it not for a deep line appearing between his gathered eyebrows whenever the needle went in or the thread tugged.

A handsome tableau they made, thought Ben with the impersonal enjoyment of one appreciating a scenic painting: Grim's defined and dusky features next to Olivia's classic profile and elegant hands, spun from material as fine as sunlight. Even her flaws—made apparent by the lateness of the hour and imperfect lighting—manifesting in a slight puffiness beneath her eyes, and a faint line slanting from nostril to the outer corner of her mouth, revealing which cheek she pressed to her pillow—even they became her like the play of light and shadow on marble.

Such observation would have embarrassed him into looking away lest he got caught staring. But to his surprise, Ben found his fixation somewhat slipping behind a simpler albeit absorbing interest in food and sleep; truly at that moment, he felt that life yielded no keener pleasures than the medley of flavors and textures: the sweet, salt, tart, crunch of every bite; and beyond it the blessed prospect of climbing into bed, replete and ripe for sleep. Still, a heady, hazy amalgamation of drowsiness and slumbering envy in him had him trading places with Grim; through half-closed eyes he envisioned himself receiving Olivia's attention and tender ministrations as she stitched his wounded cheek. The scissors would conveniently vanish so that instead of clipping the redundant thread, she would lean closer and snap it with her teeth.

There was no heat to the vision, no delectable weakness, no trace of vicarious pleasure. The ever-present fervor—youth's boon and its millstone whenever it stirred his loneliness—

seemed for once to have forsaken him. The apathy would have bothered him had it not overwhelmed all his faculties.

He was dead tired. That was all.

Not long after Olivia had finished and left, the phone began to ring. By then Ben had gone into the bathroom, all set to take a shower.

Grim, sitting at the table, picking tomato slices and other undesirables out of his sandwich, answered the phone after the first ring.

"Yeah?" he said, cradling the receiver between his right shoulder and ear.

It was Ben's first instinct to keep the shower running while he listened in on the conversation, but had to forgo it once he discovered the impossibility of hearing anything through the rush of water. Besides, what did Grim have to hide from him at this point?

He grabbed a bath towel and stepped out of the bathroom in time to hear Grim say: "Yeah, we know that *now*—No, it's not that I don't appreciate your effort, it's just—"

The senior held the phone farther from his ear while a tirade crackled, and used the opportunity to set the receiver down and switch to speakerphone.

"… I called and called but no one was there to pick up!" Harper's voice sputtered through the speakers. "I even had to rent a room in a motel just to be able to use the phone without looking over my shoulder!"

"This won't happen again. Just give us the motel's number—"

"It won't happen again cause I'm done here!"

"Just hear me out," Grim entreated. "This one's closer to your department."

"Look, I'd love to help, but I can't. I can't keep sneaking around just to make phone calls—"

"Not even for your son?"

Ben stared at Grim, then back at the phone, as though he could see Harper's expression. For once, she seemed at a loss for words. And while the revelation was hardly a bombshell, it nevertheless answered for something that had been bothering Ben ever since he began seeing Harper—why she seemed distracted on some nights, or why their dates, though intimate in conversation, were chaste in almost every other aspect. Even when her brown eyes shone into his, she seemed to keep him at an arms' length, never inviting him back to her place. Maybe she didn't want him to know she had a son, who was probably too young to be in the same program the organization had arranged for the children of staff members. Not that Ben had made any advances towards her—at least not while he was sober. But then there was his dejection, which he had hoped would move her into reciprocating his feelings. Now he winced with belated embarrassment, yet wondered whether the birthday gift was her way of apologizing for stringing him along.

She spoke after a pause of stunned silence. "This call never happened."

"He needs help, doesn't he?" Grim cut in before she hung up. "I know your son requires special care. I know someone who can help you. I'll send you their contact details, through Ben. Get in touch with them. Tell them you came through me."

Ben hung on the words "special care" though he had trouble picturing what it entailed. As far as he knew, none of his peers ever required special care, though perhaps the ones that did never remained long in the program. The retrospective scrutiny recalled one girl and two boys who acted out, fell behind, and disappeared within a month of their academic year. Their presence in his class was brief enough not to leave a lasting impression, and he briefly wondered what happened to them, whether they were taken elsewhere, or were left to fall through the cracks.

He emerged from his thoughts to lingering silence—upheld to the point where he assumed Harper had already hung up on them.

Instead, she asked with some constraint what Grim wanted.

"Duncastor," he said. "We apprehended a man there, a Dr. Bernard Carver. It's been a while so there should be a report on him. I want that, plus any information surrounding the incident. That's it, that's all I'm asking."

CHAPTER 21

"Sir?"

The room was dark. Each lay in his own cot—Ben on his back, hands resting on his middle, and Grim on his side, facing the wall—both keeping still, trying to lure sleep the way they would a skittish animal.

"Sir?" Ben softly called again. All he heard was faint regular breathing. Reluctantly, he went back to contemplating the ceiling, open to circling thoughts.

His phone sat on the desk, a reminder of duties unfulfilled. In another reality, under different circumstances, he would have stolen away to log another report; now he lay dreading the chime of a message—a stern inquiry as to why he had not reported the night before. He wondered whether they noticed the lapse, whether they expected to hear from him this evening, or whether they could not care less; he thought of the three men lined up on the floor, smiling in their sleep; he thought of sleep, which refused to come at his beck, even as he remained still.

He fought to remain still while his body was confusedly feverish and cold, the chill driving him to cover up, only to kick away the blanket a minute later.

In-between those fits were flashes of the pigs closing in on him, or leaping back as if stung. His palms pricked with sweat; and yet he couldn't help revisiting it in brief flashes, like touching a hot surface and recoiling from it before it had a chance to scorch him.

Still, sleep would not come. How could it when he burned up? And his stomach—he really shouldn't have eaten those sandwiches—should have stuck with toast and tea. Yet the dry fare would hardly have satisfied him, not when he had gone more than a day without eating. Even now, as he gnashed his teeth and twisted in restless agony, his mouth perversely watered at the thought of food.

Clutch his belly as he would, it would not be soothed. Skin stretched over a stomach rounded by something other than food, tight as a drum. Beneath his gnarled hands, his insides swelled, strained, and threatened to burst out. He rose out of bed and stoopingly staggered towards the bathroom, cradling his stomach as though to keep some leaden weight from falling out.

Nothing came of that protracted visit, yet somehow he must have tricked his mind into thinking relief came in some way; or else the comforting light and heated floor tiles must have had a relaxing influence that eased his cramps.

However his relief was purchased mattered little in the face of its tranquil aftermath: he closed the door on the bright bathroom and crept back to his cot, thinking now he could get some sleep.

But it wasn't a minute before his eyes flew open again.

Something stirred in his stomach.

A blanket covered that segment, and his hands were folded on top of it, but even they felt the brief twitch. The sensation was so new, so unlike the prosaic digestive rumblings, that a wave of cold sweat swept through him; and yet it came with a measure of doubt, even as he pressed and poked the firm convex of his distended abdomen, feeling for the spasm beneath.

All he got for his trouble was a dull ache. Then it happened again: a small pulse of two or three beats.

He started with a weak gasp and sat up, probing his stomach again as if to convince himself that it had happened while simultaneously hoping like crazy that it did not. In the dark he sat, waiting for a third repeat of the odd phenomena. Time passed with nothing happening, and as he was about to write it off as muscle twitches, a loud thud and clatter shattered his self-examination.

"Sir?" Ben called in the dark, guessing from sound and direction that Grim had either overturned his cot or fell from it. An answering groan confirmed this, and he rose and knelt by his senior's side, asking if he was all right.

"Yeah, fine," gritted the other.

"Trouble sleeping, sir?"

"No, just troubled dreams," said Grim with a sigh. "This recurring one where I'm trapped in the backseat of a car. It's parked in front of our house. Except my family was in there, and some thugs were inside waiting for them. I didn't see what happened—I just knew they were dead. Then the car started moving, with me still in it. I began slamming myself against the door, trying to get it open."

"And that's when you fell off the bed?"

"At least this time I escaped." The senior smiled with hollow satisfaction.

"Old memories, sir?"

Grim sat quiet for a second, as if he wasn't sure what Ben was referring to.

"No, no," he dismissed with a head shake. "It's just these pills, they melt in your mind—give you these weird, vivid dreams."

"Why did we take them, sir?"

"I told you why—"

"They're some form of protection, I know that, sir. What I don't understand is why you ran off."

The remark was met with silence.

"You even had the Tegmen on. Wasn't it enough, sir?"

Grim pretended not to hear. "Go back to sleep," he grumbled as he rose and turned to fix his overturned cot.

Without having to see his senior's face, Ben knew he struck a raw nerve. Evidently the same man who answered the angry horde with a savage gleam of his teeth did not like being reminded of his retreat. He was no coward in Ben's estimate, and yet the bitterness with which he met the queries reflected an inner-loathing that said otherwise.

"Sir, I don't mean to sound impertinent. I just want to understand—"

"It got too close," Grim interjected. "I was trying to draw it back to the cabin, but it got too close. What did you expect me to do? Stay and fight? I didn't have a chance. Even if I had the Tegmen—wearing a helmet does not mean you can just launch yourself off a cliff."

"I hear you, sir. But just for the sake of argument, let's say we haven't taken those pills. What would have happened?"

Ben expected a curt answer at best, or to be told to shut up and go back to sleep. So that it surprised him a little to find Grim entertaining the question, taking his time as he sat on his cot; and while Ben couldn't get a clear view of his face, judging from the way his head slightly turned, he must have been casting his eyes about the room, as if pursuing an answer.

"Let me put it this way," he said at length. "The kraken will try to draw you to it—"

"Through mimicking," Ben added.

"No, not just that. Take the pill, and you hear the banshee wail. Go without it, and it's the isle of sirens. That's one part of it. Another is…" he hesitated. "I think I already mentioned this: The pill makes you undesirable. You stink like rotten meat, or whatever the kraken would find repulsive."

"Yeah, it said something to that effect."

Grim leaned forward with interest. "What else did it say?"

"Sir, I promise you," answered Ben with a deep sigh. "I swear I didn't hear much. If I remembered something, I would have told you."

"What time is it?" asked Grim, undeterred. "We need to go back."

"Now?" Ben protested, wondering if his senior was trying to prove something by heading back already.

"We don't have time to sit around. Grab some coffee if you need it."

"I hardly closed my eyes, sir."

"Good," said Grim as he stepped into the Tegmen.

"Sir, hold up, I want to see something."

Grim, dressed to the waist, stood still while Ben tentatively touched the empty sleeve and a part of the Tegmen corresponding to the front of the torso.

"What?" asked the clad man, growing impatient.

"How did it do that, sir? I saw you getting shot at. But there's not one hole in it. And yet it's so thin and pliant—"

"So is chainmail," Grim suggested, pulling the sleeve away to slide his arm into it.

"No, it was different when I bumped into you, sir—when the kraken was nearby? It wasn't like this."

"I told you, it reacts to the kraken's presence. It ossifies. Does the same when I got shot at—just on a smaller scale."

"What's it made of?"

"Yeah, well," said Grim, sounding like he was smiling, "that info is sorta beyond my pay grade. I mean I'm sure there's a lot of work that goes into making one—state of the art engineering and all that shit. But if you wanna hear my theory, I believe it's the same material that covers the kraken. Not that they take it from a dead kraken. By then it's no good. My source says it's lab grown—you know, like growing skin for grafting. Though for all I know they've got some nightmare apparatus for immobilizing and peeling it off a kraken. Not entirely sure how I feel about it—especially when the stuff seems alive, with a mind of its own. Imagine if you will wearing some living thing's living skin—"

"Sir?" said Ben, in part to interrupt his senior's rambling, which had begun to sound somewhat deranged the longer it went on.

"Yeah?"

Ben almost changed his mind about asking but asked anyway. "What happened to those men, sir? Thane said they fell into the lake like I did. And then you said you got to me on time. What about them, sir?"

"They're beyond help at this stage," came the terse answer.

"So, what happens if they don't burn them?" Ben asked, envisioning the entire commune spread out in wake-less sleep.

"Then they made their bed and now have to lie in it. Now move. We got more urgent matters to take care of."

They locked the kitchen door and descended the outside stairway. On the landing, Grim paused when he noticed Ben keeping more than a few steps behind.

"You okay, scout?" he called.

The young man faltered, on the verge of pointing out the thin black tail switching about behind Grim's knees; but before he could say anything, the appendage cunningly wrapped itself around the senior's black-clad leg, vanishing from sight. When Ben lifted his gaze, he saw the other man still waiting for an answer, lifting his eyebrows by way of reiterating his question.

"Sir, I- I-" stammered the subordinate without having decided whether or not to bring up the matter: in spite of his protest on the lateness of the hour, a part of him inexplicably yearned to go after the kraken, and the last thing he wanted was to receive a look of concern before being told to stay behind. In a flash, he decided against saying anything, and in his haste to fill the gap left by the annulled subject, his mind seized one of many free-floating thoughts.

"I was thinking," he pursued, "whether it was right to involve Harper with us."

Grim appeared skeptical. "Harper?" he inquired as he continued towards the truck.

"That is, I'm worried she'll get into trouble over us. I mean the first time was necessary. But now I'm not sure what we're after. Plus she's got a kid."

"She's free to refuse if she wants. Besides, the file should be within her department by now. I'm pretty sure that part of the case is closed."

"What's that, sir?" Ben asked, climbing into the passenger side.

"Bernard Carver. A veritable quack, that one," answered Grim, the sound of the engine starting eerily synchronous with a flashing glint in his eyes. "We snared him outside a remote facility in Duncastor. He was breeding krakens and was reaching out to sell them—or their derivatives. Tried to escape when he realized someone was coming after him— tried to cover his tracks too: all the larvae he had in the facility were dead. All, that is, except one. They found it while they were interrogating him. One of the guards told me the good doctor was in a bad way, though at first, they thought it was all an act—even when he fell over and was having a seizure fit. Turns out all this time he was carrying one inside him, trying to smuggle it out."

The senior resumed after a quick glance at Ben, whose face puckered up in revulsion.

"Crazy, right? God knows how he hoped he'd get it out. I tell you, though, that bastard got what he deserved."

"Why's that, sir?"

"'First do no harm.' That's what the good doctor believed. He never harmed them, he just let harm come to them before having to intervene."

"I don't think I follow, sir."

"Maybe it's for the best," was Grim's cryptic reply. "What I want is a transcript of that interrogation. All the details. Maybe a list of victims or… survivors. Plus, I have my suspicions that the larva Carver was carrying is the same one we ended up bringing here."

"Why?" Ben asked before reaching an answer on his own. "Because it recognized you?"

Grim, as if aware of the desperate leap of logic this required, seemed reluctant to answer. "Well, you're the one who said it did."

"Yeah, but how would it know you if it was inside Carver's stomach when you arrested him?"

"That's what I want to know, scout."

Ben settled back in his seat, rubbing his forehead in an endeavor to calm his reeling mind.

"This all so…" he began, his pained smile wavering into a short laugh. "The more I learn, the less I feel like I understand what the hell is happening. Do we—does the organization even know what they're dealing with?"

"If they did, you'll never straight answer out of them," said Grim with a derisive snort.

"But they have to know something! How could they not when we have a whole department working with them?"

Grim gave a tired chuckle: "More like a house divided. As far as I know we've got a hung jury on its origins—could be from deep sea, or outer space, or even another realm."

"I suppose it doesn't matter then," Ben resigned, finding that thinking only spurred an ensuing headache.

Beyond his closed eyes he heard his senior say: "Doesn't it, scout? When it might answer the question on whether there's something out there besides us?"

Ben hid his smile. "You believe in intelligent life, sir?"

"Maybe I just like the idea that we're not alone. I think others feel the same way. They just won't admit to it."

"And is that—the kraken, I mean—is that the answer you want?"

Well, it's something, Grim wanted to say; and *maybe not*. The conflicting answers rendered him silent as he thought of a concise way to reconcile the two.

CHAPTER 22

— Six weeks earlier —

His hands were clean; but seeing them clasped over the white surface of the table made him question the fact. Though it could have been the stark light above that made them appear mottled and almost sooty.

Grim rubbed his left thumb against the side of his right hand—an alternative to drumming his fingers, which Winston would take as a sign he was getting antsy. Not that he was antsy—just bored. Bored and craving a smoke.

Winston was pacing behind him, drawing out the procedure. That's how they got them soft. Nervousness and impatience were two tools in a long line of ways to get someone to talk.

Robert Winston—Wendigo Winston some liked to call him. The two things prominent in his face were his eyes and cheekbones. He had a way of slightly tipping down his head, presenting the cranium, and rolling his eyes up to look at you, as if peering over his glasses, though he never wore any. The effect was a morose expression, a curious combination of intimidation and regret that seemed to say: "it would be a shame if you push me to do whatever it is I'm about to do."

Early in his career Grim himself stood guard and watched as Winston broke down one man after another. Those first sessions had haunted him for a week afterwards; even if the memory lost its color, the mark remained. Winston knew this, and by doing nothing kept the fact suspended over Grim.

The presence of guards in the room served the triple purpose of providing security, hardening or sometimes testing their mettle, and playing out a cautionary tale in front of them. One corner of Grim's mouth slightly perked as he caught the wandering eye of one of the guards.

Winston finally stopped orbiting the table and planted his bony knuckles on the white surface.

"You know, the more I think of it, the less sense it makes," he said. "The matter would have taken less than five seconds. There was no reason whatsoever to retreat without accomplishing it."

Grim returned his gaze to his clasped hands before answering.

"They signaled me to return," was all he said, keeping to the same answer he had given before. There was no point in repeating it, except he had nothing else to say.

"Why did you let him go?" asked Winston, staring down at Grim as though trying to shrink him with his gaze.

Grim contemplated repeating the answer, but held his tongue, knowing well a repeated answer could set off the interrogator. Not that he feared the inevitable, but why inflict it on himself? His stint in Duncastor made him numb to whatever Winston could inflict on him. He knew physical pain, but his body no longer felt like it was his. Where he once felt something to the quick, now an invisible barrier stood to keep it from reaching those depths. Or perhaps his soul remained tethered to his body without inhabiting it. It must be, when a dream felt more tangible than real life. It was hard to say, and harder yet to live with, losing his sorrow, and with it his joy.

At times like the present, he might have welcomed the numbness, when he wouldn't fear breaking down. But if anything, Winston's job was his hobby, and he was efficient in his ways; he wouldn't be wasting time or method if he believed it wouldn't get results, but he was not above mending a broken bone just to break it again.

"You were fit enough for redeployment," remarked Winston.

Grim couldn't even remember getting out of Duncastor and was later told he managed to contact HQ and have himself picked up. That was all he had to go on. And the team who came to collect him corroborated this by saying he was in a state. None of it he remembered, except the period that followed: debriefing, a torturous rest and recovery, and subsequent redeployment occurring within mere days.

He was put through some accelerated healing program that they were testing, with marvelous results if at some unknown cost. They told him he would be more comfortable lying down but he insisted on remaining seated while receiving his dose. Grim once asked the nurse monitoring his readings what side-effects they were looking out for, and was told something about unnatural growth or fused organs. He rose sweaty and tremorous after each session, convinced his heart would stop, yet increasingly numb to the sharp shooting pain that for a while had plagued his side.

There was no talk of redeployment then: he just happened to complete his course and was found fit enough to be sent out again.

"You were fit enough for redeployment, weren't you?" Winston persisted.

"Yes, sir."

"Then why didn't you carry out your duty?"

The monitor to Grim's left lit up as Winston began to play some footage taken from Grim's helmet camera. Flickering lights and jumpy motion played out in the peripheries of Grim's vision. He stared at his clammy hands, avoiding looking at the screen for as long as he could.

Winston knew this. That's what made him exceptional at his job, the ability to read people, coming close to forecasting their next move. They all share similar weaknesses and follies, however much they like to think themselves unique and nuanced. And sure enough, Grim could no longer ignore the still image staring at him.

Something horrible about the man. Those black streaks— something about them that Grim understood and yet could not bring himself to dwell on. It was their reality, their experience— they had lived with it. So then, why did it set off something in him, as though he had lived it too?

The onlooker struggled to reconcile with it. It passed in a flash, a lifetime packed in transient seconds. The milky white of his eyes, that look on his begrimed face that recognized death and waited for him to deliver it. Could one deny one's own reflection?

Sweat pricked the back of Grim's neck. He could not keep looking any more than he could bring himself to look away.

He looked away when a packet of cigarettes was tossed onto the table, and Grim had to unclasp his trembling hands to reach for it.

Winston placed two fingers on the packet and drew it back.

"Why didn't you shoot him?" he wanted to know.

Grim glared at him, one hand vainly outstretched on the table, his blank expression full of latent anger.

"You had no trouble shooting unarmed civilians," continued Winston, "patients, nurses…"

"The staff were complicit in Carver's scheme. They were a risk in themselves."

"You were given clear orders: secure the target; leave no survivors. You managed to follow through up to that point. Why? Why stop at him?"

Grim couldn't bring himself to look at the screen again. He didn't have to. The man's image was burned into his mind—so much so that to look at him was to stare at a blank wall. It achieved nothing, except to touch some part of him buried deep beyond the threshold of consciousness.

An arbitrary line flashed across his mind: "If you raise your hand to kill me, I will not raise mine to kill you."

Where he had heard or read it, he couldn't say. Not that it mattered when it was nowhere near the supposed confession Winston sought to hear, and moreover signified insubordination in this context.

"I just got out of that place," Grim said at length. "Seeing him—seeing him just brought it all back. So I froze." He shrugged. "Maybe it was too soon—maybe I wasn't fit to go back there after all."

The statement was the closest he had to a truthful answer without resorting to incoherent babbling. The same statement was repeated at a subsequent hearing. Something in it smacked of psychological disturbance, which was how the panel of judges regarded the whole incident, considering the circumstances preceding his redeployment.

And while Winston never bought it for a second, all the figurative or literal arm-twisting failed to wring out a different answer.

"He poked the guy with his rifle. You can see it in the footage clear as day. Grade-A horseshit is what it is," Winston would later say to an associate, adding that he would have preferred to carry on with the interrogation, not in hopes of getting a confession, but because there was only one way to deal with traitors who escaped conviction. He never elaborated, for fear of incrimination, but a pencil he held in one hand snapped under the pressure of his thumb.

CHAPTER 23

The moon had either set or disappeared behind the line of trees, leaving everything to darkness unmitigated by anything save the truck's headlights. Atwood's cabin waxed stark and forbidding, its dark windows presenting an eyeless face to the approaching vehicle.

As the engine rumble died off, it occurred to Ben that he hadn't the slightest notion what Grim planned on doing.

"Something different," said Grim, refusing to elaborate until after they entered the cabin, ascended the stairs, and from there climbed out of the bedroom window and onto the flat roof—or rather Grim climbed ahead, then turned to extend his hand and assist Ben.

"I want to see if we can draw it all the way here," Grim went on, walking near the edge. "It's relatively safe and we'll be able to see it coming."

"Then we see about opening up the pipe canal below? To draw it into the basement?"

"Ah, see? That's why I like you. You pay attention," said Grim, a beam in his voice.

"But, sir, shouldn't we check if the pipe opens up? What if it doesn't work?"

"We'll cross that bridge when we get to it. First, we need to see if we can draw it all the way here, then we'll worry about how we get it inside."

To Ben, the idea sounded half-baked, but he lacked the energy to argue; besides it was evident that Grim had some tangential purpose in mind, enough to tow him out of bed, and the excitable mood he was in was either the by-product of exhaustion, or a monomaniac mind on the trail of its target.

"Got the stones, scout?"

"Sir?"

"Stones, rocks. Things you toss and make a splash."

Ben looked around for a confused moment. "You didn't ask me to bring any, sir!"

It was Grim's turn to look around, perplexed.

"Are you feeling alright, sir?"

"Of course I am. Yeah. Why wouldn't I be?"

"You just seem a little out of it."

"Alright, alright, forget the rocks. I'll see what I can find."

He returned ten minutes later and handed Ben a wire wastebasket heavy with sundry items, from coffee mugs to small boxes of detergent.

"Ready?" asked Grim as he and Ben held an alarm clock and paperweight respectively and stood poised to throw them. At his signal, they flung them into the lake, listening to the satisfying splash they made. They did this at intervals, counting to ten before throwing another set of items. Soon the basket was empty, and Grim had to climb back down and fill it again to repeat the process.

"What if it doesn't work, sir?" Ben asked during one of the brief intervals

"It's a huge lake, scout. Give it time. It's bound to hear us at some point."

Half-way through the third basket, Ben began to feel light-headed, and asked for a short break, to which Grim agreed. They settled at the edge of the roof facing the lake in anticipation of any movement.

For a while they sat quiet, Grim idly swinging his legs over the edge, and Ben huddled with his crossed arms on his knees, the two of them listening for the faintest ripple.

"Okay, so I lied," Grim said.

"Sir?"

"I said I lied. It's not like I can't remember anything, it's just whatever I remember doesn't amount to much. Might as well be blurred photos. I can't remember all the important details—not my parents' names, not our street name, our neighborhood—how old I was when I formed those memories... I mean you'd think it'd been hammered into my mind. But it's all a blank."

Several questions formed in Ben's mind—a few reactionary ones were at the tip of his tongue. He could have easily uttered any of them, though none would have demystified the subject. But the longer he listened, the better his mind was able to connect two seemingly unrelated points; whether it was a leap of imagination or generous empathy, he began to understand Grim's obsession with the kraken's fragmentary phrases, into which he read more meaning than perhaps was warranted.

"You think it might have something to tell you," Ben ventured to say without looking at him.

Grim uttered a soft laugh. "This can of corn could start

talking to me and as long as it's saying something relevant…" he paused, staring down at the can he held in one hand before flinging it.

Ben said nothing, and provoked by his silence Grim went on to say: "You don't have to buy into it. You got your birth certificate. Me? I don't know what happened to my family. All I know is that it messed me up. That's my theory: it's locked away in my mind somewhere. But I don't have access to it. So, I'll take what I can get. If I can find something, a clue I could follow…" he trailed off, frustrated with the inadequacy of his words, and perhaps somewhat embarrassed by his partners' reticence.

Ben in truth had nothing to say, except to stare at Grim in awe, thinking how wonderful the senior still retained his ability to speak when his lower jaw had split into mandibles like that of an ant—no, a stag beetle, skin smoothly merged with black bone, now curving upwards like tusks, now curling back into great horns.

Oh my fallen friend, thought Ben, *will you never see how lies round back to pierce you?*

Grim would not hear him, but reared up, trailing long strings of pitch, his horned form a terrible vision to behold.

"Where are you?" he yelled into the night. "Why did you have to show up and throw everything off?"

Somewhere below, a tall blackened figure stood, his features hidden, apart from the half-moons that answered for the white of his eyes, implying the figure cast his gaze up at them. Ben didn't see him but knew he was there. And he was grateful for the truth, thankful Grim had finally shown his true form, and vowed to save him from himself.

O child, lorn child, lost and wayward.

Unlike him, Grim never tasted the loving strain of her arms.

Foul and fallow, she will take him, restore him, make him pure and whole once more.

Ben stood up.

He couldn't hear anything yet, but all the same strove to listen in the vacuum silence. Then a signing voice stole like approaching light. It began low, almost whispering, then rose to a fair, sweet note, delicately reverberating through his vitals, evaporating to leave behind a warm, lingering weakness. It drowned out everything, isolating him in a shell, so that when he felt himself caught by the arms and pulled back, he all but lashed out in retaliation.

Grim was his name, and he called him to... what?

The singing receded a moment, allowing Ben to return to the physical realm and Grim, who still held him fast and was saying something about walking off the ledge.

"I'm fine," breathed Ben, unable to contain a foolish grin. "Really I am, sir."

"You better be or you'll find yourself hog-tied," the other warned. "Now listen: I want you to tell me everything it says. You hear me? Everything."

"I will, sir, I will," assured Ben, eager to go back to hearing the song.

She sounded as he imagined Olivia would if she sang. The unearthly quality of her beauty seemed fitted for such a voice. And so his mind imposed an image of her with hooded lids and mouth gently open to shape a mildly wavering, softly tapering sound, melting into air like fragrant smoke. The image faded, forgotten, but the voice remained, streaming over his body, raising and stirring the fine hairs. There was a calling in it, a compelling beckon by which he must abide. More so when it waxed low and intimate. He wanted to see her, the wondrous vision. A step closer? What's a small step for a closer look?

Again, he was jerked back.

"I'm listening, sir, I'm listening," maintained Ben, trying to push past Grim who struggled to restrain him. "I promise you I'm listening," he reiterated, managing to inch them closer to the ledge.

"Like hell you are," gritted Grim, still trying to push Ben back and growing concerned with the feverish strength possessing the young man. "You keep this up and I'm gonna knock you cold."

"Wait! I think she's starting to speak."

"I swear, if you're making this up," muttered Grim, faltering a moment before adding: "Well?"

Ben paused to listen, trying again to separate song from speech, or its equivalent.

"Familiar and not," he began, conscious of his flat delivery compared to the lilting voice. "It sickens the smaller ones. Yet familiar once before. We desire it so."

"Familiar how?" said Grim in the manner peculiar to one asking a translator to pass on his inquiry.

Ben repeated the question. The words were in him and he knew he did not need to voice his answer, except he knew saying them aloud would satisfy his senior. The answer came promptly:

"It carried us, sustained us, we milked it for thin blood. Full of death stench yet we drank deep, and fell to heavy sleep."

It went on, using disjointed meanings that Ben's mind effortlessly knitted into coherent words. What he heard was "food supplier" and "false carrier", and he understood it to mean "surrogate".

"We heard the call: the progenitor beckoned; we stilled the surrogate, and bade it listen."

"What happened to this surrogate?" demanded Grim.

"Untimely severance," came the answer. "We remain bereft."

He stopped because she stopped. She had climbed out of the water. He heard it part and run down her sides. She moved towards land, towards the house, her dozen arms reaching up, yearning for him... no, for his companion. She begged him to throw down his companion, cast him to her. But the connection with her was severed as soon as Grim's fist connected with his jaw.

For the past few seconds Grim had been trying to no avail to rouse the young man from his fatal infatuation, to keep him from pushing the two of them over the edge; and it soon grew evident that shoving back wasn't enough, not when Grim released Ben a moment only for Ben to grab his senior by the throat, intent on shoving him to the kraken below. What he lacked in strength he made up for in fervor. That's when Grim decked him.

The world wildly spun for Ben before his head hit the surface of the roof. Grim pinned him facedown, by which point Ben recovered, and his arms flew back, clawing and hitting whatever they could reach.

"Get off me!" he spat out in a high, frantic voice he rarely if ever used. Soon even words failed to form fast enough and he gave into shouting incoherently.

This suited Grim, who deposited a pill into Ben's open mouth. Ben knew what it was, but just out of spite he spat it out.

"Son of bitch!" cried the senior, at which Ben grinned with strained laughter.

"She doesn't want you! She's calling me to come to her!" he raved on, granting Grim a second chance to push another pill into his mouth. This time, Ben clenched his teeth, not caring that Grim's fingers were caught between them. The fact that his senior did not cry out in pain made Ben bite down all the harder. Just as he realized the fingers were protected by the Tegmen's shell, he felt the pill rolling inside his cheek, and had to release Grim's finger to spit it out. Before he could, Grim clamped a hand over his mouth and pinched his nose with the other.

Ben struggled to throw him off, which was a mistake. In the reshuffling of priorities, breathing became a primary concern. He struggled again as soon as he swallowed the pill, moving his head to motion that it went down.

"You spit it out, and I swear I'll do it again and I won't let go till you black out. We clear?"

Ben nodded emphatically and was soon released. He rolled over, gasping and coughing. With every part of him, he loathed his senior: What did he bring him here for anyway? What did he hope to accomplish?

As soon as the coughing subsided, he noticed the hand extended to help him up.

"You alright?" Grim asked after Ben stood up on his own. The question sounded incredibly arbitrary to Ben, who felt anything but alright. But for lack of any answer, he nodded.

"Do you still hear it?"

Ben shook his head. He lied: of course he could still hear her. If Grim hoped the pill would sour the notes of her song, he was sorely mistaken. Her song had thinned but it still reached him clear. What did she sing of? It didn't matter. Her voice could turn vile, lurid lyrics into radiant psalmodies. As though the lake waters were soporific, her song waned to sleep; and she, heavy with her drink, through black waves sank deep.

CHAPTER 24

Not long after, they climbed down into the bedroom window, making a brief stop while Ben disappeared into the bathroom, convinced he was about to throw up; in truth, he was tempted to stick his finger down his throat for that relief, but knew Grim would hear him and again coerce him to take another pill.

After that, they left the cabin to find dawn had crept up on them in the interval, greeting them with skies several shades paler than what they saw on the roof. On the shore were visible tracks left by the kraken, going up the slope to the side of the cabin, where wide, wet streaks glistened in the coming light. Evidently, the creature had sidled up to the wall, but whether or not it was able to scale it was hard to say.

"If we can summon it here, we could draw it into the basement," Grim summarized with a nod of self-satisfaction. "Just need to see about opening that pipe tunnel."

"She won't fall for it, not without bait at least," said Ben, earning him an odd look from his senior, who nevertheless was obliged to agree.

"Hm. Think we can score a fresh body somewhere?"

"She seems drawn to you, sir," the young man quietly implied.

Again, Grim looked askance at him, but refrained from remarking.

"Let's go get something to eat," he instead suggested. "It's been a long night. I'm sure we'll figure out something over breakfast."

He went ahead, leaving Ben to a lingering look at the lake. The still surface presented a faded reflection of bluing skies, hiding stagnant waters beneath. It all sat strangely with him, and he felt like he had caught the world unawares in a moment of poetry—heady and burgeoning with possibilities. There was a certain heaviness to the truck's interior, much like how the encroaching light deepened the shadows of its nooks and corners. Yet Ben felt himself weightless within it, the heaviness having little to no bearing on him, no more than water would bear down on a body floating a meter or two below surface. The sky's flush was in his blood, and he fancied himself a thing of dust and air.

Whether his perception of time was altered or whether Grim took a different route, the drive back took longer than he remembered. It was light by the time they parked behind the Tea House, where white smoke rose out of the chimney pipe. They crept up the stairs, and Ben waited while Grim changed into civilian attire pilfered from Atwood's wardrobe before trying the connecting door.

Olivia had locked it the night before, and discovering it was presently unlocked, the two men descended, assuming the shop was open for business. They found the owner busy setting tables, and she was quick to point out that the Tea Room was not yet open.

"Though I suppose there's no rule against serving boarders

before customers," she ruminated out loud just as the two men were about to turn around and head back upstairs.

They sat at their usual table while she fetched them a pot of coffee. At this hour, sunlight shone directly through the front windows, and seemed to repose on the floor amid empty tables and chairs. It gave a silken glimmer to the stream of coffee being poured, caught and amplified the mist rising from the filled mugs. Fresh and scalding, Ben took frequent sips of it to numb his prickly throat. He knew he was going to descend from his elevated mood at some point or other, but he was determined to enjoy every swoop and glide on the way down.

"What do you think?" said Olivia, setting down a slice of green cake.

Grim folded his arms, cocking his head to one side in a contemplative manner. "I say it's time to throw it away."

"It's supposed to be green," she answered.

"Why?"

"I'm testing recipes using ingredients you can forage. You know how I give out food at the end of the day? Sometimes the commune people try to pay me back with mushrooms, and herbs, and stuff they gathered. I'd tell them to keep it, but they insist and I don't want to hurt their feelings or anything. But it's more than I can use, and it'll be a waste to let it go bad."

"So, make a salad or an omelet, or something," Grim suggested, sliding the plate away from him.

"Well, what's wrong with cakes?" said Olivia, nudging the plate back in front of him. "Red velvet has beetroots in it. And I've heard of people sneaking spinach and broccoli into cakes."

"It's not weed that makes the cake," Grim pointed out. "You still need flour, eggs, and sugar."

"They got chickens, and a sack of flour or sugar will keep.

Besides, I'm just experimenting here, I don't plan on adding it to the menu."

"Of course not," Grim scoffed, "it's not edible."

"Oh, come on," she persuaded, nudging his shoulder. "Try it."

"I'm not your hamster," he countered, looking up at her with an expression that could only be described as mildly offended.

"You mean guinea pig?"

"No, I mean those rodents people keep—feed them carrot peels and newspapers."

"Would I feed you garbage?" she airily asked, placing her hands on her hips.

Grim stared at the cake, petulantly keeping his arms folded. "It's green and unholy."

"I thought you said you were a cake man."

"I prefer my cakes plain and in natural shades of white, yellow, or brown."

"I'll try it," Ben broke in, pulling the plate towards him. "I'm sure if you made it, it must be good."

"You're a braver man than he is." Olivia smiled with satisfaction.

"Now you've done it," Grim muttered to no one in particular.

By the time the Tea Room was open for business, both men had already finished their meals and gone upstairs. Grim was set to head out again, except Ben begged a moment to use the bathroom, closing the door in sweaty haste before his insides exploded. Much like the night before, nothing seemed to come out of the painful spasms except endless, excruciating minutes of doubling over the toilet. And when he finally dragged himself to the sink, swaying a little as he rinsed his hands, he considered telling his senior to leave without him.

Except, by the time he got out, he found Grim asleep in his cot, feet planted on the floor from sitting on the edge of the bed; and it was evident from his uncomfortable position that he sat there waiting, with no intention of laying on his side or closing his eyes, only gradually yielding as the minutes went by. The unexpectedness of finding him in that state almost moved his subordinate: How vulnerable he looked, lying there with his eyes closed, softly snoring through parted lips—how easy it would be to find the hollow between his ribs and sink a knife there.

Ben started back from his thoughts and stared at the sleeping man, finding scant reassurance in the fact that he hadn't done anything besides stand there and...

And what? Plot? Dream? A blink was longer than the glimpse flashing behind his eyes, and into which his entire being was submerged, as though he had dipped into a different reality where the foul deed was done. He continued to stare without moving, making sure no part of his senior was disturbed or injured. It seemed imperative to establish the fact with open eyes, especially when whole realities seemed to pass whenever they closed—realities separated by a membrane as thin as his own lids.

Satisfied his partner lay undisturbed, Ben extracted the truck keys out of Grim's hand and stole out.

He plugged his phone into the truck's console to charge, but dreaded turning it over to check for messages. They were there and no doubt: yesterday, when Grim dictated some contact information to send to Harper, Ben caught sight of his inbox and the eight new messages waiting for him.

Presently his heart sank when he found two inquired after his report, the rest being memos of nominal importance. And while the repeated inquiries were mildly-worded reminders, he knew a polite front does not signify lenience. The latest one was sent a few hours ago, tempting him to respond with a quick answer. Yet his fingers remained suspended over the keypad, stalling as he composed a vague yet adequate answer. None sounded satisfactory. And after a few tries, he tossed the phone onto the passenger seat without so much as a second glance.

He started the truck, determined to have something ready for them come evening.

The morning was fine, with azure skies and a lively wind that whipped the milk white clouds, and bore him all the fresh air he needed to fill his lungs. Even the sedate forest surrounding the lake was animated by its gentle influence.

On reaching the cabin, Ben stepped out of the truck, but stayed behind the open door while he looked about for signs of danger, a repeat of yesterday's ambush. The tail of his borrowed plaid shirt flapped in the brisk air, which likewise stirred the surrounding bushes; no shadows darted out of the ongoing rustle, and at length, he felt secure enough to walk over to the edge of the lake and the shaded spot where Grim had shown him the other end of the pipe. Since they managed to draw the kraken here, all they had to do was lead it down the pipe tunnel and lock it in the basement. The plan was deceptively easy that he could not scrutinize it long without coming across a few hitches: Baiting the kraken into entering the tunnel was one thing, but first and foremost was the issue of opening up the pipe.

So Ben began by descending into the basement to investigate the console unit. There, he tried a set of switches he knew Grim had overlooked in favor of trying to activate the security doors and electrified floor. It took about a minute of fiddling before Ben heard a great rush of water gushing out of the pipe; soon after, he learned which buttons were responsible for opening and shutting valves within the tunnel pipe, allowing him to control the flow of lake water or cut it off. So elated was he at his progress that he bounded up the basement stairs and ran towards the lake to watch the water swirl into the pipe, then rushed down again to see it stream out the other end, almost flooding the enclosure's shallow pool. His exhilaration might have been complete had he not discovered that one of the valves was faulty and would not close all the way.

But before he had time to dwell on the matter, his phone vibrated with a message from Harper, alerting him to the fact that she was going to call within the next five minutes.

Ben stopped short of shooting an automatic "OK," recalling at the last moment that Grim was fast asleep, and would likely be awakened by the incoming call. Having begun this business with the pipe, the young man preferred to wait until he figured out how to resolve the faulty valve issue on his own.

With that in mind, he answered Harper's text with Atwood's phone number, and shortly thereafter answered the phone on the first ring.

"Hey," said Harper, reciprocating his greeting with a slight inquisitive accent, perhaps surprised to hear his voice on the other end instead of Grim's.

There was an uncertain pause, through which Ben calculated several responses before settling on a noncommittal: "How are things?"

"Good, good," she said with artificial cheer.

The fact that she was beset by similar constraint puzzled Ben, who could no longer stand the awkwardness of their situation.

"Listen, Harper, I just wanted to say I'm sorry."

The abruptness caught her off-guard. "Sorry? Sorry for what?"

"I don't know what it is I said or did—but whatever it is, I just wanted to apologize if I upset you in any way."

"Ben, what the hell are you talking about?" she asked after an appreciable pause, during which he anxiously sucked in his lips.

"I don't know," he said, starting to regret his decision. "Except in the last two calls, you sounded angry with me for some reason."

"I wasn't mad at you! What made you think that?"

"Well, I thought maybe I owed you something, you know, like a favor for giving me the birth certificate."

"Why? Do you usually pay for gifts?" she asked in a flat tone, sounding annoyed.

"I just..." he floundered before sighing deeply. "You know what? Forget it. It's just a stupid thought."

"Listen, Ben. If I wanted something, I'd have said it to you straight. And if I sounded pissed off—well, I was just going through a rough time. It's nothing personal."

"You're right, I'm sorry."

"Oh, good lord, Ben, please don't apologize. It just makes me feel worse. Look, I'll be honest, I was mad at anyone who wasn't in my life sharing my struggles. I felt isolated and resentful, especially when everyone expected me to go on as if life was normal."

Ben wasn't sure how to answer; and perhaps sensing his unease, she quickly added: "But, hey—thanks to your friend, things might be looking up. Grim's an opportunist, but I'm grateful for what he did all the same. Where is he by the way?"

"Oh, I'm letting him sleep in. We both had a rough night.

But I'm glad you called. I wanted to ask you something—" Ben shifted the phone to his other ear—"hypothetically speaking: what are the chances of finding his file in your department? Anything on his background, maybe a birth certificate, or something. I promise to pay you this time."

For a while there was no answer, so much so that he wondered whether she was still on the line.

"I'm with you, I'm with you," she reassured him. "It's just that…" She paused again. "Look, it's not that I don't want to try. But chances are his file is either buried somewhere, or it could be beyond my reach. Yours is comparatively recent, and was easier to access. But I'll keep an eye out, and if I find anything, I'll be sure to let you know," she concluded. "Now, do you want the report?"

"What? Oh, yeah, the report," he said, suddenly remembering why she called in the first place.

"Just so you know, I couldn't find much on survivors. Most of what I got was on Dr. Carver and the bug they found in his stomach."

"Bug?"

"Sorry—the larva. That's what Grim was asking for, right? Well, the larva they found wasn't implanted in there. According to the report, its size or developmental stage did not match where they found it. They suspect he was trying to smuggle it out—"

"H- Hold on," stammered Ben. "What do you mean implanted?"

"You don't know? That's how krakens have their babies. I don't know how well you remember your natural science, but you know how some species of parasitic wasps inject their young into a living host? Same method."

"You mean... inside people?" he whispered, horrified.

She laughed and proceeded with morbid relish. "If you think that's nasty, listen to this: At that stage, it starts to lose its protective mucus. Meaning it can't stay in the stomach—you know, because of stomach acid. Usually, it moves on and settles in other cavities while it continues growing. So, all this time it was trying to eat its way out, causing major damage. What's weird was that he'd been quiet the whole time. They never suspected anything until he collapsed in the middle of questioning."

"Wh- How?"

"According to the transcript, he confessed to farming larva to extract some opioid or something out of them. My guess is that the larva had him doped up while it chewed its way through, and the only reason he confessed to anything was 'cause he kept complaining about not feeling well, and they promised to let a doctor see him as soon as he told them everything. I'm sorry, was that too graphic?" she asked when Ben remained quiet on his end.

In truth, he had his eyes closed, and was holding a fist to his mouth. "How do they even handle these things?" he managed to say once he swallowed back something acrid. "And you say they breed them?"

"I never said that," Harper was prompt to point out.

"Oh, right, that was Grim," said Ben, pinching his eyes shut as if hoping to crush a small mass growing between them. The lack of sleep was starting to get to him.

"Well, this empties the bag, I guess."

"Wait! That's it? What about victims or survivors?"

"I already told you I didn't find much on them. Though between you and me, I heard they raised a stink over some slipping by. They could be tracking them down, though you won't find anything on them in Archives."

"One more thing," said Ben. "Grim had this theory that the larva they got from Carver is the same one they sent here. Do you know anything about that?"

"Nope. I don't have the report with me, but I'm pretty sure they didn't mention that. Those documents were filed away weeks ago."

"So the larva would have been too old—no, wait. I think they can slow down its development," muttered Ben, more to himself.

"I don't know," said Harper, already tiring of the subject. "Look, I gotta go. I'll be in touch if I find anything on Grim."

After they hung up, Ben returned to the basement and the more pressing problem of the impaired valve. He supposed it didn't matter, as long as they succeeded in luring the kraken before making a hasty exit. But then, they would still need to turn the valves off to keep it from crawling out again. Moreover, the valve issue might be a slight one, a mere case of obstruction or debris keeping it from closing all the way. And with both valves working, they had a better chance of capturing the kraken, closing off one and then the other to trap it inside the pipe.

With that in mind, Ben turned to the small, three-shelf bookcase, hoping to find a technical manual or some diagram that would shed light on the subject.

CHAPTER 25

They all saw it, they read it without intending to, in the uneasy silence, in the constant, restless shifting of seated positions, in heads turning expectantly without knowing what to look out for. The tension, multiplied by the number of people present, was moreover magnified by their empty stomachs. Many had not slept, or had fallen into a troubled sleep, and rose to a stark morning of resentment and frustrated anger. Some families, urged by their hungry children, got up early and contrived to make a meal using whatever they could snatch from the pantry.

A community, no matter how seemingly harmonious, can never indefinitely keep its congenial state, not while it remains made up of individuals, many of whom move in his or her own direction, following wants, needs or notions that don't always align with that of others. In the past it had taken their leader's rallying words and promises to unify them into reconciling their differences. For all that, hairline cracks continued to exist in the form of unexpressed opinions some members cherished regarding Thane's poor choice of real estate and, in reality, not aligning to the glowing hopes they had of a bucolic Eden. Such cracks preceded the shock of finding three members afflicted with an unknown ailment, and grew deeper when Thane failed to resolve the matter in a satisfactory way. Even to concede to what the outsider had said—to take a firm stand, however difficult, by killing and burning the three—would have brought some form of closure preferable to letting matters escalate as they did. A guard was killed in the shootout, two suffered injuries, and a woman was trampled on when everyone scattered. Worse yet was the possible threat of a contagion, if the outsider was to be believed. A handful of members did— enough to flee the commune before dawn, absconding with an ample share of the provisions they were meant to guard.

Strangely enough, some members saw the unprecedented incident as a test, and said as much to their fellow members; having no lives outside the commune to return to, nor visions of an alternative future, they held fast to hopes of an imminent promised land, and their fervor was either met with acquiescence from members who sought that much reassurance, or answered with looks of mute dejection from others. To the latter, Thane was no longer the deliverer of their hopes for a small, happy community. Still, even the skeptics looked to him to soothe and inspire steadfastness; even to admit his oversight would have won them over.

But presently their ba'al sat in the eye of their semi-circle, staring them down, as if directing his anger at them, or perhaps daring anyone to say anything. It was enough for parents to anxiously hush their children, some of whom began to fuss and complain out of boredom or hunger.

Ten minutes ago, before Thane had walked amongst them to take his seat, the lobby was alive with discourse. The subject of the past couple of days was freely discussed and argued among groups of threes and fives, agitated with doubt and uncertainty. What disease befell those three men who floated back to shore that night? Was the outsider truly invincible as the guards claimed he was? More than half saw him rise again after being shot at point-blank, and while several men scoffed at the idea, none volunteered to go after him.

Thane knew all this without having heard their talk. He saw it in the expectant glance a few lifted to him before breaking eye contact to drop their gaze. Old habits, formed in his childhood through a father that always took his frustration on the party that least deserved it: on a wife in his path, a dog at his foot, and a child caught unawares, who at the time never understood his father's anger. Would that he could, Thane would have kicked his people in a body for their collective cowardice. Not a single martyr or brave soul in their midst. All were small; all cherished their selfish lives.

A look of weariness passed over his face, softening the hard look. He shifted his weight to lean more to the right.

"How very much I loved you. How very much I tried to give you the life you deserve," he began, sounding weary—so much so that those seated in the middle and back rows had to lean forward to better hear him. "Against all my effort to shelter you from the world and its many reaching hands, two outsiders made that impossible. It's impossible to ignore and forget what has happened. They are like the ravenous wolves culling the herd. When we came here, we vowed to be self-sufficient, to thrive on our own. Like mighty trees digging our roots deeper and deeper into our beloved mother, the giving earth. We sought to live by our own principles, for 'Man is born free, but he is everywhere in chains.' We would have stayed happy with our lot, but they proved to us it's not enough, this lot. This small corner? It was never enough!"

Here he rose from his petulant slump, growing more emphatic as he continued.

"And maybe we should thank them for opening our eyes. They envy us our freedom, our numbers. They look at us and see a threat. We outnumber them. That is why they won't offer us anything. But they will give us scraps when we beg for them. Why? To subjugate us! To feel a sense of dominion over us! To feel less inferior, sitting all day and growing fat, while we work hard and grow strong—what is that caterwauling over there?"

All eyes turned towards the back of the room, where women with infants and young children often sat for easier leave-taking in case a child was too inconsolable to stop crying. This time however the mother sat cross-legged, vacantly staring at nothing in particular, while in her lap a baby continued to kick and wail.

"Someone see to that fussing child now," Thane demanded just a man approached him.

"Thane we humbly beg for permission—"

Thane raised a hand to cut him off. "I will have no begging amongst us."

"Then we ask your permission to leave."

"You know you don't need my permission to leave," answered Thane, masking his irritation at being interrupted over trivial matters. "The mothers may take their children to calm them—"

"I meant me, Thane," said the doleful man.

"What for?"

"My wife's been in a state since yesterday. I don't believe she's fit to look after our child."

Before he could answer, another man approached Thane.

"Thane, I humbly ask for permission too. I need to go foraging. My children are hungry and there's no food left."

"There were plenty of provisions when I last checked."

The man hesitated to deliver the news. "Some three or four members ran off with them. We only found out this morning. They were supposed to guard them, but they—"

Members with similar complaints rose as well, seeking leave to see to their families, wearing down Thane's patience, though for the time being he could only scan the semi-circle of tired, bleating faces.

"If that's how you feel then bind your stomachs and listen! I was about to tell everyone what I had in mind in that regard before I was interrupted." He cast about admonitory stares until everyone sat back down, and the woman with the baby was covertly escorted out. Then he too took his seat to resume.

"I was about to say this: winter's close upon us. We haven't had much luck in growing things. We don't have time to start over, but that shouldn't be our concern—not when there's plenty of food to go around. 'You are undone if you once forget that the fruits of the earth belong to us all, and the earth itself to nobody.' Take old man Howard, now," he said, jumping ahead, knowing well-enough any elaboration would be lost on a restless crowd. "What does old Howard do? Every night he goes and dumps milk into his sink. Perfectly good milk! Gone to waste cause the government told him to dump it on a given day! And he can't give it away cause the government won't allow it. 'Rules and Regulations' he'd say. Nothing goes to waste in nature. It's only in corrupt societies that one excuses iniquity as 'Rules and Regulations.' But does he care? Of course not. He would rather see it pour down the drain than give it. If he can't sell it, no one can have it."

He paused for effect and was satisfied at the indignant mumblings that rose.

"What does he care?" Thane repeated, charged with his theme, "as long as he's not obliged to do his part and share the wealth. He grows fat while our children starve. Shame on him, I say! Shame! Shame! Shame!"

Every reiteration was met with growing scorn, and the crowd's culminating roar was enough to restore Thane's self-assurance; his smug smile waned a little when he spotted a hand waving for attention.

"Why don't we just slaughter the pigs?" a woman suggested.

"The hogs are our last resort," Thane answered evenly. "When we hit rock bottom, I will be the first to slit their throats. But we're nowhere near it yet, I promise you that."

Another hand went up with another suggestion.

"Miss Olivia never begrudged us anything before. Why don't we go to her and see what she can give us?"

"Yes. 'Why don't we go to Miss Olivia?'" Thane wearily repeated, annoyed by questions focused on gratifying their immediate needs and furthermore tamped down the flame he tried to kindle. "Anyone want to answer that? Anyone?" he challenged, his opaque eyes sweeping the semi-circle.

Knowing he had a specific answer in mind, no one ventured to guess, or risk sharing the censure coming the inquirer's way.

"You know what I heard Howard say to Olivia the other day, when he thought I was out of earshot?" the leader began, seeming to go off on a tangent. "He was warning her against giving us anything. Called us bums and moochers. Worse than that: He went as far as to threaten to report her if she didn't stop. You know why? 'Cause it kills him each time a potential customer gets something for free. It gives him an ulcer to see people not spending money. Now we never set out to make an enemy of this man. But did he leave us alone? Or did he try to sever our ties with the one good person who sympathized with our cause? Why, it wouldn't surprise me if he did report her, and sicced the authorities on us. Because he can afford it.

Because it pleases this fat, selfish man to see us driven away. Because he's loathsome and hateful!"

Thundering the last few sentences, Thane stirred a responsive blaze from the crowd that satisfied him; they had their sights locked on a new target, and an easier target at that. He would deal with the other two in due course. Maybe it was a mistake to rely on Olivia. His people certainly had grown complacent with whatever she gave them, and the complacency took the beast out of them. That's why they scattered like sheep at the first sign of danger. They knew it, and none dared to look him in the eye. Hunger and humility made them keen for blood, and they were raring to prove themselves to him and their families.

"But why wait for him to bring the fight to us?" Thane raved on. "I promise you this: we will tip the scales, and give him a taste of his own medicine! He will rue the day he crossed paths with us!"

For the pining crowd, this had the tantalizing promise of looting, and not a few of them imagined leaving Howard's Store with armfuls of goods they desperately needed—far better than the handouts they received and had to divide amongst them. After the cheers died out, someone close to the front row mumbled something.

"Come again?" said Thane.

A balding man in faded denim stood up, raising his voice a little as he reiterated: "I said a couple of days ago we noticed Howard had placed a 'Help Wanted' sign and spoke to him. He said he's opening up a store in the next town over and offered to hire a few of us to sweep and bag groceries."

An electric silence followed this disclosure, made more uncomfortable by Thane's unblinking eyes.

"The weather's turning," the man went on, carried by the momentum of having stated something irrevocable, "and there's no time to grow things. Soon we won't be able to forage or hunt. It's just to help us get by this coming winter—"

Thane stood up, frightening the speaker into silence. "Whose idea was it?"

The man hesitated. "It'll just be temporary, Alpha. Just until we're able to—"

Thane fixed him with a look as he quietly repeated: "Whose idea was it? I know you, Pete. You're always one for talking, but you never take initiative. Whose idea was it?"

"It was m- mine, Th-Th- Thane," stuttered a second man, Pete's younger brother, Henry. Despite being his junior in years, Henry stood a head above Pete, but stooped whenever he was near him as if to hide the fact.

"The way I s- see it," Henry went on, in spite of his speech impediment and the dead stare directed his way, "why k- k-kill a goose when we c- c- co... while it lays golden eggs?"

Thane stared up at the workhorse of a man. "And pray-tell what do you want to do with those golden eggs? Fry them up? Make a giant omelet to feed everyone?"

"Some of us already work part-time for Miss Olivia," Pete chimed in. "This won't be any different."

"Olivia is an exception. Howard's a capitalist pig who wants to make little walking banks out of all of you. He'll work you to the bone, and whatever meager coin he pays you will go back into his pocket when he charges you for his overpriced goods."

Henry came to his brother's aid. "I mean, s- sir, we—"

"What now?!" cried Thane, flying into a sudden rage. "I see their programming is kicking in—all that brainwashing coming back online. You need help, my friends. You need me to show you how to fly!"

He did not realize he had smacked Henry until he noticed the tall man holding his cheek with a cowed angry look.

The look only served to further infuriate Thane: instead of toughening them, life out here had enfeebled their minds and souls. The empty claims, the praises he sang in the past for their supposed hardiness and vigor were not testimonies, but words meant to cultivate those qualities. In his eyes, he had behaved like a parent encouraging his child to adopt stoic standards by commending him on every trifle, hoping they would yield more desirable traits. There were times when he even marveled at his own patience and forbearance, as if he drew them from an infinite well. Now that well was dry and empty: He had been good to them, and now they repaid him with doubts and complaints.

"Go ahead then," he granted. "I never set out to enthrall you. You go back to the world there and they'll enslave you, drive you to toil until you die. If you want that, then you're free to go. But you're no longer welcome here. You're to leave with only the clothes on your back."

The brothers have evidently made up their mind then and there. And seeing them make for their spouses and children to take them along, Thane added: "The children are staying."

Henry and Pete glanced at one another and at their respective spouses, not quite sure what they had just heard.

"The children are staying," Thane repeated when neither parent let go of their children.

"Thane!" Pete exclaimed, almost laughed through his nervous smile, as if imploring him to be reasonable.

"They're members of the same commune that took them in, which makes them ours as much as yours."

The space created around the brothers to let them leave now began to close as more members stood up. The motion confused the four adults, who could not read whether the crowd about them moved to detain, or whether they rose in sympathetic protest. Things were happening so fast that Pete's wife, Gertrude, saw her younger brother approaching, and in her bewildered state relinquished her daughter to a pair of outstretched arms. The act was as automatic as a reflex, brought on by months of living in a society where parents trustfully handed their small children to one another to free their hands for interminable duties. It was moreover incited by the little girl leaning towards the hands that reached for her.

Arms now empty, Gertrude's heart dropped when she turned and saw her daughter being carried off by Thane. Her soft cry of protest belied the frantic energy that seized her as she lunged forward only to be held back by the same group that surrounded them. Henry, meanwhile, pulled his son closer and hid him behind him.

"Please," entreated Gertrude, her outstretched hand incapable of closing the small gap between her and Thane.

"You still have a choice, Gertrude," said Thane, taking a step closer to entice her. Pete pulled her back from the restraining crowd, encircled her thin shoulders with his arms as he whispered something in her ears. Her pained look remained, though her lips pressed together, and it was evident she was trying to muster some resolve.

"We don't want anything," said Pete to Thane. "Just let us leave with our family. We're willing to stay and share the wealth if you just let us."

"What guarantees us you won't squirrel some away while you live off our land? Theirs is a corrupt system. And if you're unable to see it, it's because you are within the system."

"We just want to get by, Thane. That's all we want, I swear," Gertrude contended in a quavering voice.

"Are you sure, Gerty? How do you know Pete didn't put you up to this? Go back and work to pay for his drinking habit?"

Thane went on. "What does he care if you work a late-night shift—when it's just you and Howard? What does he care if his fat little hand creeps up your leg?"

"You shut the hell up," gritted Pete, whose turn it was to fling himself and be restrained. Gertrude's reaching hand fell as she began to sob.

"Oh, now don't be like that, Gerty," gently spoke Thane. "You can still stay with us, right, honey?" He turned to the girl in his arms, who was idly running her little finger along his beard. "Right, baby? Tell Gerty to come stay with us."

"Gerty come stay," repeated the girl as she rested her head on Thane's shoulder. It was then that she noticed Gertrude's anguish.

"Gerty cry," observed the child.

"Gerty cry because Pete wants to leave."

"Why?"

"Because he says they need to go back and work. Do you want to go with them? Hm? They'll take you back to school. You know what school is, darling? It's where they make everyone sit all day on hard chairs and study. Do you want that? Hm?"

Lifting her head, the little girl looked at him, thinking it over. All she knew was that the idea of sitting all day sounded unappealing, and for that she shook her head.

"No, of course not," Thane smiled back. "You want to stay here with all your friends and family. And later on, I'll take you to the forest and show you where the deer sleeps and the squirrel hides his food."

"He hides food?"

"Yes, but we have to keep it a secret. Just you and me."

This all sounded most enchanting to Henry's son, a boy of

four who moreover coveted the special attention. He slipped his hand from Henry's slackened grasp.

"I want to stay too!" he cried out, running after Thane before Henry could catch him.

CHAPTER 26

Ben sat sprawl-legged on the white floor of the basement, holding a manual in his listless hand.

The manual was little more than a sheaf of papers with the edges stapled to make a booklet. It sat in Atwood's meager library, sandwiched between similarly slim volumes, most of which were references, guidelines and technical handbooks.

Now and then, Ben would emerge from his daze to revisit the makeshift manual, flipping back and forth between a few specific paragraphs and their accompanying illustrations.

The larva, drawn next to an adult hand to scale, had a protozoan appearance: an oblong body with one tapering end, no discernible eyes or head, and small stumps capable of stretching into long, thin tendrils. Whoever made these drawings spend more time lovingly rendering the infants as opposed to adults, delineated with an abstract outline resembling that of a hydra.

A bizarre read, though not quite as unsettling as the pages that followed. Harper's report on Carver's fate seemed a precursor to their content: To find out that such things occurred was disturbing to say the least; to read about the symptoms and pore over the gradual change detailed in pages was a shock he had yet to process. And while he could pull back from lurid descriptions, or keep from staring at diagrams illustrating the developmental stages of the larva, where in the body it nestled, and worst of all what cruel and irreversible deterioration it wrought on its host—while he could turn a blind eye to all that, he could not ignore the possibility that he might be carrying one.

At first blush it did not seem to be the case since nothing in the manual directly informed him of the fact. An implanted host would instantly fall into a period of heavy sleep, from which they neither rose nor stirred, except to present a faint smile. The smile is thought to occur in the proximity of the parent kraken, as hosts kept in a separate building never bore such smiles. No explanation was provided for the phenomenon, apart from one theory that speculated the progenitor sang to its progeny, and that the reaction reflected on the host was really that of the larva.

Word for word, the text seemed to describe the case of the three men, for whom Thane demanded a cure. And yet, Ben couldn't help wondering whether others—unaffected persons, sober and awake—might also hear the kraken singing to them. Grim certainly couldn't hear it, though he was fixated on hearing what it had to say.

As he read on, Ben came across a line that made him pause.

"The ovipositor barb also injects a mix of secretory products to paralyze the host or protect the egg from the host's immune system. In many cases, a large welt appears on the host's side..."

The young man stared through the words, and then read them again. Without looking, his hand reached under the borrowed plaid shirt to check for the inflamed spot. The swelling had gone down, though he still felt its residual ache, like a day-old insect bite. His vacant gaze dropped back onto the page, skimming over blocks of text for words like "treatment" or "cure" before being arrested by a short paragraph set apart by its bold font. It was recently added, according to the parenthesized date, but it was a certain sequence of numbers that drew Ben's attention.

"The testimonies of one agent (ID No. 6753-2) state that an implanted subject can regain consciousness when given a dose of the prophylactic, INH-1015. Manufactured to prevent implantation, INH-1015 is currently being studied for its potential in temporarily inhibiting the larva's development, or in some cases, as a larvicide. Please note that several adverse reactions have been reported in such cases, including psychosis, auditory and visual hallucinations, dizziness, nausea, stomach cramps, hematuria, nosebleeds, petechiae, bruises, and excessive bleeding from cuts and wounds."

Time and again, Ben went over the same paragraph, one hand covering his mouth as he passed through the threshold of denial. Though he could attribute his stomach complaints to ingesting contaminated water, there was no explaining away the welt—nor the fact that the ID number belonged to Grim.

Grim knew about it, then—knew what he was doing when he gave his subordinate those red pills—knew it all and kept it to himself, going as far as to slur vital details to keep Ben from discovering the truth. The tormenting question was why—what possible motive induced him to do so? Was he looking out for him or was he moved by some self-serving purpose? The latter seemed unthinkable, yet taking Grim's duplicitous nature into account, Ben could never wholly beat back his doubts.

The hand covering his mouth dropped, followed by the one holding the booklet, and he remained in that state for an indefinite period, till his unfocused eyes settled on a blur of a figure descending the stairs.

Expecting to see Grim, Ben's gaze fixed on Thane's small face instead.

"So you found it," said Thane, including the entire room in a wandering gaze.

Ben stared back without answering, or so much as shifting his position.

"Radney showed it to me days ago," Thane went on, a slight awe in his voice. "Long before you arrived here. He told me everything. I thought he was out of his goddamn mind until I saw it."

He smiled after his roving gaze rested on Ben. "Kill him?" Thane scoffed, refuting an accusation Ben never recalled making. "Now why would I do that? I never killed anyone, I never even hurt anyone."

"You threw me to the pigs," answered Ben with growing resentment that had little to do with that incident.

"Pigs?" said Thane, then gave a wheezing laugh. "Pigs! Pigs?" he jeered, narrowing his eyes under furrowed brows at the outrageous accusation. "So what? I threw you to the pigs. What are pigs? Ham? Bacon?" His derisive expression abruptly turned grave. "Would you rather I threw you to the mob? They wanted to tear into you, they did. But I didn't want carnage. I wanted answers. I had to do something to get an answer. To satisfy them. I owe it to my people. That's what fathers do: promise and deliver..."

"What about the ritual?"

"What about the ritual?" Thane nodded, appearing thoughtful. "You agreed to it, didn't you? Or are you blaming me for the foul-up? You're the one who chickened out. You're the one who kicked off the raft and caused a ruckus. If you kept your cool and went with it, none of this would have happened—and I wouldn't have lost members to you and your partner. There's blood on both your hands!" he added, slamming the top of a nearby table at the word 'both', causing Ben to flinch. "They have every right to get back at you. And maybe I should let them."

Whatever acrimony Ben tasted at the sight of Thane now was gone. The look of dull resentment had lost its edge, try as he would to return stare for stare.

Did he slide down the wall? Why was Thane towering over him, throwing an endless shadow?

"I'm sure we can work something out," said Ben without forethought, words tumbling down a loose tongue.

"Then leave."

"We will. We're leaving. You have my word."

Thane scoffed at that. "Oh, your word! Your word might have amounted to something. But I know as soon as you go back to your partner, it's his will against yours. And we know whose will is dominant."

Ben shook his head. "That's not true."

"He's poison, Benny boy. He's poisoned the minds of my people, ruined our once harmonious commune. He's not above poisoning your mind to get his way. But don't take my word for it. You could always ask him. Ask him, for instance, what was he doing here the other day, dragging a rolled-up carpet and dumping it into the lake."

For once, Ben was able to break contact, his round eyes drifting to stare vacantly ahead. The revelation was tremendous enough that his first instinct was to deny it; and yet he could not deny that Grim had indeed gone back to Atwood's and returned with the unsettling report that the body was gone. The sinister nature of irrefutable half-truths is that they often feel more solid than established truths. So here now was another secret startled wide open, spilling its malodorous entrails.

Ben turned to Thane but found the room empty. He went up the stairs, passed through the kitchen into the hallway, and stopped. The front door stood open, and a hazy form darkly filled that bright rectangle, humanoid in outline, showered in airy disks that flashed and winked, thwarting Ben's capacity to identify it. He closed his eyes to reset his vision, but the outline remained nebulous, looming large as it approached.

And then he understood what it was.

She came to him soft, covered in fine scales, her smooth, bone-capped head sprouting hair at the brow—shiny black hair, midway parted and falling sleek over her eyes like drapes. Her arms and neck stretched out like that of a snail, befouling the air with her fishlike stench, though she shimmered all the more when she threw her arms around his neck, cradled the base of his skull, and down laid her slippery head on his chest. How gently she did this, how loving her ensnaring touch, bidding him open his heart and be kind, telling him to bring her what she needs—for she never wants, but needs, needs, and needs—burrowing her head into his chest all bridal-like, and... oh, her endless needs...

CHAPTER 27

Ben returned to the apartment above the Tea Room in a daze, not registering where he was until he opened the door and found Grim seated at the desk staring intently at the apartment phone.

"Got a death wish, scout?" muttered the latter, keeping his eyes fixed on the phone. The question served to jumpstart Ben's faculties, pulling him out of a distracted state, though it took him a moment or two before he could process his senior's words.

"I came back, didn't I?" answered the subordinate, scratching his earlobe and finding it coated with a thin layer of crust. He stared down at his fingers and the flaky traces of dried blood wedged under the nails; more traces of it were found inside his ear, and though the bleeding had stopped, there was no mistaking it originated from an inner source. Yet somehow the discovery did not trouble Ben, who merely observed that he must have lost his capacity for shock or surprise before wiping his hand down the front of his shirt.

Grim said nothing: he had yet to glance away from the phone, as if focusing all his mental powers on making it ring. And while he continued to disregard his subordinate, Ben mused on what it would be like to tell him what he had learned in the past couple of hours—whether he should say it straight or pay it out in hints and insinuations, unspooling it line by line just to jerk him around.

"I went to check the pipe control system at Atwood's, sir," he began, then paused for a response.

"Any progress?" Grim asked, muttering against the thumbnail he was chewing.

Not having settled on which approach to take, Ben gathered up his implications, keeping them at the forefront of his mind to mentally thumb like a concealed dagger while he delivered his report. If the past few days taught him anything, it was to stay on his guard around his senior. Though Grim was on probation, his latest call with Harper—and the fact that he knew about her son—proved the man still had a network of informants and a few strings to pull. Nothing would be gained from confronting him just yet—far from it: one false move, and he (Ben) could unknowingly set some detrimental scheme in motion.

Meanwhile, the report he gave covered his brief trials with the controls and prompt success in opening up the pipe, leaving out the part about the faulty valve; later he would wonder whether he had subconsciously planned this from the start. At any rate, Grim was impressed enough to favor him with an approving nod and one of his half-smiles, which Ben found infuriating.

"In essence, sir," the young man concluded in a detached tone—his sole means of expressing contempt without betraying it—"once the kraken is in the pipe tunnel, we can shut one valve behind it and one in front, thereby capturing it without putting ourselves at risk."

"You think?" said Grim, rubbing his chin. "I don't know. Sounds too easy."

"Well, we still need some bait," offered Ben, as if presenting the one hitch in an otherwise foolproof plan. "Either we get a corpse, like you said. Or..." he trailed off, baiting his senior, who echoed the last word as a prompt to continue.

"Or you could dive in, sir, and lure it after you. I mentioned this before, but for some reason it seems drawn to you." Grim dismissed the notion with a dry laugh, but Ben kept on, unperturbed. "I don't pretend to understand it, sir, but it could be this whole 'familiar' thing it keeps bringing up around you. Isn't it why you asked Harper to look into the Duncastor report? By the way, sir, if you're waiting for her call, I already had her call me at Mr. Atwood's while I was there."

Something in his cold, formal manner must have finally roused Grim's suspicion. Or else the senior might have been more concerned with what Harper had told him, whether she revealed something vital, or said more than she should have. Whatever the case was, his smile faded as he said: "I wish you hadn't done that. We're not even sure if the line there is secure."

"She texted me prior to calling, saying that she was going to call within five minutes. You were asleep at the time. Even if I drove back, I wasn't going to make it on time. So I had her call me there."

Grim continued to examine Ben. "So, what'd she have to say?"

"It was a replication of what you told me regarding Dr. Carver and the larva. As for survivors, she said there wasn't anything on them."

"Nothing?" asked Grim with the dashed hope of one shaking a bag upside down and finding it empty. "Nothing at all?"

Ben shook his head, and the look of quiet dismay that weighed down Grim's gaze was so plaintive that under different circumstances, Ben might have felt sorry for him.

On their way back to the cabin, Ben peered into his reflection in the passenger window, against which he leaned his head. The gentle vibrating glass cooled by the morning's chill made his forehead feel warm by contrast. Too bad he couldn't say the same for his hands and feet.

"I'm doing the right thing," he said to himself, allowing the thought to rise once to the surface before sinking it again.

At the cabin, he briefly demonstrated the pipe opening and shutting, manipulating the controls to make it seem like he was working two valves instead of one. It helped that Grim's attention was more drawn to the result than the process itself, fixed by the brown and frothy deluge that came pouring out at controlled intervals.

Satisfied with the demonstration, he tossed a rock down the mouth of the pipe, then ran down to see it fly out with the rushing water after Ben opened the valve. He demanded a repeat, this time proposing to use something bigger than a fist-sized rock.

"Like what?" asked Ben, nervously thinking the senior was going to try jumping down the pipeline himself and discover the faulty valve. Thankfully, the polluted water was enough of a deterrent that instead Grim began assembling a makeshift dummy, stuffing a shirt and pants, and using a rolled-up towel in place of a head.

"Think we can bait the kraken with this?" he asked, propping up the dummy for comparison.

Ben pretended to busy himself with finding the switch to drain the few inches of water accumulated in the cell. "I wouldn't know, sir. You're the expert."

He half-expected the dry, remote tone to provoke Grim into asking if something was wrong, but he went on securing the dummy's limbs to keep the arms crossed and the legs pressed together.

"I'm pretty sure they go by heat or scent," said Grim, answering his own question. "But I sure as hell don't want to take a dive until I have to. That's where you come in," he added, holding up the dummy as if addressing it, and making it nod in answer.

The lack of concern did not bother Ben. Ever since his return to the apartment, he was aware of a stillness and clarity of purpose, unclouded by sentiment. It worked better that way. Still, no person, however detached, liked to be reminded of their insignificance to others.

The dummy slid down the tunnel with no issue, and Grim had to carry it sopping wet to repeat the process, this time to try trapping it between the two valves. Ben simulated this by closing the one working valve to trap the water with the dummy, opening it to let them through, and then closing it again to make it appear as if nothing more than the trapped portion of water was being flushed out. For all that, the perceptible delay was noted by Grim, and Ben opined that the presence of trapped water affected the response time of the valve, causing the delay.

"Well, as long as it stays closed when we need it," mumbled Grim, turning his attention to another minor issue. "We just need to pad the floor and maybe those walls in there…"

A surprising, draining sense of relief washed over Ben, underneath which was something akin to awe at the extent of his senior's trust. And when the subordinate looked down to find the button responsible for removing water out of the cell, he found his own hands clutching either edge of the console in a vice-like grip.

As water gurgled into tiny drain holes, he noted a quality of silence that made him look up in time to catch Grim regarding him with an expression of faint perplexity; and fearing lest his face would betray him, Ben excused himself to run to the bathroom, where he locked the door and stood panting over the sink, avoiding his ghostly reflection while he waited for his heart to slow to its regular rhythm.

According to Grim, the kraken was less likely to show up during the day, and therefore he insisted on waiting till late afternoon or early evening to try and summon it.

The rest of the day passed quietly: they arranged a landing nest in the enclosure using a mattress, sofa backs, pillows, and cushions; they ate a modest repast of coffee and whatever they found in Atwood's kitchen; then at last, they went to work putting the rest of the house in order. To wait was torture, and the agony was magnified by pretending that everything was alright. Yet somehow Ben managed to maintain a calm front incongruous with the hornets' nest humming in his mind.

Thankfully, the day was short, and before long, the sun-absent sky drew furnace-red bands that melted purple against the encroaching night.

Grim, cuirassed in his Tegmen, stood on the shore, staring out at the lake.

"Scout?"

"Sir?"

"You ever had one of those moments when your life was reduced to a single point? When nothing mattered except for one small thing—small in the eye of the world, maybe. But for you, it's all you see?"

He had his back turned as he posed this question, sounding as though he was speaking to himself. Ben hesitated, uncertain what sort of answer he was expecting—whether he was expecting one at all, or was content to just share a passing thought. The uncertainty turned into an odd foreboding as he wondered whether Grim guessed the truth or even suspected something.

"Where'd that come from, sir?" asked Ben.

Grim looked down contemplatively at the helmet he held in his hands before putting it on.

"Nowhere, scout. I'm just stalling."

In the basement, Ben stood before the console, one hand poised over the switch, the other holding a cellphone to his ear.

Nerve-wracking minutes passed while he stayed on the line with Grim, listening to him toss one large stone after another.

Finally, the order came like a gunshot: "Now!"

Ben flipped the switches, heard the water gurgling down the tunnel, then ran for the stairs.

Not ten seconds after the water began gushing out, Grim shot from the tunnel, slamming into the soggy nest arranged to soften the impact.

As he scrambled to his feet, he marked the relative dead quiet, and turned to find the water had stopped pouring out of the pipe—or rather had slowed down to a mere trickle.

"Did we get it?" he wondered out loud, fearing that Ben might have closed the valves too soon, locking the kraken out before it had a chance to enter the tunnel after him. The Tegmen was in its ossified state, though given his recent proximity to the kraken he could not count on it to determine its presence.

The answer came soon enough when from the depths of the pipe came a slippery skidding sound, which Grim—after leaning in to better hear through his helmet—took for a positive sign that the kraken was inside. But before he had a chance to turn away, a giant hand shot out of the pipe's mouth, catching his helmet with such force that he staggered back. His hands automatically clasped the thick, bony wrist in vain, trying to wrench it off his helmet. It held fast, wet palm spread flat against the shield. Straightaway, the rest of the kraken poured out of the confining pipe, water-slicked sides swelling to their prodigious size as it emerged into the open. While Grim still fought to pry it off, the bony hand lifted him kicking off the floor, and held him suspended in mid-air.

He gave up on prying off the kraken's hand and reached to undo his helmet's chin strap. The process was retarded by the stinger striking his sides, which while failing to break through the Tegmen's guard still had the bone-rattling effect of a physical blow. His upturned head meanwhile inadvertently exposed a gap between helmet and the Tegmen's high collar, attracting the kraken's attention to it as a strip of heat. So that when the stinger next struck, it went for the uncovered bit of throat. His entire body gave one slight convulse before his jaw fell slack and his arms sank down to his sides.

The kraken held him up while it sought its accustomed spot, feeling for an underbelly or flank into which it could deposit a polyp or two. Yet as he remained sheathed in a tough shell, the kraken found no viable access to his vitals.

It laid him down on the soaking mattresses, a safe distance from the streaming water, determined to continue its task, feelers sweeping every surface in search of heat or the taste of skin. Soon it discovered the hinging shield of his helmet, and pushed under it towards the mouth. But there it recoiled, detecting something faint which it did not like. As if mistrusting itself, the kraken went on appraising, thin feelers crowding under the helmet's visor, all but smothering him, only to determine the same red odor that colored his breath was present in the beaded moisture issuing from his skin.

It hesitated to leave, lingering a moment to broodily nudge him. Then, deeming him undesirable, the feelers curled back from his lips and withdrew as the kraken sullenly retreated into the tunnel pipe.

CHAPTER 28

Thane ducked behind a tree to hide from view. Twenty feet ahead, he saw the cabin and Ben stumbling out through the front door. The boy came to a stop as he turned to face the cabin and stood panting, apparently on the watch for something, unable to keep still as he wrung his hands and restlessly shifted his weight from foot to foot.

A minute passed without anything happening, leading Thane to wonder whether whatever spooked the boy had already taken place. Then he heard a faint slosh of water, and a great bubbling preceded a hump rising from the water below the cabin—so close it almost appeared as if the building was unfurling its hidden appendage. Even from a distance, the black gleam could be seen troubling the reflected image of a rosy sky, drifting for a moment or two before the monster dove down whale-like, lashing the air with its trailing tentacles as it dipped below the surface and vanished.

The sight so arrested Thane that he forgot about Ben until he turned and saw the boy, too, had disappeared. He went into the cabin, presuming Ben had re-entered it, and made his way into the kitchen without bothering to turn on the lights. The hatchway was open, and from its depths he heard shallow splashes, followed by echoes of pathetic grunts as the boy struggled with something.

"The hell you got there?" Thane demanded halfway down the basement stairs, startling Ben, who dropped the black mass he was dragging. A closer scrutiny showed Thane that it was a lifeless body in black the boy was trying to drag out of the flooded enclosure, though his face was hidden by a dark helmet. Then, recognizing the uniform, and realizing it was his primary source of nuisance, Thane approached the two, his wide eyes fixed on the supine figure in disbelief.

Ben all but shrank back, hands twitching as though he could not settle whether to hide them from view or let them stay in plain sight for fear of rousing suspicion. Meanwhile, Thane knelt down to remove the helmet, ignoring Ben's weak mumble of protest, then stood back, staring down at the lax features, the unresponsive half-closed eyes and threads of hair plastered across Grim's face.

Ben's face, ruddied by the effort of dragging Grim's body, lost its color at that instant. He picked up the helmet intending to replace it only to drop it when Thane jerked him back up.

"How'd you do it?" demanded Thane.

For want of a reprieve, Ben stammered through a confused summary, hoping the confession would alleviate the sickening feeling that plagued him.

"Why you sneaky little shit!" Thane laughed, clapping the back of Ben's neck. "I didn't think you had it in you!"

The timorous boy said nothing, turning to retrieve the helmet which he tried to place back on Grim's head, if just to cover his eyes. Thane smiled down on Ben, watching him fumble with the chin strap, thinking how easy it would be to kill them both then and there. But for his own design, he wanted the cabin and its vicinity clear of bodies—dead or otherwise. To facilitate this, he helped Ben carry his friend back into the truck and saw them drive off.

Ben was perhaps all the more glad to see the cabin shrink in the rearview mirror and disappear behind the line of trees. He forced himself to look ahead, trying to rally his scattered thoughts and put them in order. The flashing low-gas signal caught his attention, and after a frown of annoyance, Ben decided they may as well stop for gas.

Did he have his wallet? They would need to stop at the Tea Room and settle the bill. But no, Grim paid ahead. They didn't owe anything, did they? There should be enough cash left, and he still needed to collect their things...

His heart petrified at a long dry wheeze issuing from the passenger side. The figure in black slumped in his seat, head propped against the passenger window, hair falling in untidy clumps over his face. No other sound escaped through the relaxed mouth when Ben felt brave enough to glance its way.

"Just asleep," the young man reminded himself, reaching over a few times to check if Grim was still breathing before snatching his hand back at the last moment.

"Just asleep, just asleep," he repeated, a nervous tic tugging one corner of his mouth. He wished the helmet had stayed on. Maybe he could put it back on when they stopped for gas— no: the Tea Room, then gas station. And then it's back to HQ, finally! Heading back to HQ.

The exhilarating relief was paltry, brief as the wavering smile that flashed across his face and fell. He was almost sure he had a story prepared to explain everything, from the delay in his report to the incident at Atwood's.

What if he told them the kraken broke out, killing Atwood

in the process, and that he and Grim had attempted to return it to its enclosure? But then in such cases they should have contacted them to contain the problem. Why hadn't they?

The wheel felt uncomfortably moist in his grasp. He unclasped and clasped his hands, concentrating on airing them, in part to ignore a perceptible shift in the passenger side: Grim presently sat up, his drooping head gently bobbing to the motion of the vehicle rolling over the uneven road.

The tires gave an abrupt shriek as Ben realized he missed a turn and had to wheel the truck round to take it. Though the incident gave him a fleeting jolt, he began to yawn in its aftermath, as though the jarring spike begat a sudden crash.

He dragged a hand down his cheek before slapping it to keep himself awake. He needed coffee, and to fill up the gas tank. Where was the station, anyway? The roads looked so different at night, sparsely lit by jaundiced lights.

In the meantime, he still needed to answer why neither of them contacted HQ, and it occurred to him then that he should have closed off the valve to contain the problem, trapping both the kraken and Grim in the basement; at least then he would have partly solved the issue, and the kraken could do no worse than what it already did to him. Besides, why should he care what happened to Grim when Grim himself didn't give a damn what happened to him?

"Son of a bitch."

Ben's eyes were wide open, though he couldn't bring himself to turn towards the source, and instead shook his head to deny it.

It can't be... it couldn't be him. He was incapable of anything now.

What's the first course of action when you're in deep shit?

Denial. Deny everything.

Once more he tried another approach: Atwood released the kraken when no one was looking, then disappeared. They wasted two whole days looking for him, and on the last day tried to recapture the kraken, which ended badly. It was satisfying until he recalled they could have contacted HQ since day one, or was it two? Not to mention the larva he carried—when did that happen? They would know, they could tell. Shit! Why was he incapable of aligning his thoughts?

Ben closed his eyes a moment, pressing a palm to his forehead to ease the tension. Still the image from the manual intruded into his thoughts: larvae attached to his organs, like suckling infants—small, faceless and ever-feeding.

Two blinding lights shone on his face, and he swore as he swerved, marginally avoiding collision with an oncoming vehicle, whose horn kept blaring long after it had passed by.

Ben beat the steering wheel in spasmodic anger. He shouldn't blink, shouldn't close his eyes. He was going to be sick. But he had to hold out until he found the gas station. Wasn't much left in the tank. The sharp turn caused Grim to list to his side. Ben pushed him away, catching sight of his face under passing street lights.

Those closed eyes. Why did he have to face him so? Even sitting as he did, Ben was sure those eyes were trained on him.

Stop at the gas tank. Fill up coffee. Pick some gum. Why didn't you call? Sir, it was Grim's idea. I did what I could. It was the right thing.

"I did right, I did the right thing," Ben drowsily reiterated. "You're gonna make it, Benny boy. Just keep your eyes open. As long as you don't look at him, you're gonna make it. Keep talking, just keep talking. Can't remember his own family. Well good for him! My parents were crummy people. They left me—or sold me—or they just didn't give a damn whether

I went out the door and never came back. They're not even worth looking for in a rubble."

The words poured out slow and heavy. Outside him spoke another drowsy voice. "You know what they say: One man's trash is another man's treasure."

The remark triggered an involuntary hissing laugh; and deciding it was no use ignoring it, Ben answered: "Amen to that, sir."

"Why'd you do it, Benny boy?"

"'Cause you kept it from me, sir," answered Ben, sounding hurt. "'Cause you never told me the whole truth." A pause. "So, I went and did the same."

"Well, shit, son. I guess that makes us even."

There was nothing remotely funny in that, no reason to fall into rasping brays that disintegrated into feeble giggles with every moment of waning energy. Except he was tired—dog tired—tired enough not to pay any heed to the white light blazing ahead.

Outside the cabin, Thane heard the crunch of gravel and turned to greet the group of exiles.

Before the conclusion of that morning's meeting, Gertrude had succumbed to attrition, and was rewarded by being allowed to hold her child again; her husband, Pete, his brother, Henry, and Henry's wife were all cast out. But though they were exiled in the eyes of the commune, Thane was never one to give up on his wayward children; which was why he invited them back to discuss matters on neutral grounds, far from the tension-filled air of the commune (and more importantly, the eyes and ears of its members).

"Let's talk inside," said Thane, pushing the front door open. The wood-paneled foyer, warmly lit and furnished with paintings of mallards, was not disarming enough to persuade the wary ex-members to step inside.

"We're fine talking out here," said Pete.

"Listen," began Thane, clapping his hands together, "this morning—well, it was hard on all of us. We've been through a rough night and woke up to nothing but trouble. Tempers were bound to flare. But you have to understand, I have everyone's best interest at heart. There were dubious things taking place here—things that you don't know about—things that led up to the calamity that befell us. I didn't invite you here just to give a tour of the cabin. If I told you what took place here, you wouldn't believe me. You need to see it for yourself to better understand where I'm coming from."

While he spoke, his eyes sought theirs with an earnest light, so much so that all three exchange looks of doubt. As they had only one reason for agreeing to see him—that is, to have him release their family members—they had assumed that he likewise had one purpose in mind: to try and coerce them back into the fold. But if anything, the statement made his intentions all the murkier; moreover, why show up to a secret meeting alone, which by anyone's estimate put him at a disadvantage? No one moved, yet Henry held out his arm to bar the other two from entering, indicating that he was going to check the premise for any signs of traps or ambush.

While he was searching inside, Pete turned to Thane. "Look, I'll be honest, we're not sure why you called us here."

Thane, spreading his arms in an expansive gesture, said: "I thought we could discuss things."

"No, no. There's nothing to discuss. We're not going to change our minds. We just want our families.

"Your families?" said Thane as if no such thing existed.

"My wife, my daughter, and my nephew—Henry's boy."

"If you want them, you can come back. That's where they are now, and that's where they chose to say."

"No," Pete insisted, straining to keep his temper. "They don't want to stay."

"Maybe they do."

"Did it ever occur to you—" Pete interrupted himself to attenuate a flare of anger—"Have you even considered the possibility that they don't want to stay? I know you did. That's why you pulled that trick."

Thane scrutinized him for a length of time, allowing Pete to do the same, observing that never before had Thane's eyes appeared so small and mean as they did then.

"If you knew what I knew," soberly iterated Thane, "you'd understand why I don't want any of you leaving. It all comes back to here. This place hides its share of sinister secrets."

Pete peeled his eyes away and stuck his head in the cabin. "Find anything in there, Henry?"

Henry's heavy tread drummed down the stairs, skipping over the last couple of steps in his hurry. He answered in the negative with a shake of his head.

"So we're good to go in?" the older brother asked.

Swiveling his head for one final survey, Henry nodded.

"Awfully quiet today." Thane smiled, and whatever Henry might have said in answer was better expressed in the dirty glance he cast down on Thane.

"Leave the door open," was Pete's mandate as they stepped in.

"I'm sure Henry already told you in his own way," said Thane as he led the group into the kitchen, "nothing seems out of order. And so it is on the surface. But here—" opening the hatchway—"here is where things get interesting. Smell that? Yes, that's lake water. Watch your step now. See, I knew the poor soul who used to live here. A man of science, he was, sent all the way here to study the quality of water here. 'So what?' you say. Ah, but that's not all. See those aquariums? They're not meant for fish. Or frogs, salamanders or any recognizable creature. Not at all. See that big cage there?" he pointed to the enclosure. "What do you think that's for? If I told you the truth, you wouldn't believe me. But why tell you when you can see for yourselves."

Here he pulled out a stack of books and manuals, sifted through them for the right volume, and opened it on a choice page full of lurid illustrations and diagrams before presenting it to Pete.

"What the hell is this?" said Pete in a confused and horrified undertone, staring at an image of a dissected cadaver, whose insides were overlaid with something resembling a deflated balloon in outline and an organ in its porous texture.

"You're wondering what happened to those three men," Thane answered enigmatically. "I say we have our answer right here."

Henry and his wife looked over Pete's shoulders at the bizarre drawings, skimming over the explanatory paragraphs which did little to demystify what they saw before going back to the image, trying to make sense of it on their own. Their first instinct was to write the whole thing off as a sick joke. But the lab, the equipment, the strange cries in the woods, and the outsiders just yesterday warning them to burn their dead—all seemed tied to one big knot.

Pete flipped to the next page, and then the next, trying to get to the heart of the matter, forgetting Thane's presence until he heard a heavy creak, and all three turned in time to see the hatchway swing shut.

CHAPTER 29

The car sped with him inside it. He was no longer a boy, but that didn't matter, not when his arms remained useless at his sides as they had when the kraken held him up. He couldn't see past the bony fingers and wet palm glued to his face shield, but he could tell what it was doing, raking its short nails down the Tegmen. That done, it gently laid him down and began to peel off the shredded suit, one strip at a time.

A scream was lodged in his throat as he opened his eyes to darkness, and a body that would not respond. The first impression was that of a thin mattress and a thin pillow, and the sensation was familiar enough to quicken his waking. He dry-swallowed, eyes frantically roving about with pupils dilated to split the all-encompassing black into a spectrum of pitch and coal. There was a whiff of antiseptic, and soon a high ceiling came into view. If he rolled his eyes down, he could make out the edge of a folding screen used to divide the beds.

So far, all signs pointed to the infirmary at Duncastor's facility; and yet how could that be when the building itself was reportedly burned down after he and his company left the site?

Or had his memory been false? With nothing to refute it, the possibility settled inside him like a block of ice, yet to thaw into coursing panic.

His arms felt as they had when he accidentally slept on them and cut off the circulation; a sensory blindness, moving without the inner feedback he had long grown accustomed to and took for granted—except during moments like these when every ungainly movement was like the fling of dead meat. Legs were another matter: no force of will could kindle them into motion. His entire body may as well have been concrete.

All the same he kept trying, attempting to move one leg and its corresponding foot before alternating with the other. His face was flushed and glistening by the time he managed some semblance of a response, which came in the welcome form of a thousand needle stabs, and an arm he could lift. Such was his relief, that his weak pants were punctuated with one or two soft laughs.

The door to his room opened a crack, letting in a thin wedge of light. No one entered, but he heard Olivia's voice as she spoke to someone outside his room.

"We'll ask him about it when he wakes up," was all he could catch before she moved away from the door. Her presence merged past with what he knew was near-present, deepening the mystery.

Why was she here? And where was here if not Duncastor?

With his eyes, Grim followed the slim line of light, which shone on a cream-colored wall, a midcentury desk, and a white lab coat hanging from a wooden coat hanger. Lifting his head a fraction more, Grim saw he still wore the Tegmen, and the sight of it confused him more than clarified his situation. He knew what it was, could remember wearing it in the recent past; but all events were mingled that he wondered why he had it on now.

With his head still raised, Grim made out a second voice, deep yet vague in its distance. He went on trying to sit up only to fall back when the relevant muscles failed. After a failed second try and a long huff, he decided it might be easier to roll over to his side.

To that end, he threw his right arm over to his left side, and the maneuver revealed the narrowness of the bed as he toppled over and landed face-down on the tile floor.

Progress was progress, he consolingly thought, muffling a pained groan. Thankfully the impromptu bodyslam did not get Olivia or her companion's attention; all seemed quiet outside his room.

His legs, though showing signs of response, remained unreliable as means of conveyance, and he perforce had to crawl towards the door, flinging one arm ahead to pull forward and repeating the same with the other. The distance to the door was short but taxed him more than he anticipated. He rested his head on the crook of one arm and lay prone, heated breath misting the cool floor as he waited for his strength to return.

The voices returned, floating in from the outer room.

Grim lifted his head and inched closer to the door, craning to peer through the slit between its hinges. He caught sight of a seating area, and a lean, white-haired man with a slight paunch, who came into view and sat in a brown leather three-seater.

"Well it's a switch from your pro-bono cases," said he in a low gravelly voice that nonetheless carried clear. "It's always something broken, abandoned or feral with you," he grumbled on, evidently trying to provoke a response from Olivia, who eased herself into an adjacent sofa. From there, Grim was only able to see her crossed legs.

"Thought you'd like a change," she returned.

The white-haired man's tentative smile grew broad and impish. "Well, you didn't mangle them too badly this time."

"I swerved to avoid collision," Olivia coolly modified. "They're the ones who ran into a tree."

Grim mentally withdrew to reflect on her words, comparing them to his own memory, or lack thereof, before giving up in favor of eavesdropping for more hints. The conversation progressed without him in the short interval, and when he returned his focus on the two, the hoary gentleman's smiling furrow was replaced with a solemn look.

"I'm not sure I like the idea of boarding strangers," he said.

"It's over the shop, Dad."

"Doesn't matter. What if they rob the place?"

She laughed. "What's there to rob? The worst they could do is raid the fridge."

"Liv," the father murmured in tender protest.

She leaned over to clasp his hand. "Every night I check the alarm system and make sure everything is locked up. It's just... business can be slow sometimes. And I'm just doing what I can to get by."

"You should've closed that place and moved on."

She said nothing, still holding his hand, which he turned over to reciprocate her clasp as he went on: "I'll be fine, Olivia. I got my life here. You don't have to stick around just 'cause I'm posted to this spot."

"Well, maybe I like running a tea shop in the middle of nowhere."

This drew a skeptical grunt from her father. Then reaching

into his pocket for his phone, he said: "What time is it? I need to make a few calls."

"What for?"

He indicated Grim's room with his phone. "That one's got a nasty bite on his neck," he said, prompting the hidden onlooker to touch the side of his neck; the skin was numb, though beneath it he felt a raised bump that sent memories of the basement encounter flooding back. Time must have yawned out at that instant, since once he blinked himself back from an open-eyed stare, Grim saw the old man point in another direction, presumably towards a second room, continuing to speak without a perceptible break in his account.

"That one's more concerning. The driver, wasn't he? No signs of serious head trauma, but…" He trailed off, cursing softly when he realized his phone was out of charge.

Grim meanwhile cast about for the nearest standing structure, happened on a steel trolley, and began his slow crawl towards it. He had little time to consider his next move beyond standing himself up. All he knew was that he had to keep them from taking Ben away or running any tests on him. He clasped the top tray of the trolley and tried to pull himself to his feet, then fell in a clattering heap as the upset trolley toppled over and spilled its load.

This time the noise drew the attention of his neighbors, and when Grim lifted his head off the floor and found the two of them standing at the door, he raised his hand and made an unintentional broad sweep to wave hello.

After they made sure he was alright, and Olivia introduced her old man as Eugene Warren—former army surgeon turned country doctor—the three of them sat in the waiting room, Grim staring across the square coffee table at two faces bearing varying degrees of concern and doubt.

"No hospitals," he calmly told them.

"They'll only examine him," Olivia persuaded.

"What they'll do is run tests he doesn't need. Can't afford run-arounds like that, I don't have the insurance to cover it."

"Don't worry, we won't bleed you dry," said Eugene half-humorously.

Grim slowly bobbed his head, as if to give one forbearing nod that would ward off all future inquiries. "I appreciate it, doc, but I'd rather not impose on your kindness. We'll pay what we owe, and we'll be on our way."

"It's not about the money," Eugene muttered, somewhat affronted but with a tinge of concern. "We just wanna see what's wrong with your nephew."

"Nothing's wrong with him. He's probably just exhausted," said Grim, too drained to come up with a convincing reason or fabricate something to explain Ben's state; not that there was any need to when he knew well there was nothing they could do to detain them should he elect to leave. "Look, I can see the clinic's closed, so how about I just take him home, and if there's anything alarming, I'll give you a call—or take him to the emergency room myself."

"I'm not sure you're in any state to drive," remarked Olivia, pointing out his nervous rush to leave.

"You got an ID or driver's license?" added the doctor.

Grim frowned at the second. "Sure I do."

Eugene leaned forward in his seat. "Could you show it to us?"

Grim in turn smiled and leaned back, tried to cross his arms but was clumsy enough in his endeavor to favor letting them fall into his lap. "I don't have to show you anything."

"And I can't release him into your care unless you prove you're his next of kin."

"Oh, don't start with this…" Grim shook his head. "Olivia, you know me and Ben. Please tell him I'm next of kin."

Instead of corroborating his story, she surprised him by saying: "We're not gonna report you or anything, Grim. We just want to be sure."

Grim's smile grew tense. "Report me? Report me for what?"

"Your nephew was driving under the influence," Eugene said. "Almost ran into my daughter. Instead of calling the cops, she brought you over here. I'm not exactly thrilled, but I say that at least earns us the right to know what the hell is going on."

"He wasn't on anything! Listen, I'm sorry about our near-collision, but nothing weird is going on. I fell asleep, and I guess he did too."

"Except he's not waking up now," Eugene pointed out.

"I said I'll take care of it."

The doctor paid him no mind, but turned to Olivia, telling her to call an ambulance. She rose, but lingered a moment, as though to give Grim a chance to reconsider.

What he considered instead was taking Ben away by force. If he could past them, take care of them in some way…

Grim chuckled to himself, semi-aware of the concerned glances he drew. Who was he kidding? Take care of the two of them with his clumsy arms and a pair of legs that barely functioned? When he couldn't even make it to the waiting room without assistance?

Yet the clock kept ticking, and presently Olivia moved towards the desk to call for an ambulance.

He had to stop her—say anything to stop her. *Think, dammit, think!*

Something stalled Olivia from calling. He heard the receiver leave its cradle, but heard no soft clicks of the numbers.

What arrested her was the sight of him leaning into his hands, eyes all but pressed into his palms, splayed fingers buried in his hair. Between them, the suspended breath came out shuddering, not because he wept, but something long held was bound to bring about a tremulous release.

He finally knew what he had to say, but needed time before he said it.

CHAPTER 30

To the young couple, the open door was as good an invitation as any. Jerris Moody, all nineteen years, stood in the doorway of the lakeside cabin, appraising its interior as the new owner. He may as well be, seeing no one was around to claim the spot. And going by Thane's example, no one would be coming anytime soon. But the young man was savvy enough to know that if there were any valuables to be had, he'd better root them out before other folks with the same bright idea came barging in. After Thane sent those ex-commune members packing, Jerris decided that he'd be better off keeping his distance, do some thinking, maybe start his own faction and claim this turf; it was certainly a damn sight better than that overcrowded, weed-choked complex.

But now, there was cash to sniff for. Dearly departed Atwood, gone in such a rush that he surely left something behind—hopefully something along the lines of a cheap strongbox, or wads of cash sewn into a mattress... maybe some frozen assets in the freezer, if not a fat roll stashed in flour or a coffee can.

"I'm going upstairs," he said to Madlyn, who wandered in behind him, making a slow turn to look around as if seeing the place for the first time. "I'd say the kitchen is your designated area."

She rolled her eyes and made a sound of disgust. "Oh my god, you did not quote your dad just now," she grumbled in her half-hearted way.

He lifted a hand in the manner of one absolving himself of the ugly facts he was delivering. "Excuse me, I thought that's what he had you here for. It's not like that drooling whey-face could get up to anything."

Madlyn detected a hint of jealousy behind the careless remark and was pleased. Sweeping him a knowing smile, she said under her breath: "More than you could, anyway," before drifting into the kitchen. She stopped with a sharp cry when a fistful of her hair was caught in a pitiless tug.

Jerris shoved her against the kitchen counter, twisted one arm behind her back, and still clutching her hair, forced her head down, stopping short of slamming it against the granite.

"That's all in the past. And now he's worm food," he jeered through a pernicious grin. "What is he now, Maddie? Huh?" he insisted, accompanying his question with a painful twist. "What is he?"

She fought to free herself, but every struggle only made him press harder.

"Alright, fine! He's worm food!" she conceded, if just to keep her shoulder from popping out of its socket.

Satisfied, Jerris released her and backed out of the kitchen, leaving Madlyn to fight back tears.

Why was she like this? Why did she constantly provoke him into hurting her?

With him out of sight, she grew bold enough to turn around

and glare at the narrow stairs, tempted to steal after him, push him in the bedroom door and lock the door. But then he'd just jump from the window, land in the bushes and then there'd be twice the punishment to pay.

So she returned to the cupboards, mechanically opening and peering inside every container while thinking of the late Radney.

He was middle-aged, and a little gross sometimes, but he was a whole lot more fun to be around; at least he never behaved like he owned her; more than that, he was grateful for her presence, his whole sad face lighting up as soon as she walked into the room, and she couldn't get enough of his adoring attention...

Her wandering mind returned to the present once she began to move about the kitchen and perceived something different about it. She examined the corner responsible for that impression and decided that yes, something was different about it—or rather something missing—maybe a rug that was once there and now was gone. The bare floor showed a faint outline of a hatchway, reminding her of Howard's trapdoor and the underground warehouse beneath it.

She stole a swift glance to make sure Jerris was nowhere near, then smiled to herself, thinking she finally found where Radney Atwood stored the good stuff.

Following Grim's disclosure on Ben's condition, the doctor went back to reexamine the young man, probing his distended stomach for a solid mass. He found it in the lower right quadrant, the very spot where Grim had told him he would feel it. And while Eugene remained wary of this black-garbed stranger, it was hard to deny that something was there, especially when it throbbed in protest, each time he chanced to press on it.

"How long has he had it?" he asked Grim, who slumped in the brown leather sofa, his gaze absently fixed on the varnished surface of the coffee table.

"Coming up on forty-eight hours."

"Judas Priest," murmured Eugene in mild shock. "Was he waiting for it to pop out on its own?"

Grim hesitated. "He doesn't know."

"But you did?"

A half-hearted nod.

"And you never did anything about it?"

Grim stopped short of saying, *I had it under control*, knowing well it would generate at least ten more questions. Instead he said, "You wanted to know why he's not waking up? Why I didn't want you or anyone else examining him? Why I'm semi-incapacitated for the time being? Same answer applies to all of the above."

"So you have it too?"

The question smote Grim in an unexpected way. He was almost sure he wasn't impregnated, else he wouldn't be up and talking—at least not without someone giving him a dose of INH-1015; but the attack left a lingering doubt in his mind that he couldn't quite shake off.

"No, but I had a run-in with its mother. She left me with this hickey," he added, hooking one finger into the lip of the collar to reveal the reddish lump—in a way wanting to reassure himself that the kraken had left him with just that and nothing more. "We were trying to trap her—it," he acerbically corrected. "It went down as badly as you might expect."

"Right, right," nodded Eugene, uncertain as to what to make

of all this, whether Grim's reticence was due to him knowing how crazy the story sounded, or whether something more unsavory was at the heart of the matter.

"Is Atwood involved in this?" inquired Olivia, lifting her head from its contemplative bend.

Grim glanced up at her, and then regretted it, though it needed no look of surprise on his part to betray the fact that she was onto something.

"He is, isn't he?" she said, fixing him with her inscrutable gaze.

Though they couldn't pry the truth out of him, Grim knew the smart thing to do was not resist, but pretend to yield something in the guise of the truth. If anything, it might satisfy them and keep her from heading to the lakeside cabin to investigate on her own.

"Yeah, yeah, he was," said Grim, placing a slight emphasis on the last word.

"Was?" she echoed, catching the hint.

"Maybe I'd better start from the beginning," he said, shifting in his seat. "See, Ben and I—we work odd jobs here and there. I got hired by this client to deliver a container to Mr. Atwood. I can't tell you who the client was, though they probably took care to mask their identity, approaching me in the guise of a workaday bureaucrat, with a briefcase full of papers and a generic business card. They didn't tell me what the cargo was, just that it was nothing illegal—"

"And you took their word for it." Eugene nodded in the reproachful manner of the elderly watching some youthful folly unfold a mile away.

Grim turned to him with a ghost of his usual smile. "I'm not stupid, doc. If for some reason the client can't tell me what's in the box, first thing I do is bring two sniffer dogs before agreeing to anything. As far as I knew, it was clean."

This failed to impress Eugene, who did little to hide his skepticism. "Seems like a lot of trouble just to send something that is not illegal when they could hire a real courier or send one of their own vans."

"Hey, I'm just as good as any courier company—I get things done," answered Grim with a convincing mixture of pride and indignation. "I can't speak on my client's behalf, but I imagine they might have rivals or enemies or something. Maybe they thought a nondescript truck wouldn't get as much attention as, say, a vehicle with a logo."

"I bet that suit would, though," said the doctor with a slight jut of his chin to indicate the Tegmen.

"I bet it would too," Grim agreed, "but I'll get to that in a minute. Anyway, we made the delivery and called our contractor to notify them. But things weren't to their satisfaction—they didn't like the fact that Atwood had company, so we were told to stay and keep watch, letting no one inside the cabin, not even us. I agreed, as long as they understood that I kept the meter running. So we went and bought the gun, you know the shotgun?" he added in an aside to Olivia, "And camped out in Atwood's yard, taking turns keeping watch. The boy, bless his heart, he's not used to guard duty. He won't confess to it, but I suspect he dozed off, or got distracted with his phone or something. Anyhow, next morning, when we went to check on Mr. Atwood, we discovered he was gone."

Grim paused, surveying their faces to see the effect this had on them.

"So all that time you said Radney was there…" Olivia began, without the hint of surprise Grim expected to see, as though she suspected something all along—or more realistically, reached that conclusion while he was telling his story.

"Being just the two of us there," he offered apologetically, "you can see how it might look. Plus we were supposed to keep an eye on him and keep everyone off the property."

"But how did you know he was gone when you weren't supposed to go inside?"

"The front door was left ajar. We knocked—we tried calling—but got no answer. It all looked very wrong and we began to suspect something was off. We had no choice but to go against orders. He wasn't anywhere inside. I knew he was on friendly terms with Thane, so we went to see if he was at the commune—that's when we came by for and bought those provisions. No luck, we couldn't find him there, either. But we stayed on, in case he showed up."

He stopped to let the events settle in their minds while he organized his own thoughts. So far, he avoided involving Thane as much as he could, eschewing the impulse to paint him as the prime suspect in case Olivia decided at some future point to inquire any member of the commune about it and hear a different story altogether.

"Meanwhile," he resumed, a trifle hesitant, "meanwhile, we went in to investigate—see if we could find some clues or something to point us towards where Atwood had gone. No such luck. However, we did discover his cabin had secrets of its own. He had this hidden basement with all kinds of shit—excuse me, stuff—a small lab with aquarium tanks, instruments and a big cage or cell made of shatterproof glass. Only it was empty, and the thing it meant to hold was no longer there."

"Meaning that thing that attacked you," Eugene supplied, jumping ahead.

Grim nodded, raising his eyebrows and murmuring with sepulchral humor: "And how! We didn't see it when we first went in, but it was still in the basement, laying low, probably waiting for a couple of clowns like us to walk in, leaving the door open. That's when it got Ben."

"You called it 'the mother,'" the doctor remarked by way of inquiry.

Pensively thumbing his lower lip, Grim decided they may as well call it that or stick to similarly vague appellations if just to keep them from using the same name the organization bestowed on the creature.

"The thing tackled him and escaped," he began. "We didn't take it seriously at first, seeing how Ben seemed fine after the attack. Our main concern was that thing we set loose. It hadn't gone far, but it was cunning and elusive. I started looking through Atwood's documents. This rig here—" he gestured towards the Tegmen—"was in the basement with the rest of the stuff. I wore it thinking it might help before we tried again the next night. Maybe it did. I got jumped the second night, but it wasn't the same as Ben. By then he was starting to show symptoms. Turns out the mother did not attack him so much as laid something inside."

Eugene involuntarily glanced in the direction of Ben's room, as though comparing this with the ventral pulse he'd observed just minutes ago. In the brief hush, Grim caught the low whistle of the wind outside and an imperceptible shiver ran through him despite sitting in a relatively warm room.

"Why you didn't tell him?" asked the doctor, turning to the man in black, who stared ahead in moody abstraction.

"I wasn't going to stay quiet about it. I thought we still had time," he said without premeditation. "I needed him to stay focused and work with me. We were this close—this close to capturing it. It's bad enough Atwood disappeared on us without our trespassing and losing what could be some precious specimen. The client might let us off on the first without paying—the other two?" he shook his head. "I think you can see why I was cagey about the whole deal," he added, sounding weary even to his own ears. "We were supposed to keep the whole matter hush-hush. I doubt our client will be thrilled to hear it's closer to FUBAR."

Olivia broke the ensuing silence: "But why would Radney disappear just like that?"

Grim feigned his bemusement in a slight shrug. "Maybe it ate him. There weren't any signs of an attack, but, for my own sake, I wish I knew."

"How big is this thing?" Eugene wanted to know.

"I didn't get a clear view, but I'd say it's about the size of a grizzly."

"You mean you drove miles with a container the size of a grizzly and you never suspected anything?"

"Who said we did?" rejoined Grim with an innocent shrug. "The box we brought was this big—" holding up his hands to illustrate—"big enough for equipment, maybe, but too small for big momma to squeeze into."

"Maybe they didn't bring it all the way here," Olivia suggested, this time addressing Eugene. "Radney mentioned he's a limnologist," she said, going off on a tangent that involved her and Eugene puzzling over the creature's origin— whether or not it came from the lake or its peripheries—and whether that was the reason behind setting up a lakeside lab as opposed to an isolated facility, with staff and security guards.

Grim said nothing, but watched while the two speculated, satisfied that they seemed thrown off the scent. He knew that sooner or later the organization would dispatch someone to investigate the incident at the cabin, and wanted to keep Olivia and her father from saying or doing anything that would draw the organization's fatal attention to them, marking them as individuals who knew too much. Eidercrest might not turn into a mass grave like Duncastor, but calamities can visit in other faceless forms.

Grim knew there was no going back to HQ, not with the mess he was leaving behind; no amount of glibness could save him from this. As for Ben, the organization might fix him, or they might keep him as he was to make up for their loss; whatever the organization decided, it wouldn't be kind for either of them.

He was roused from this cheerless line of thought by Eugene's inquiring what he planned on doing now. The doctor's voice almost sounded as if it traveled down the depths of a well to reach him; and after a surprised glance, Grim dropped his gaze again and thought it over.

"First, things first: the kid needs medical attention," said Grim without looking up, rubbing his palms crosswise in slow, nervous strokes. "Can I trust you to take care of it here, in the privacy of this clinic?"

Though he expected the request was coming for some time, Eugene still hesitated to agree right off the bat.

"I have no qualms operating on him and keeping it between us, but there's still that thing on the loose. You might think you're covering your traces now, but I wouldn't be surprised if more cases like your nephew's turn up. I think you should inform the local sheriff or call animal control service—"

"Leave it to me, I'll handle it," interposed Grim. And looking up to find Eugene regarding him with a hint of doubt in his lifted brows, he iterated: "I'll take care of it," not wanting to give himself a chance to back away from his decision.

CHAPTER 31

Thane took the long way back. Starting from the lake cabin, he walked all five miles to Main Street, wanting to stop by Howard's store, the Tea Room, and Caleb's Sporting Cabin, in that order.

There was plenty of time, now that he managed to get rid of a couple of thorns in his side. Already he was making plans regarding the lakeside cabin, wavering between returning the next day to strip it of its furnishings, or leaving everything there and annex it—it would serve as a rendezvous point, a home away from home, a base for trysts—a mini palace of possibilities, complete with its own oubliette. On that note, he had to wait until the three prisoners in the basement lost their strength and could no longer pound the trap door, calling for help. Not that anyone would hear—the only answer they'd get was a visit from that thing in the lake.

Somehow the memory of that black mass swimming away took the savor out of his plans. He brushed it aside. The evening was fine and the long stroll did him good; and how glad he was to take a break from his people and their nonstop demands.

Though he kept an old nag of a station wagon, chiefly used for conveying members to and from the Tea Room, what little gas it had left would be better spent on their next outing.

To that end, he entered Howard's store, curious to see if troubling news had reached its owner. More than half a day had passed since Pete and the other two were kicked out of the commune—surely they had time to see Howard about the job offer and warn him about his (Thane's) implied threat?

He wandered down the fluorescent-lit aisles, idly handling overpriced goods while sideways eyeing Howard, who stood on the other end, dusting and rearranging the items on the top shelf. Thane decided if the grocer started or appeared nervous, that meant he knew. But the portly man went on dusting and reshelving boxes of cereal, aware of Thane's presence but choosing to ignore him: no grocer was ever so absorbed as to resist sizing up a potential customer; either he heard nothing, or did but deemed it little more than bluster. Even in the face of warning signs, people are apt to be incredulous than take any form of action that would disrupt their routine.

Having fulfilled his purpose—and perhaps lulled Howard into deeper complacency by showing up and leaving without incident—Thane left the store and crossed the street towards the Tea Room.

Though the large windows showed a dark interior, Thane went round to the back, convinced Olivia would still be inside tending to some business in the kitchen. He pulled the handle, but only managed to rattle the locked door. His insistent knocks summoned no movement or apparition behind the glass, and in a way, he was thankful his unanswered calls were made at the backdoor instead of the front, in full view of Main Street. But it was unlike her to close shop early, unless she had an errand

that required her immediate attention; she might have noted
his or his people's absence and decided to visit them herself,
bringing along whatever she could spare.

He smiled at the thought. What a woman—a shining
example to her kind. Though she never subscribed to their
lifestyle, she was sympathetic to it, which to Thane was less
than a convert but almost as yielding as one. He was fond of
Olivia in his fashion, though he never put any serious effort
into proselytizing her: she served him far better where she was,
even if she was on friendly terms with Howard. Deliberating on
this, Thane mused over robbing the Everything Store at night,
once everyone had closed shop and left. That way he could
fulfill his promise without risking antagonizing the owner of
the Tea Room; kind as she was, even she had her limits.

Meanwhile, he was hoping to see her about dinner and a
ride home...

Caleb's Sporting Cabin was his last stop before heading
back to the commune. Besides stolen provisions, the defectors
took with them three indispensable rifles and several boxes of
ammo. It almost surprised Thane that, what with all the stolen
goods, they left the station wagon alone; then again, he always
carried the keys on his person, and perhaps not one of them
knew how to hot-wire the car; or perhaps they feared the noise
would draw unwanted attention before they had a chance to
escape. Let them be for now, he decided. They'll get what's
coming before long.

Once again, Thane tried a door only to find it locked. The
interior of the Sporting Cabin was well-lit, and through the
display window Thane could see Curtis manning the register.

He pulled the door again, but it remained shut fast. Like
Howard, Curtis tried to ignore Thane, who stood at the window

waiting for him to look up. At length he did, but when Thane gestured at the door, Curtis shook his head before returning to whatever task occupied him behind the counter.

Thane turned away in disgust and began his trek homewards. Not that he had enough cash to buy anything since he relied on Olivia's paying Curtis on his behalf and eventually settling his debt in his own way, but the dismissal rankled, more so since he had no plans of retaliation to satisfy his resentment. And so, the length of his walk was taken up with schemes that now included the Sporting Cabin—schemes that were providently divided over a period of time, starting with robbery, and ending in arson. In his mind, he dined and dined on both businesses, driving them to eventual ruin while allowing Olivia to thrive—going as far as suggesting she takes up the empty lots vacated by the other two to expand her business. The more he thought them through, the more his machinations warmed him with a satisfied glow; as the day had proved, none was equal to his cunning. So intoxicating was his hubris that he whistled tunefully through the final stretch, in a way announcing his arrival some distance before the wrought iron gates finally came into view.

As expected, he heard and then saw two figures bounding towards him—likely that of the guards, concerned over his long absence, if not happily reporting that Olivia had come by with food and provisions. Too late he perceived the aggressive motion of their sprint and the familiar shape the figures took, though not ones he expected to see.

Just as Thane was wheeling round to take off, Henry and Pete tackled him and pinned him to the ground with their knees while they twisted back his arms and bound them.

Thane never stooped to call for help—would never stoop

to that. Instead, he laughed at them, laughed through the bag
they placed over his head and kept laughing as they carried
him off.

Grim paced the anteroom trying to limber up his legs. His
gait was stiff and awkward, but he progressed past requiring
the wall's support to lean on while he moved from one end of
the narrow vestibule to the other. After a dozen or so circuits,
he carefully lowered himself on the wooden bench to rest a
minute with outstretched legs, letting the stirred blood work
through them.

Beyond the thin walls, the wind whistled through needled
branches, amplifying by contrast the empty stillness of the
clinic. And with nothing but his own thoughts to occupy him,
the quiet jangled on Grim's nerves. It had only been fifteen
minutes since Eugene went in with Olivia as his assistant.
The doctor had estimated the procedure would take at least
two hours, maybe less if the damage wasn't extensive. Grim
tried comparing this with his own procedure, which might
have lasted ten minutes or ten hours. The intrusive memory
rekindled a biting phantom pain so vivid that his hand
unthinkingly cradled his side.

At least Ben was in good hands. Eugene had even offered
to let Grim join them and watch, if just to put his mind at
ease; the latter declining on the plea that they probably knew
their way around and did not require his hovering presence.
He did however advise them to keep a large, wide-mouthed
jar nearby.

"To hold the larva," he explained. "Preferably one with

a secure lid. Who knows how long that thing's capable of surviving outside the host? Might need to build a fire to burn it," he added before asking their permission to dig a small pit in their backyard for that purpose.

As he rose to see to it, Olivia, gowned and masked, poked her head through the swing door, asking Grim if he knew Ben's blood type.

"Everything is fine," she quickly added, "but just in case we need to set up a transfusion. If you're not sure, we still have a few units of O negative…"

Grim answered that he would check and get back to her. She withdrew, and he limped towards a nearby cubby shelve, where Ben's clothes and few personal effects were stashed in a small heap.

The young man's phone had slipped out of the plaid shirt's breast pocket, and Grim caught sight of a brief flash, notifying its owner of a recent text message.

"Any recommendations?" wrote Harper. "All the places I know are closed."

The long-haired man frowned for a moment before recalling the code in which the three of them communicated. He stared at the phone and almost set it down without answering. And yet, why go to the trouble of trying to reach them unless she had something important to say?

As quietly as he could, Grim hobbled over to the reception, copied the clinic's contact number from the business card display, then switched the front desk phone to silent mode in anticipation of the incoming call.

"Where's Ben?" Harper asked soon after he picked up.

"He's asleep," replied Grim in a low-voice.

"Already? Must have been a long day."

Her cheerful, bantering manner led Grim to believe she had nothing urgent to report. "What's this about?" he asked, partly wondering whether she and Ben had reconciled when they last spoke, and this phone call was for him only.

"Oh, it's…" she faltered. "It's just that Ben asked me to look into something. But I guess it's just as well I got you instead of him. Does the name Greg Shaw mean anything to you?"

"No," said Grim, idly swiveling the office chair. "Should it?"

"I thought it might be your name or, you know, one of your aliases."

"What gave you that idea?"

"The gentleman in the photo looked a lot like you," she answered.

Grim stopped spinning in the office chair. "What gentleman?"

"Well, you know how you asked me to look into Duncastor files? Back then, I came across something of yours. At least I thought it was. The box containing transcript papers also had a clear plastic pouch with a wallet inside. According to the document it was found on your person the day you returned to HQ from Duncastor. You don't remember?"

"No… no, I don't." He glanced over the top of the desk, thinking he might have heard someone call his name. "I don't… I can't remember. I know I was in someone's shoes and civvies when I was picked up…"

"Yeah?"

"I just don't remember whose," he muttered helplessly, and he could hear her incredulous smile as she echoed: "You don't remember?"

"Yeah well, try telling me what you had for lunch last Tuesday—and that's your mind without drugs or days' worth of sleep deprivation," he shot back, exasperated. "I'm pretty sure my mind's clocked out by then and I was just a couple of klicks north of dementia."

"Alright, fair enough," she conciliated. "According to the document, the wallet was in the jacket's inner pocket. Are you saying you never took it out?"

"I very much doubt it. What else does his license say?"

"I don't have it on me. Ben asked if I could find something on your profile, you know, birth certificate and all that. I told him not to hold his breath: When you gave me your ID number and I stole a peek at your file—part of it, at least—all I found were aliases, fake IDs. Nothing like a real name, just codenames and handles."

"Hm." Grim smiled sardonically. "Well, you know how it is. Tools like us don't have names, just handles."

"Still, sometimes they use your first name, right? Greg Shaw seemed like the closest thing to an actual name, so I thought 'maybe,' you know?" She paused, waiting for him to comment, and marking the silence on his end, she asked: "You there?"

"Yeah," said he, miles away from his voice. "Did you..." he stopped to clear his throat. "Did anything else come up under that name?"

"You mean Greg Shaw? No, not that I know of. Are you sure it's not one of your aliases? You looked a little different but that's definitely you in the photo. I mean when you think about it, it's more likely they issued you that license and you just forgot about it."

"As opposed to happening across someone with the same face," he owned. "But then why keep it as evidence?"

She mumbled something in lieu of a shrug. "Maybe they wanted to keep track of which ID you used for which mission. I could take a second look at that license and call back tomorrow during lunch break."

Grim caught himself before he gave in to an involuntary agreement. What the night events would bring, he could not divine; but come morning, he and Ben would drive by Lake Penumbra, fling their phones into the murky waters, and then drive on to the nearest bus station, buy two tickets and disappear.

Greg Shaw.

He faltered into a short laugh, half-covering his face with one hand, knowing well what he was about to say yet hesitating to commit to an answer. "No. There's no need for that."

"You sure? Could be something. Well, if you change your mind, you know where to reach me."

"I will. Take care," he said and hung up, remembering afterwards that he forgot to ask her if she knew Ben's blood type.

Not long after he returned to the wooden bench in the vestibule, Olivia came out, holding a half-gallon jar that contained a blood-soaked mass. The raw-looking thing shone under the anemic light, unmoving, though it trailed an unclean streak down one side of the jar. She handed him the jar to hold on to, and as if relieved of her burden, sat on the bench, keeping some distance from him, even after he put the unsightly specimen away.

There was something stony and disapproving in her silence, and in the way she kept her gaze averted. Grim had a feeling she was still suspicious of him. Well, as long as she didn't interfere in some way—

"Shouldn't you help him close?" he suggested.

"What do you know about surgery?" she asked with a trace of her rare smile, albeit one tinged with disdain. They spoke in low voices, as though conspiring not to disturb the patient next door.

"Not much, except that I sat through one," he said.

This failed to move Olivia from her absorbing weariness.

"Honest to God! I even got the scar to prove it," he elaborated, placing a hand on the lower right portion of his abdomen.

Slowly, as slow as a few seconds could pass, she understood: her green eyes and the bright sweep of lashes went from their downcast slope to staring ahead while she listened again in her mind to the last few sentences.

"Like Ben?" she asked, glancing his way.

"Like Ben," he agreed. Why he said this, he wasn't sure—why drive a hole in a story he worked hard to weave, was incomprehensible. Except nothing made sense to him anymore, and that was enough to put him in a reckless mood—that, and the fact that he would have to tell them the whole truth at some point.

Olivia looked away to consider this. After so many falsehoods, it wouldn't have surprised him to see her get up and return to surgery without giving him a second thought. But she stayed, and her next words were: "Well I like to think dad's patchwork is fine enough not to leave a scar."

Grim frowned playfully at that. "No, give the boy something to show off."

She acknowledged this with a token smile and he fell quiet. Then his clasped hands began to shake in sympathy with his tapping foot.

Olivia, thinking he was concerned for Ben, said: "He's alright now."

Grim nodded, deciding to keep his concerns to himself.

An hour later, they were out in the backyard, where Grim crouched before the fire, whittling a stick and tossing the shavings into the leaping flames. Now and then he would glance up at Olivia and the jar she held; whenever he did, she would follow suit and look at it as well, perhaps nervously imagining its contents had moved or did something that warranted attention. But the grubby thing in the jar barely if ever stirred; and if Olivia was nervous, she hardly showed it.

"Is it dead?" she asked, holding up the jar for closer scrutiny, perhaps tempted to shake it.

"Might be playing dead," said Grim, shifting his gaze back to her. She had removed the surgical cap and mask but kept the stained, linen-white gown on. The light of fire, warming her face with a flickering glow, caught the thread-like wisps of hair that had escaped her crowning braid. Her presence lent a mystical charm to the scene, and Grim felt moved to encapsulate the general air of ambiguity and tell her how much she resembled a witch; yet recognizing the inadequacy of the remark, he kept it to himself.

She surprised him then by answering him with a subtle smile, more apparent in the crooks of her mouth than a spreading line, as though he had spoken out loud. But perhaps she read his face more than his mind, and in the hidden alchemy of her thoughts, smiled for a reason independent of him.

He returned her smile and motioned her to hand him the jar, biting down on the sharpened stick to receive it. He sat cross-legged, setting the jar down in the hollow created by his encircling legs. He tried not to think about the others that would follow: within weeks, the area surrounding the lake would be crawling with nymphs, their numbers multiplying as long as they had living bodies—something the nearby commune had in spades. That alone made contacting HQ necessary.

Perhaps he should make a call to tip them off before disappearing on them. Or perhaps he needn't bother: the radio silence on their end was getting far less reassuring now than it was a couple of days ago. Was it a couple of days? His grasp of time was slippery at best, though he knew lack of communication on their part meant they were ready to spring a surprise visit—maybe within a few hours. He would have to warn Olivia to keep her distance until the whole thing blew over. Either that or feign ignorance if ever outsiders showed up and began asking strange questions...

Twenty-odd thoughts dashed through his mind—so much so that he briefly forgot about his present task until Olivia called him, and following her gaze remembered the jar resting between his knees. Slowly, he began undoing the jar's clasp, trying not to disturb the sleeping creature—or rather alert it to the fact that its glass prison was unsealed. The larva remained inert, and it was hard to say whether it twitched, or whether the wavering light gave the illusion of animation. And while he puzzled over its lethargy, he did not hesitate to drive the sharp whittled end of his stick straight through its spongy flesh.

But the instant he delivered the fatal jab was a strange one, for he felt a duplicate twinge twisting his insides. The act had cheated him into an unaccountable sorrow, and two tears fell from his eyes, as though it was one of his own he had speared.

Outwardly, and to Olivia, nothing seemed out of the ordinary when Grim pulled out the stuck larva and pushed it into the fire. Black spots now blinked all over the smooth surface as the larva curled onto itself. She averted her eyes and looked to Grim, who for once wore an expression compatible with his name.

CHAPTER 32

Remarkably enough, the truck was in working order despite its dented front. The fact that it had missed the curve of the road and skidded off into a clearing must have slowed it down before a slender tree brought the rolling vehicle to an abrupt stop.

Grim was no mechanic, but as long as nothing leaked, and the truck started without complaint, he saw no reason not to extend its use. Presently he sat in the driver's seat, trying to ignore the low gurgling rumble while he checked the area map on his phone. The coverage here was weak at best, and while the phone labored to load the map, Grim took a peek inside the glove compartment, satisfying himself that the brown bottle of INH-1015 still sat there intact.

Since the last pill he took was earlier that afternoon, he deferred taking one for another hour or so. Under normal conditions, their side-effects were deemed marginal, but he knew from personal experience that a double dose, or doses taken in quick succession, might still blur his judgment. One traffic accident was more than enough, and he would do well to remain clear-eyed until he reached his destination. Fortunately for him, the cabin was but a few minutes away, and as soon as he got his bearings, Grim backed the truck and guided it rattling towards the road.

In the passenger seat sat Grim's mute partner, a makeshift spear fashioned from a chef's knife duct-taped to a broom handle.

Never having had any practical experience in bringing down a kraken, Grim figuratively shook his head at how one's training could fit them with blinkers to overlook the obvious—and the obvious in this case was that the kraken, invincible as it was, still bore the proverbial crack in its armor. Where the idea came from, and when it had crystalized, he wasn't sure, though he suspected it was an amalgamation of his most recent encounter with the kraken, and the tormenting memory of that one Duncastor inmate, whose begrimed state could only be described as having crawled out of the belly of the beast. A rifle or shotgun would have better served his purpose, going against his early claim; but Eugene kept no firearms at the clinic, and at this hour, he could not hope to get one from Caleb's Sporting Cabin. True he could wait till the following night, but could he trust himself to maintain enough resolve to carry out the task, however well-prepared the next night saw him?

As the truck treaded over the wooden bridge, he thought again about the larva, seeming half-dead, and ruminated over the possibility of it being sickened by polluted waters. The adult kraken seemed to thrive, but that didn't mean it was entirely unaffected. More curious—if less close to his immediate thoughts—was the stab he felt when he lanced its progeny. He had heard of cellular memory transference, a peculiar phenomenon observed by recipients of donated organs, who besides the organ itself, apparently inherit some of the donor's traits or memories. And who was it that told him pregnant women kept souvenir cells from their fetuses, whether or not they complete a pregnancy? Of course, the kraken's larva was in no shape or form like an organ or a human embryo. Moreover, he was not the one who carried it. But then, parasites were notorious for influencing their hosts; who could say what lingering effects remained after carrying one, however brief?

Was this what the kraken had recognized in him? And all this time he was mislead by some private hope that it knew or was somehow connected to someone who might have been his blood kin?

Just as he was about to turn into the cabin's driveway, the Tegmen began to ossify. Not a second later, the truck's headlights discovered a great roadblock, and Grim's foot mechanically stomped the brake pedal.

His initial, unfocused impression was that of an asphalt mound, mysteriously rising from the road. But as the black, light flecked mass moved, unheedful of him, he soon saw it was the broad side of the elusive kraken, which had unexpectedly crept all the way out into the open. Either Grim had caught it at an inopportune moment, just as it was transitioning from one hiding place to the next, or something had drawn it out. Soon enough he saw it was the latter when, leaning forwards a little and peering beyond the scope of lights, he spotted one of many trees, set apart by the unseasonable fruit it bore.

A hanged body depended from one of its high branches, slightly rotating at the end of the rope. The departed's face was concealed by a burlap sack, though his stature, his calico shirt and pointed boots gave a fair indication of his identity. The body was not going anywhere, yet the kraken thought it necessary to secure it by seizing the head with one claw-like hand, a sight from which Grim almost recoiled, thinking the claw-hand was about to rip the bag off the man's head;

instead, the kraken's tendril-like arms stole up the body's lifeless legs, roping around them before it began to pull him down, as though trying to pluck him from that tree.

At that instant the futile horror turned sympathetic, and determined to distract the kraken, Grim flashed the trucks beamers at it. That did the trick, and the kraken released the body only to turn on him, charging towards the offending light.

He threw the truck into reverse. The engine revved and the back wheels spun, issuing fumes of heated rubber and a thwarted flight: The kraken had seized the truck's bumper, and was now dragging it towards it, rearing up to meet with arms spread, taking the front in a grotesque embrace.

So positioned, the kraken presented its underside, revealing a portion of its long, dripping mouth, which by turns dragged wet streaks across the windshield and moistly adhered to it. On either side, its tendrils covered the windows in a writhing lattice, the worming heads of which were determined to pry through the glass; and overhead, the thickest of the tentacles beat and hammered on the sunroof. Hardy as the truck was, it began to suffer under this assault, groaning under the weight bearing down on parts not made to handle such load.

All this occurred in the span of seconds, and snapping out of a transfixed state, Grim once again floored the accelerator and peeled back with the kraken still hanging on. He spun the truck around in a semi-circle, hoping to throw the creature off. But the kraken's hold was secure, and failing to shake it off, Grim sped the truck down the road and began to fishtail, twisting the wheel left and right in another futile attempt. Worse yet, though he could not see the road, he knew he had veered off and was tearing through the brush. But he couldn't stop, not when the kraken began to slip and seemed struggling to maintain its hold.

A large rock or patch of raised earth rolled beneath the speeding truck, surprising it into a leap that further compromised the kraken's hold. Then suddenly the truck's nose made a sharp dip, and for a wild, stomach-sinking moment, Grim imagined they were about to roll off a cliff. But too soon came the jolting impact.

When the rattling had ceased, Grim opened his eyes to precarious stillness, and the sense of being dangerously close to spilling forward and landing face-down on the windshield. His loose hair fell over the sides of his face, and he tucked it behind his ears to survey his dark surroundings.

From the angle of the cabin, he gathered the truck had fallen into a trench—or in all likelihood, a deep ditch through which flowed a thin stream.

The running engine kept its grouse, replacing the gurgling rumble with a rattling pant. And while the headlights were still on, they were muffled by the surface pressed up against them.

With slow care, Grim strained his neck to peer over the dashboard. But if it was the kraken he wanted to see, he got his answer in the form of a stinger angrily striking the passenger window. The barbed point left a pockmark as it withdrew before striking again, each thrust accompanied by a spasm that originated from the front of the truck—or rather from the kraken pinned lengthwise to the ground by the weight of the vehicle.

Grim sat with one hand holding the grasp handle, one thrown behind his seat, and his two feet braced against either side of the pedal pit, nervously grinning at the kraken's current predicament.

"Yeah, how about you stay down, you son of a bitch?"

On the passenger side, the stinger slid down in what might have been a spell of exhaustion and seeing his chance, Grim reached for his helmet and strapped it on, knowing he had to act now before the kraken gathered enough strength for a second attempt at overthrowing the truck.

With his makeshift weapon in hand, Grim cautiously opened the door, trying not to provoke the kraken into a fresh furor. But just as he climbed out, he remembered the pills and recalled that he had yet to take a fresh dose. It was but a moment's hesitation, but it was enough for the kraken to demonstrate its reach, as the other appendages now found and seized Grim's ankle. The violent yank surprised him into dropping his spear to grab the door frame, holding on for dear life. But having secured one part of him, the other flailing arms lashed onto his legs and waist, pulling against his resisting grasp, until he was drawn straight as a bowstring. His hands trembled, and the laboring growl rose to an agonized cry as every joint screamed under the strain. The kraken might have carried on like this, but lacking energy to spare, all strands gave a mighty twitch that forced Grim into letting go.

Instantly he was slammed face-down into the ground. What little he heard through his helmet suggested the kraken was trying to strike him with its stinger—except a truck's broad side was in the way, clanking with every jab, as if catching sniper rounds.

Growing frustrated, the kraken dragged him by the ankle and threw him up against the driver's side of the truck, perhaps attempting to bring him closer to the stinger; failing that, it once again brought him down hard, and whaled on him with its tentacles, intent on beating him to a pulp.

At some point during the volley, his helmet began to crack, all but splitting open; and by the time it stopped, Grim was half-buried in the soil.

He opened his eyes, feeling himself a pile of disjointed parts, and that in order to get up, he needed to reassemble himself bone by bone, and joint by joint. The task seemed daunting enough that he put it off as long as he could. Fortunately for him, the punishment was not without its cost, and the inflicter seemed more exhausted than ever. What's more, Grim discovered as he began his painful crawl towards the spear, lifting the shield to breathe a little easier, though each breath delivered a fresh kick to his ribs—what's more, the air was replete with the stench of raw meat—a stench he knew from experience indicated the black sap, a vital liquid that was the kraken's proximation to blood. As a guard, he would catch whiffs of it whenever a kraken smeared the walls of its enclosure—an act that the organization's science team argued over, some claiming it was a form of bloodletting, and others attributing it to nesting behavior. Only now his hope was that the crash had inflicted some internal damage on the creature, bringing him that much closer to accomplishing what he had set out to do.

He kept the visor up, though it made little difference in terms of seeing where he was going in this thick dark. Instead, he used the engine's rattling growl as a guide and crept towards it, one inaudible groan at a time.

It seemed miraculous to him as he reached the towering truck that it continued to doggedly hold down the kraken. He knew the inanimate thing wasn't sentient enough to care either way, that it was locked in place more by sloping land than any steadfastness on its part; but as his wandering hands found the spear, and he leaned on the shaft to raised himself to his feet, placing a steadying hand on the truck just below the dangling side mirror, he couldn't help giving it a small affectionate pat before pushing off.

Some of the wilted tendrils twitched at his approach, but the kraken had yet to find its second wind by the time Grim went round to it. The truck's headlights shone close on the kraken's side, and he caught a masticating movement that hinted at the creature's underbelly mouth—at least, he hoped the heaving portion was the kraken's underbelly, figuring that since the stinger was over there, and the arms were over here, the kraken now lay in an awkward position, partway between its side and back. Observing this, Grim theorized that if he hadn't tried to shake the kraken off, and the vehicle landed in the same position, the creature might have ended up choking down the entire front of the truck, hood and all. The bitter thought hurt him in other ways as he tried to chuckle and produced a faint, dry wheeze like the rattling remnants of a departing soul. He nursed his ribs, trying to gentle the sharp pain into dull throbs.

Fumes radiating from the truck mixed with the kraken's stench, and made the air almost unbreathable. And with the Tegmen's protective albeit suffocating squeeze, Grim had to remove the helmet if just to keep himself from passing out. That done, he slowly and methodically scaled the mound-like side of the kraken, reached the top, and rotated the spear to point its sharp end down, using it to probe the underbelly for the slit mouth.

Like him, or rather like his Tegmen, the kraken's hide was invulnerable on all sides, except the edge or lips of its mouth. The surface was uneven and treacherous, rising under one foot and sinking under another, like a slow bubbling. Compounded by his lightheadedness, it threatened to throw him off, as did the tendrils that languidly twisted and eeled up his legs. It took but a few seconds to find its mouth, and placing each foot on either lip, he pried them apart. Only a small gap was made, but it was enough for Grim to raise his spear and drive it down.

With a towering black spray, the kraken quickened to life and thrashed. Grim held on to the lodged spear, shutting his eyes against the racking pain and fountain of black blood while he waited for the violent reaction to die down. And after a swift wipe he regained some vision, and plunged his spear again, eyes ablaze with terrible whiteness. The black stuff gushed again, greasing its lips and making it difficult for Grim to keep his feet anchored in place—something the kraken was only too aware of; in a swift move that sent pitch-like strings flying, its jaws opened and snapped shut.

One of his legs got caught, and the other shortly sank after it. And having lost his footing, Grim fell on his hands, but wasted no time in trying to pull himself out. The spear's handle tilted out of reach and was besides firmly lodged as well. He grabbed and clawed the kraken's blood-slicked side to no avail: besides holding him fast, the insides of its mouth were lined with undulating rows of pine teeth, each pine raking down his legs, catching the thin gaps between the Tegmen's raised slabs to effectively pull him down like a grinder.

With the truck bearing down on it, the creature's stomach was crushed to a third of its capacity, keeping it from swallowing him whole. Even so, it was no less determined to devour him—to mill him down into that scant third, or else keep at it until he bled through his eyes.

Hand after hand, Grim kept clawing, pulling against pull. It was a losing battle: he knew it in the way his thrown hands landed an inch closer to its mouth, and in how deep his legs sank in, hips soon to follow. Though half-blinded by the last spray of black blood, Grim looked ahead at the sloping turf, and his squinting eyes made out a blur of a crouching figure, extending its hand towards him. No one could possibly be there, but in his desperate state, Grim extended a flailing arm, trying in vain to bridge the gap between his unsteady hand and the outstretched one.

Meanwhile, the spear's handle broke, but its blade remained

stuck inside like a thorn, which the kraken felt with each movement of its gullet. Unable to withstand it threw up everything in a terrible shriek; but the paroxysm failed to loosen anything, except the black sap that came pouring out, blood veined with blood.

CHAPTER 33

The lights were still on in the small room by the time Olivia returned to the clinic.

Patients were rarely if ever allowed to stay overnight— even the commune mothers, whom Olivia secreted here to give birth in a more sterile environment than their dilapidated rooms, had to leave before Thane suspected anything. A firm believer in home births, he only made allowances whenever Olivia insisted on looking after them, believing she acted as a capable midwife. Where he got the idea, no one knew, though Olivia correctly surmised he invented the fiction to save face in public and in private. With enough hardships plaguing his people, a bit of leniency where it counted went a long way, and a mother coming home with a living, healthy baby was a source of brief and tempered joy. But if labor went into the small hours, a separate room was sometimes set apart, usually one adjacent to the operating room. Eugene often groused over receiving expectant mothers, reminding Olivia that he was not a practicing obstetrician; but he had yet to turn a case down or send her away.

Olivia found her father seated at Ben's bedside, still in scrubs, arms crossed and chin tucked into his chest, issuing an uneven, buzzing snore. It broke off with an abrupt snort as soon as she laid a hand on his shoulder.

Eugene looked about in a blinking daze, then winced as he reached to rub the back of his neck and shoulders.

"Back already?"

"Just dropped him off," answered Olivia.

"Stubborn fool should've waited till morning to call animal control."

"How's Ben?"

"He'll be fine. Go back home. He'll probably be up tomorrow expecting pancakes or something. I want mine sunny side up with plenty of coffee."

"Sure, Pops," she humored as she helped Eugene out of his seat. "Two dots and a dash—double Java, high and dry, with wheels on."

"That's my girl," was his dozy response.

"Put it on your tab, Pops?"

He paused to look at her, one eyebrow raised over heavy eyes. "Now you're just talking nonsense," he muttered and went on his way.

After he left, Olivia brought a second chair to use as an ottoman and settled down to read one of the few dozen paperbacks she found while cleaning out the apartment above the Tea Room. A carton of them sat in the trunk of her car, waiting to be sold to a nostalgic buyer, if not a collector with a penchant for lurid covers.

The books had their own worth to her and her classmates in middle school, freely circulated during recess or between classes to be read under a desk or behind a propped-up textbook. She supposed in retrospect one or two teachers must have spotted the hidden tomes, rolled their eyes and looked the other way, though some enjoyed catching and confiscating what they deemed was trash. But where there was once absorbing intrigue, Olivia now found comfort in the brown-edged pages and predictable plot, in the funny, dated vernacular, hackneyed prose, and earnest claptrap writers invented to conveniently arrive at their conclusions. Yet so heady was this tour of the past that she considered taking the next day off, spending it here to help around the clinic, skimming over this and other titles while she manned the desk during the receptionist's lunch break; she may as well, since she planned on staying up with Ben, and would likely sleep in the next morning.

She glanced over at the patient, wondering if he had read any of the titles. He may be a few years younger, but they were close enough in age that he likely read some of the same pulpy classics. At any rate, it would be a nice diversion for him to spend the day going through the entire box.

Grim, of course, would either be sleeping off his nightly expedition, or—not having succeeded—would take Eugene's advice and call animal control. Somehow the matter seemed less dire when she saw the homespun weapon he fashioned for his hunt, lending a quixotic aspect to the situation that would have been humorous (and perhaps mildly troubling) if it weren't for the bizarre thing they pulled out of Ben. But Grim seemed to know what he was doing and was likely capable of handling the situation...

The paperback lay face-down on her knees, when she heard Ben murmur: "I'm dreaming."

Against the surrounding hush, the abrupt remark unsettled Olivia with a shiver. But the odd feeling began to dissipate as she turned towards Ben, who lay there with his eyes partly-open, showing signs of coming round.

"How're you feeling?" she asked, hastening to bring about a sense of normalcy.

Ben's eyes made a slow turn towards her.

"Hi," he whispered, more from lack of energy than trying to keep quiet.

"Hey," she answered in the same low tone, pulling her chair close.

"Where…" he began, his dry lips barely moving.

Olivia rose to fetch him a glass of water, from which he took a few sips. She recalled the question he tried to form and guessed he either wanted to ask where he was or where Grim was.

"We're at a clinic," she said, answering the former. "Do you remember what happened?"

His unfocused gray eyes sleepily fixed on her. "Clinic?"

"Do you remember anything?" she repeated.

His gaze shifted as he thought about it before slowly moving his head to indicate a negative answer.

She tried to help him along. "You were driving your uncle's truck."

"My uncle?" he mumbled, almost childlike, and then: "Oh yeah, my uncle."

"Right. You were driving his truck, and you must have fallen asleep at the wheel. You almost ran into me. No one was hurt," she promptly added. "But that's why I brought you here."

"Oh, wow, that's really nice of you," he murmured with touching sincerity.

"Hey, don't worry about it," she said a careless shrug, thinking that perhaps it would be best to leave the rest of the evening's events for Grim to recount.

As if reading her thoughts, Ben asked: "Where is he?"

"He?" she echoed, feigning ignorance.

"My uncle, Grim."

"He... stepped out," she answered, underestimating the young man's capacity to catch the note of hesitation.

"Where'd he go?"

Olivia stopped to think before deciding a direct answer was favorable to dancing around the subject. "He went to hunt down that creature..." she began, still hesitant to say more. It was not that she was afraid of upsetting him as much as worried he would choose to stay up instead of going back to sleep. Already her answer roused him from a drowsy apathy.

"Creature?" he echoed.

"The creature from Atwood's basement," she clarified.

His eyes opened a little wider. "He told you?"

"He had to. He wanted us to help you," she explained, not quite sure what to make of Ben's growing alarm.

At this, Ben began to sit up, grimacing at the incision which he vaguely acknowledged by placing a hand on the site as he looked about with absent horror. "Why'd he do that?"

"Do what, Ben?"

"It's treason!" he arbitrarily broke out. "Why'd he do that?"

The word struck Olivia as odd, even if she understood that Grim broke some form of NDA or client confidentiality by explaining the situation. "Ben, it's alright, it was necessary. We had to know what we were dealing with so we could help you."

But Ben was too absorbed to hear her. His gray eyes, magnified by standing tears, searched the room as he worked through something.

"Why'd he have to go and do that?" he repeated in a thick voice, arriving at the same mystifying point. His face gathered in a painful expression as he weakly began casting his arm over his head and drawing it back down again, in some confused way seeking a physical outlet for his laments.

"I blew it," he moaned, covering his eyes with the back of his hand as he bitterly sobbed: "Oh, God, I blew it!"

But just as quickly as the sobs came, the young man sniffed and composed himself.

"Where's my phone?" he asked, erasing his tears with furious wipes.

Olivia, attributing his sudden mood swings to a mixture of grogginess and fatigue, patted his arm and told him to get some sleep. He ignored her compassionate touch, bending his eye on her as he quietly insisted: "Where's my phone?"

CHAPTER 34

At the center of the formidable committee reviewing the case was a man who still read the report, presenting a shiny pate while he weighed events against evidence. On either side of him was a line of men and women who sat with hands clasped or resting over their own copies of the report, apparently content to wait while the head of the committee continued to flip back and forth between a specific set of pages until something caught his attention.

"And you say the specialist was involved with the commune?" he asked, lifting his filmy eyes to the seated young man.

"Yes, sir," answered Ben, refreshing his straight-backed posture. "When we arrived, we found Mr. Atwood in the company of their leader—a man called Thane—and a young woman who, to my knowledge, was a town local and a new recruit."

"And where does this play into the events that followed?"

"Sir, if you read the report—"

"I've read it enough times to recite it from memory," the old man flared. "I don't care what the report says. Answer the question."

"Yes, sir," answered Ben. "As you know, sir, we were ordered to keep Thane off the property and succeeded in intercepting his attempts up until the second day—or rather evening. That evening, he descended on us with a group of armed men and overwhelmed us. It was pandemonium. They tied us up—that is, Mr. Atwood, my senior partner and I—and carried us back to the compound."

"And what did he hope to achieve from this?"

"From what I've seen, sir, Thane was a megalomaniac, who no doubt carried a grudge ever since we stepped in and kept him off the property. Whatever benefits he reaped from associating with Mr. Atwood, he no longer had access to them. He was also fond of rituals which he used to maintain his hold on his people. He began with Mr. Atwood, slitting his throat to commence the public execution he planned for the three of us, and tossed the body to the pigs to get rid of any evidence. As he said at the time: 'Whatever the pigs won't eat, we burn.'"

"Obviously he never got to you," said the head of the committee, who oddly enough did not seem disturbed on hearing the story. Then again, from where he sat, every report had the detached unreality of fiction.

"No, sir. Nor my senior. We both managed to escape before it was our turn, though I was shot and injured in the process. My senior partner then drove me to a clinic in the next town to get treated. That's when I last saw him. By the time I woke up, three whole days had passed. I tried to call him as soon as I could, and waited six hours to hear back from him. When he didn't call back, I contacted HQ to report the situation."

"And why did you wait six hours before contacting us?"

"My apologies, sir, but I presumed he might have called to report in the interval while I was out of commission."

"I see," said the head of the committee, shuffling some papers with self-important dignity meant to cover up his mild embarrassment. "According to your file," he continued, "you were sent to observe him and report his conduct."

"Yes, sir. I managed to call in the first night to submit my report while he was asleep—that is to say, during my shift, when it was my turn to stand guard. After that, the ensuing events kept me from making any updates on my report."

"And your verdict?"

"Sir?"

"The report you couldn't submit—let's hear it."

Ben shifted slightly in his seat as he surveyed the other members, who, detecting his uncertainty turned to him from their various attitudes of disinterest. His face grew warm under their attention, and from having to come up with something to say on the spot.

"I would—that is—I never had a chance to prepare one."

"Improvise, then," coolly answered the head of the committee.

"I–In summation," faltered Ben, then coughed to clear his throat, "he was a man dedicated to his duty, first and foremost."

No one spoke for several moments, and Ben, seeing they expected him to continue, added: "That is all, sir."

A disappointed silence received this, apart from the head of the committee, who allowed himself a dry chuckle at the paltry report.

"I suppose there are matters of higher priority," he muttered with a lingering smile, and Ben was sure the old man was getting back at him for an imagined slight.

"Indeed, sir. The two agents dispatched after I had called HQ drove me to the site of the cabin, where we came across the unusual sight mentioned in the report. Near a small bridge, we found both that unidentifiable creature and the organization's truck. And further ahead, just outside Mr. Atwood's cabin, was Thane's dead body hanging from a tree."

"You said this Thane was a leader of a cult, revered by his followers. How did he end up like that?"

"Sir, as the two other agents have attested, it seems that conflict broke out at some point in the commune. The commune itself is no longer. It appears most members have fled—perhaps the sight of the monster scared them off." Ben threw in that last part knowing how it rankled with them that there were witnesses out there beyond their reach. He himself was not supposed to know about the kraken's existence, and was extra-careful not to call it by name lest they discover he was acquainted with more than he was privy to.

"And your partner?" the head of the committee pressed.

Ben dropped his gaze. "I never saw him again. The agents who went to investigate never told me anything, except..." He trailed off, pressing his lips together.

"They brought you shreds of clothes to identify," the old man finished for him.

"Yes, sir," Ben owned without lifting his head. "I wasn't allowed to disembark when the agents stopped their car at the site so I couldn't get a close look. But I could guess where they got them from."

The committee members had their collective gaze screwed on the young man, who only sat quiet while he waited for the next question. The inquest went on for some time, but with not much left to go over, Ben was eventually told he was free to go, and soon after, they adjourned.

Grayed white walls and a dimmed white ceiling were the first things that came into view when Grim opened his eyes. He closed them again, not yet ready to see what else awaited him. Somewhere below came the muffled sound of a door closing, and the sound, curious enough in its remoteness, decided him that he may as well take in his immediate surroundings before determining whether or not to shun them.

His eyes had yet to focus, which many a morning had worried him about the future of his vision, but even a bleary-eyed glance was enough to tell him where he was. The question was, who brought him back to the apartment above the Tea Room?

A heavy fog rolled outside the wide window, shrouding the world in penitent white.

"Scout!" he called, and then winced under a barrage of aches, as though canes beat down on every rib. In a flash, the pain reminded him of last night, and he realized Ben must still be laid up at the clinic.

But then so was he, Grim realized as he began to take stock of himself, throwing back the blanket and surveying with a mixture of mild horror and fascination the blue and purple patchwork of bruises covering his body. A splint invested his right foot, while the left was encased in a long cast.

Soon the penetrating cold got to him and he covered himself again.

The table and chair, which once stood by the window,

were pushed close to his bed, bearing a pitcher of water and a flannel robe. With aching bones, he grabbed the robe, causing a folded paper to flutter to the floor. He ignored it, concentrating on slipping his arms into the sleeves as trouble-free as he could manage, then pouring himself a glass of water, both mundane tasks now formidable in his twinging state. Every sudden move and pressure bore the threat of a painful snap. After a few accidental splashes, he succeeded in maneuvering the stream to fill the wide-mouthed glass before gritting his teeth to set down the pitcher.

The glass was empty in less time than it took to fill it, but thirsty as he was, Grim wasn't in any hurry to fill a second glass.

It's too quiet, he thought, staring at the window and wondering at the hour. There was something funereal in the subdued glow of the sun and the rolling fog that carried the sharp, sable scent of pine and fir.

His phone was nowhere to be found, though to be sure the Tegmen too was gone. And it was unlikely his wallet or the keys to his truck would be there. Did they just leave him here to wait for someone to come by with his things?

He didn't have long to ponder, as soon the door connecting their apartment with the Tea Room swung open.

"Oh, good, you're up," said Olivia, coming in with a tray.

"How's Ben?" Grim asked.

"He's fine," she answered as she whipped out a towel to mop up the spilled water. "Didn't you read the note?"

"What note?" Grim asked, not remembering the folded paper. And as she took the glass from his hand, he asked for a refill.

"The note on the table," she said, pouring him a glass with enviable ease.

"I don't see a note there," he observed, receiving the filled glass.

"Your partner wrote it for you before leaving for headquarters," she said, causing Grim to choke and cough. He stooped over, molding a hand against his ribs with pained groans.

"That's right, I should get you your painkillers," reflected Olivia, plucking the glass out of his loose hand.

"Wait," he brought out in a frayed voice. "What do you mean left for headquarters?"

"Yeah, funny story that one." She nodded with a distant look and faint smile of reminiscence. "See, he woke up asking after you, and I explained to him how you told us everything. Of course, he thought it was, you know, everything-everything. So, he went back and told us... well, everything."

Grim turned away with another pained groan, this time at his partner's stupidity.

"I would have been less forgiving about your feeding us a pack of lies if you hadn't kept your word, and then some," said Olivia, noticing the folded paper she accidentally kicked before stooping to pick it up. "Trust Ben to spill your secrets!" she added with a light laugh. "But you have to commend his loyalty. After all, he's the one who tracked you down and showed us where to find you. Maybe see what he has to say."

With this, she laid down the note between Grim's hands and left to fetch his medicine.

Curiosity got the better of him and he unfolded the note, penned on a sheet from Dr. Eugene's prescription pad. In it he read:

"We found you early that morning. You were almost gone, but Dr. Eugene tells me you're stable and will recover in time. If you're reading this, that means he was right. There's no avoiding calling HQ, but I've arranged things so that they don't find you. You looked after me and now it's my turn. They'll pick me up from the clinic, where I've been supposedly laid up, recovering from an injury I sustained days ago, meaning I don't have the slightest idea what unfolded after that. They can inspect the site and reach their own conclusions. As far as they're concerned, you were swallowed up by that black thing. I don't even have to tell them. The evidence I planted will speak on my behalf. You always did say a good, simple cover story is my best bet. I don't know how they'll feel about finding their precious specimen dead, but as you and I know, there's more where that came from. I told Olivia and Dr. Warren about the three victims from the commune. I hope they manage to find them. I'd rather the organization not know about them and have three more kraken babies. It's enough for me to want to go back, rise up in the ranks, and maybe see about closing down that program. But that's between you and me. If you taught me anything, it's accountability. And a bit of duplicity, let's be honest. I intend to put them to good use. I've never had a father figure or an older brother, but you're the closest thing I had to either one. Thank you. For everything.

Take care and good luck."

Grim went back and read the note again, then laid the paper down and looked out the window, waiting for the information to sink in.

There was no gladness or relief at the end of that rumination, no peak of sudden excitement. Just an emptiness as vast and overwhelming as open skies. On some level he knew he was free—as free as someone with almost nothing to his name— and whatever he felt, it was tempered by the fact he didn't know what to do with himself now.

Then, slowly, he smiled to himself, remembering something: a name that was as good a starting point as any.

9 781733 885454